ROOFTOP
DIVA

Other works by D. T. Pollard:

The Trophy Wife Network

ROOFTOP DIVA

A Novel of Triumph after Katrina

The Trophy Wife Network Series

D. T. POLLARD

iUniverse, Inc.
New York Lincoln Shanghai

Rooftop Diva
A Novel of Triumph after Katrina

iUniverse books may be ordered through booksellers or by contacting:

iUniverse
2021 Pine Lake Road, Suite 100
Lincoln, NE 68512
www.iuniverse.com
1-800-Authors (1-800-288-4677)

This is a work of fiction. All of the characters, names, incidents, organizations and dialogue in this novel are either the products of the author's imagination or are used fictitiously.

First Printing

ISBN-13: 978-0-595-40234-2 (pbk)
ISBN-13: 978-0-595-67788-7 (cloth)
ISBN-13: 978-0-595-84611-5 (ebk)
ISBN-10: 0-595-40234-8 (pbk)
ISBN-10: 0-595-67788-6 (cloth)
ISBN-10: 0-595-84611-4 (ebk)

Printed in the United States of America

To survivors of catastrophes large and small everywhere.

Preface

Rooftop Diva is about the capacity of the human spirit to survive and thrive even in the midst of unthinkable tragedy. Often the true test of resiliency comes after the tempest has passed and the task of rebuilding looms ahead. Very few things in life are more daunting than being forced to start over in life when the circumstance was forced upon you. The main theme faced by the central character is even after surviving nature's fury, you will still have to contend with and overcome storms that will come your way in everyday life going forward.

I wrote this book to focus on life after whatever rooftop moments people have had to overcome, whether it was a natural disaster or a personal loss. There is hope on the other side of life afterwards.

The factual basis of this novel was the catastrophic Hurricane named Katrina that hit New Orleans, the Mississippi and Alabama gulf coasts in August 2005. I have tried to remain true to the factual underpinnings of this work of fiction by reviewing various elements relating to the actual timeline and settings in which the events took place.

Survivor's Song

To those that hunger where the crops don't grow
I will remember you
To those dying where the cures don't flow
I will remember you
To those whose lives have been washed away
I will remember you
To those fleeing as genocide marches their way
I will remember you
To those braced against the roaring wind
I will remember you
To those fighting chemical demons within
I will remember you
To those involved with the conflicts of man
I will remember you
To those dying by their brother's hand
I will remember you

Written by Danny T. Pollard

One

Hurricane Katrina hit New Orleans as nature's weapon of mass destruction, but Monique and her grandmother stood fast. Then the levees failed and washed her old life away while she emerged through the roof of her house like a butterfly bursting out of its caterpillar's cocoon. When she was scooped up by the arms of a rescue worker and flown away by helicopter blades that served as wings to a new life, she knew things would never be the same again.

Her name is Monique Devareaux and she was called the rooftop diva by the man that saved her, but she never knew his name. She must have passed out because the next time her eyes opened she was surrounded by a throng of people at an aid station. A kind lady gave her a cold bottle of water. Reality started to settle in that all she owned was clinging to her in the form of the clothing she wore.

"Has anyone seen my grandmother Martha Devareaux?" she inquired.

All that met her was a blank stare and a shake of the head for no. Deep down inside her mind, she knew her grandmother was floating in the water that swamped their house. It came in so quickly. By the time Monique realized what was happening it was up to her neck. She called for her grandmother, but at eighty years old and wheelchair bound, there was little chance she survived. Not only was she homeless and destitute, she was also alone.

She struggled to her feet and said, "What's going to happen to me? I don't have anywhere to go."

The aid worker replied, "Hi, my name is Wanda, what's your name?"

"I'm Monique."

"Monique, I need you to fill this out and when that is done, we have a bus that will take you somewhere you can stay and get some help."

Wanda gave Monique a form attached to a clipboard and she began to fill it out and asked, "Where will I be going?"

"I don't know exactly, but either Houston or Dallas, they have some shelters set up for you there."

As Monique gave the clipboard back to Wanda, she was directed to a waiting bus filled with people from New Orleans. Their faces registered shock and disbelief at what had happened over the last week. Once on the bus she began to come to grips with her situation. Even though her head was spinning, Monique knew she was a survivor and would find an upside in the midst of this sea of misery.

With chapped lips, sunburned skin and scraped legs as reminders of her three day ordeal on top of a small shingled roof, now she was headed into the unknown. The smell of filthy clothes and unwashed human flesh that had been baking in the sun was omnipresent. Her own putrid scent offended her personal sensibilities but for the time being that would have to do.

At the age of twenty-eight she had moved back in with her grandmother because her other options had run out. Her boyfriend decided to move out and go back to his wife and children. She had no one to turn to in Chicago since she had left her high technology sales career when she met David and his promises to take care of her. In debt and jobless, Monique felt she had to pack up and go back home to New Orleans for a fresh start. Now the ultimate tragedy had occurred with the storm hitting and knocking her down again.

Even in this setting, she was a stunning woman with skin as smooth as glass and haunting green eyes. In the old days of Jim Crow she would have been called a Mulato, Quadroon or some other designation to indicate a mixed race parentage. When completing the form before boarding the bus, she checked the box by race that stated white. Monique reasoned if her old life was washed away then let it be completely swept out to sea and she would emerge on the other side as completely different person.

Soon the rhythm of the bus and hum of the diesel engine rocked her to sleep. But even sleep was not a respite because it just gave her mind a chance to replay the horrors of the past week of carnage through her dreams.

"Hey, are you all right over there?" a man yelled from a roof three houses down.

"Yeah, I'm okay," Monique yelled back.

Monique knew she was alive and that counted for a lot under these conditions. But there were two people in her house and her wheelchair bound grandmother wasn't on the roof with her. Tears streamed down her face because she knew the water swallowed Martha Devareaux, her Grandmother, after the levees broke. The ravages of diabetes had claimed Martha's legs years ago and that sealed her fate when the water came rushing into the small home.

Monique walked to the edge of the rooftop and looked down. She could see her car submerged under the water and thought, how could this happen. She then saw someone float by swimming in the filthy water using a discarded tire as a flotation device.

Her mind then jumped to the first night. The long hours of being awake were taking their toll. She nodded as she sat on the angled roof and then slipped a couple of feet.

"Oh!" she exclaimed as she bolted awake and stopped her slide by flattening her legs down to the shingles to gain traction.

That traction was paid for by giving up some of the top layers of skin on the calves of her legs as the shingles had a surface like sandpaper. She started to cry and wondered what she had done to deserve this sort of punishment. Was this her admonishment for sins of the past, if so, why destroy an entire city just to get to her?

She felt the bus lurch as they came to a stop at a roadside park and the driver announced they were in Texas and stopping to let everyone take a bathroom break.

Monique was about to get off and asked, "Where are we going?"

"We're going to Dallas, they have a shelter set up for the refugees," the driver said.

"Refugees! We're not refugees, we're Americans."

"Excuse me, Miss, it's just a term that's been thrown around."

"Well, they need to throw it away," Monique said as she got off the bus.

The driver watched her five foot eight inch frame walk away in a gliding fashion that was somehow elegant even in this sobering setting.

After using the bathroom and walking about to stretch her legs on the green grass near some pine trees that were common in this part of Texas, she surveyed the crowd of people. There were three busloads and she wondered how this happened in America. Monique had to really focus to believe this wasn't some nightmare she would soon wake up from and everything would be back to normal when a voice rang out.

"Hey, Miss, you want one?"

Monique turned and a slender young black woman was holding out a pack of cigarettes towards her in an offering gesture.

"I usually don't smoke, but I'll take one, thanks," Monique replied as she took a cigarette and the woman lit it.

"I'm Sonja," the young woman said while reaching out her hand.

"Monique," she said in response as they shook hands.

"Can you believe this is happening? It seems like a bad dream," Sonja said.

"I know, I don't really know what to think about this," Monique replied. "One minute I'm in my bed and the next minute, I'm chopping my way through my roof."

"You got any family on the bus with you?" Sonja asked.

"No. I don't think my grandmother made it, how about you?"

"Some of my folks made it to the roof, but we got picked up at different times. I don't know where they are," Sonja said.

Sonja started to cry and shake and Monique grabbed her and held her tight, but the vision of her grandmother floated in her head and she couldn't shake it. They both sat down on the grass and held each other.

"How old are you Sonja?"

"I'm eighteen. What's going to happen to us?"

"It'll be okay. I'm sure we will be taken care of, we're in America and they're taking us to get some help."

"But, it took three days and nobody came for us, why didn't they come for us? We were right there and the interstate was still open, they could have driven up to the edge of the water and got us some help. I felt like they didn't care if we lived or died. There was an old lady, Mrs. Harper, on the roof across from us and she died after two days on that roof. I'll never forget that."

Just then the call to load the buses came and Monique grabbed Sonja by the hand and led her to the bus. She sat with her for the rest of the trip. She looked out of the window and made note of the curious sight of vehicles with multiple gas containers strapped onto luggage racks.

Monique asked the driver, "Why do those cars have plastic gas containers strapped on top of their luggage racks?"

"I've heard a major pipeline that goes to the southeast isn't working and there are fuel shortages in that part of the country. Travelers don't want to take any chances. They're stocking up and taking their gas with them in case the stations are out," he answered

It occurred to her that she had been in a virtual news blackout for a week. Monique really didn't know what was going on in the world outside of her own experiences.

"Do you think they couldn't get to us? I just don't understand why it took so long. It's not that far to Baton Rouge, that's where the state capital and all of the state government is located? I mean, my dad and I were there in about ninety minutes driving straight up Interstate 10 when we drove there one day," Sonja lamented.

"Look Sonja, you'll drive yourself crazy if you try to figure out why it took so long. We all know that help should have come sooner, but now we have to try to pull our lives together. That's going to be tough enough as it is, but if you can't get past what happened right after the storm, then it's going to twice as hard," Monique advised.

"But I feel like garbage that was thrown on side of the road and nobody even cared enough to pick me up until they couldn't stand looking at it any longer. Then they scooped me up and threw me on this bus. I was hauled off like the trash truck does with garbage when it comes through. This ain't no bus, it's a trash truck. I don't even know where the rest of my family is," Sonja started to cry and laid her head on Monique's shoulder.

She held her until her sobs subsided and blended into a deep sleep. Monique really pondered when someone would hold her again in a comforting embrace to give her strength. How did this girl figure she had any more strength of will than anyone else? They were both plucked off roofs and taken away on the same day. Their situations were the same except she at least had the hope of seeing her family again. Monique was not a totally singular figure in the world as she did have an uncle she had not seen since her mother's funeral when she was fifteen years old.

It had been a long time since she had thought of her beautiful mother, Margaret Lacroix Devareaux, the most stunning woman she had ever seen. Her mother was a belle of the first degree, she loved to walk with her head high and her back with a certain sway to it. Red was her favorite color, she wore it well and almost always was adorned with a grand piece of feathered headwear. Her skin tone was a very light tan. Her face was exquisitely sculptured with high cheekbones, full lips and penetrating brown eyes.

It was said from an early age she could cast a spell over any man to get her way. That must have been the case with Monique's father, a prominent white physician in town. He did more than just administer medical care when she went for office visits at the age of sixteen. Her mother would often tell her that her father was an important man around town. She never knew who he was until her grandmother told her at the side of her mother's deathbed. Her mother died at the age of thirty-two. She was used up by life and suffering from the effects of a prolonged cocaine addition until her heart couldn't take it anymore. At her deathbed was Monique, her grandmother and her Uncle Albert who she hadn't heard from in thirteen years. She gave up with Monique holding onto her hand as she took her last breath.

Three years after that awful day, Monique went by the office of the man she was told was her father, Dr. John Morgan. She was eighteen years old and got an unexpected response.

"Are you my father?" she asked.

"Yes," John said. "Your mother said she didn't want any help from me and I blame myself for taking advantage of a young girl. Look, my wife doesn't know about this and I would rather she didn't."

"Why didn't you ever visit me or even let me know I was your daughter?" Monique questioned.

"It just wasn't proper, I mean, look, I'm sorry," he said.

"What do you want to do with your life? I know you have done well in school. Do you want to go to college?" he asked.

"How do you know how I've done in school?"

"I know your high school principal. He knows who you are and kept me informed."

Monique felt a rush of anger that she was the only one in the dark while her principal and unknown father kept tabs on her.

"What do you care, how I did in school, you didn't care enough to come around when I was growing up? I didn't know who my father was until my mother was dying and where were you?"

"Did you ever wonder how you were able to live the way you did when your mother only worked a minimum wage job? I was around and made sure you had what you needed. You may not want to hear this. If you want to go to college, go to the First Community Bank and ask for Fred Moore. Show him your driver's license. There is an account there in your name, and since you're eighteen now you can get it on your own," he said.

Monique stood there stunned and took a business card with the name of Fred Moore on the front with an account number written on the back. She left and never spoke to her father again. The bank account had fifty thousand dollars in it, and it was all in her name. Monique knew this was her ticket out of the lower ninth ward and she headed for Chicago to go to school for business administration.

Soon sleep overtook her again on the bus and when she next opened her eyes the city skyline of Dallas was in sight and growing closer. The bus went just south of downtown and exited onto Interstate 35 North and pulled around into the parking lot of Reunion Arena. The former pro basketball stadium was now transformed into an evacuee shelter. Monique couldn't help but look up at the ball on top of the shaft next to the silver hotel. She had seen this structure a thousand times on television reruns of her grandmother's favorite show. Looking at that landmark gave her hope for the future in some odd way.

The bus stopped. They began to unload and were led into the parking lot where general instructions were given as they lined up outside of the cavernous structure. Sonja stuck close to Monique as she had developed somewhat of an attachment to her. Honestly it did give Monique a sense of worth to feel important to someone else at such an uncertain time.

Now they were in the human cattle call as rows of buses pulled up. She could smell the odor of diesel emissions and heat from the engines only served to add to the oppressive Texas temperatures. She surveyed the vast concrete parking lot surrounding Reunion Arena and looked upon faces of despair as they stepped onto the scorching surface. Then the gravity of this situation became clear. This was part of a great American migration, only this time it wasn't the great drought, or great depression but the great storm that destroyed a city.

The gleaming skyscrapers of Dallas were just east of them and the bustling freeway interchange was to the west. The rhythm and speed of the city continued unabated around them while their world was in limbo. This place smelled different. She couldn't smell the water from the Mississippi River and there wasn't any texture to the air, it was thin and dry.

These were her neighbors and all of them had been ripped from their daily lives in a display of nature's wrath compounded by failures of man's foresight. Monique watched and thought these people had been broken, not by the storm but by the aftermath of anarchy that followed. Some of them had languished on hot rooftops, waded in foul floodwaters or survived shelters fraught with dangers as they waited for help to arrive.

"I need all of ya'll with last names of a through m to line up on this side, if you have family members with a different last name of course you can stay together," a red haired volunteer worker said at the front of the group.

She fell in line with the group with Sonja's hand in hers and marched towards the sports arena turned makeshift shelter. This was the most impersonal aspect of the ordeal. Monique was transformed from an individual into a member of a group and her sense of freedom was altered. She knew she was free but in order to participate in receiving the support she required there was a relinquishment of normal autonomy for a kind of institutionalized freedom. She signed up for aid, clothing and sleeping space. It was akin to joining the military service or some other structured group.

They were eventually assigned cots to sleep on and given a toiletries package of essentials like soap, toothpaste and shampoo. There was an issue of a standard drab uniform to wear before they headed for the bathroom area to clean up.

This is where Monique understood where she was in life at this time, because nothing seemed more luxurious than the feel of a toothbrush and toothpaste in her mouth. With each brush stroke of the toothbrush over her teeth and around her gums it felt like she was removing years of buildup and bringing herself slowly back to the human race. As she brushed and rinsed her mouth out she had the most peculiar thought that she was now kissable again and looked in the mirror and viewed her clean teeth with a smile.

Then she got in line for the shower and didn't even think about the fact that she would be naked in the open with total strangers. When it was her time to enter and the hot water started cascading over her naked flesh, it was the most exquisite sensation she could recall. Monique reveled in this simple pleasure as much as someone might a full day spa treatment. The feeling and smell of shampoo and soap was unlike any experience she could remember compared to the last week of human sweat stained skin, clothing and the pungent aroma they emitted. All too soon she exited the shower and dried off. She put on her clean issue of clothing, looked at herself in the mirror and although clean, she was like unfinished furniture. The designs and underlying beauty were present, but without the varnish there was no shine and texture to bring out the features and nuances.

Now Monique's individuality, style and singular sense of self began to blend in with thousands of others dressed similarly and milling around the floor of a basketball arena. Somehow she would have to reclaim that which was unique but for now it was better to be safe, clean and fed. To her it felt beautiful to just be clean again and she made her way to her cot. Before she fell off into her first full night of sleep in a week she made a vow to herself to overcome any and all obstacles in her path and reach heights she has never seen before.

Sleep helped rest Monique's exhausted body, but her mind continued to replay the past week of images throughout the night in her dreams. As she slumbered her mind began a journey starting with struggling through the small opening in her ceiling into the cramped, hot crawl space between the ceiling and roof of her house. Following the hurricane preparedness directions that were issued there was a small stash of water, bread and various other snacks to tide two people over for a couple of days. Her late grandfather's trusty old wooden handled axe had been placed on the rafters if the worst happened and the levees failed. The idea for the axe being there was from something she heard on television as a worst case fallback if going through the roof to escape was the only way out.

It was too late. Her grandmother could not be seen or heard and she barely was able to keep her head above the rising water when she made her way into the crawl space. Trying to balance in a hunched position with her knees on spaced out beams while swinging an axe was not a skill most people would ever practice. Now her very survival made this something she had to master quickly.

Trying to swing upward didn't have much effect. The heavy axe head at the end of the long handle was preventing any real force from impacting the plywood decking of the roof. With panic fast approaching she gathered her thoughts. Sweat started to sting her eyes and her clothes were drenched from perspiration. Then it came to her and she maneuvered onto her back for more leverage and could then swing the axe with both hands. She grasped the handle with both hands and swung. The blade bounced off of the decking with little effect. Catching her breath and with a grunt she swung again. This time it caught a piece of decking near the edge of where it was nailed to the rafter. The blade dislodged the sheet from the rafter as age and oxidation had exacted a toll on anchoring nails and they snapped from the impact. Pieces of brittle shingles split and a ray of sunlight came through like a beacon. Monique crawled over to the spot and used the axe blade like a hammer by banging it up against the weakened board.

Her lungs were on fire and with the stifling humidity she was drenched in sweat. She pounded upwards until her arms ached from exertion and finally the board broke free. She pushed up with her feet and punched through. Monique then placed her small amount of provisions on top of the roof and half of them had fallen into the water that now was up to the beams in the ceiling. With her remaining strength, she placed her hands on the rough shingles and pulled her drained body on top of the roof and into the sunlight.

After her eyes adjusted to the sunlight, her thoughts disconnected because the sights around her couldn't exist in reality. There was a vast lake of water surrounding her dotted by rooftop islands with stranded castaways yelling and waiting for some kind of rescue and reason. The picture became even more foreign as random boats would go by, or someone would swim by using a piece of wood or a beverage cooler as a flotation device. She scanned the horizon for possible salvation and nothing was to be found. Suddenly thirst made its presence known and she looked down at her two gallons of water stored in plastic milk containers. She took a long drink from one of them. Monique was tempted to wash her face but decided not to since she didn't have any idea how long she would be stranded and that turned out to be a critical decision.

After a couple of hours her kidneys did what kidneys do and they filled her bladder with fluid that needed to exit the body. She looked around and realized this was a problem that needed a solution. There were people close enough to see her and she didn't want to urinate in full public view, but something had to give and then she spotted the hole in the roof.

Monique positioned her body over the hole and lowered herself inside and straddled two of the beams. She then pulled her panties aside and found relief and descended down another rung from where she had been only hours earlier. Going back up to the roof she sat with her head resting on her knees and began to cry as the hot shingles burned her buttocks. Now things taken for granted before would be a great luxury because she would revisit the opening over the coming days as her body required.

No one came and the reality that she would be stuck here when night fell was frightening to say the least. Slowly the day gave way to night and around her was a sea of darkness except for occasional lights. She reasoned these were flashlights shining with the hope of attracting the attention of a rescue crew. Then she heard sounds that caused her skin to crawl as the crackle of rapid gunfire rang out in the distance. She didn't know what was happening but understood that wasn't a good sign. This was to be a time of nodding off but restful sleep would not come this night.

The next day dawned, the sound of helicopter engines and blades could be heard. She could see off in the distance the coast guard aircraft hovering and lifting people from below. Some expectation of salvation filled her and she could see others shouting and waving from perches on their homes. There was even a flyby but they did not stop, for in priority order the old, sick and otherwise infirm were first. Otherwise healthy individuals were at the back of the line. In her current state she had no understanding of any priorities other than her own.

Day two came and went and one thing came out of it and that was to use the board she dislodged as a partial shield from the sun as it beamed down relentlessly throughout the day. The water that surrounded her was a stagnant stew of many different ingredients. More toxic elements were pouring in every day from human waste to substances leaking from everything submerged underneath. The city acted as the pot and the sun was the heat source but the aromas were far less than inviting. That night she did sleep but carefully and in short bursts and always aware that rolling off the roof could be disastrous.

By mid afternoon through day three her water was gone. Then she heard the roar of the turbine engines from the chopper and a line descended with a man secured by a harness. He reached for her and attached a belt around her waist and she clung to his neck and was lifted to safety. Sometime after this scene her mind rested and began to slumber in concert with her tired body.

The next morning she woke up and looked at the vast space above and her mind reset its bearings concerning where she was. Her sleep last night was healing, even in a room with hundreds of strangers laid out in neat rows, but it was better than a roof or bus.

Sonja came to her and said, "Monique, let's get cleaned up and go eat, they're serving breakfast."

Monique got up and this day was a long one of forms, instructions and asking questions. The next day was one where the promise of a debit card worth two thousand dollars was the task of the day and hopefully she could start to figure out her new direction. Later that morning she went outside and gazed at the reunion tower ball thinking this is where she would rebuild her broken life.

Two

Near the end of her second day in Dallas a familiar voice sounded out, "Monique, is that you?"

She turned and said, "Cynthia, oh my god, you're here too?"

The two women hugged.

"Girl, I haven't seen you since high school," Cynthia said. "I didn't know you had come back to town."

"Yeah, I'd been back for a while, I don't even know what to say. We're in a shelter, what happened to you when the storm hit?" Monique asked.

"It was just crazy. The storm hit and we thought we were fine and then the water started coming in so fast that we barely got out. My mother lives with us. She has heart trouble and was in the hospital. I don't know what happened to her. We can't find out anything. I just don't know what we're going to do. My two boys were just starting school and now we have nothing," Cynthia said. "What about you?"

"I'm really just here. My grandmother didn't make it out and I guess she's still in the house," Monique replied.

"I'm sorry about your grandmother. This was just awful. I couldn't believe what we saw after the water came in," Cynthia said.

"I hope you find out about your mother," Monique said giving her old friend a hug.

"Thanks, I wish we had run into each other under better circumstances than this," Cynthia said.

"Yeah, I know," Monique replied and bid her goodbye.

It was a strange feeling to meet an old friend in this environment and know the situation is dire without asking. What do you talk about, what can you say that matters? That would not be the last familiar face she saw, but they were going in and out at a rapid pace but she was still there.

While she was standing outside on the third day she asked one of the local volunteers about some of the landmarks around the arena.

The man whose name was Robert was a retired postal worker told her, "Over there is Dealey Plaza where President Kennedy was shot."

"Really, I'm this close to where that happened?" she said.

"Yeah, there's the building the shot came from. Right behind it is the West End. There are a lot of restaurants, movie theaters and such over there. They built that so people would come downtown at night and on the weekends. There was nothing to do down here after work, so everybody just went home. Straight up the freeway is the new basketball arena that replaced this place. Across the freeway there is the county courts and jail, you want to stay away from there. That road there is Interstate 30 and it goes to Fort Worth and it goes by the bulk mail center where I worked until I retired. Now you go south on this road, I-35 and I live down that way in Oak Cliff, a lot of black people live down that way and my family has been there for generations," he said.

"Thank you. I feel like I know where I am a little better now. You know I didn't ask your name," she said.

16

"Robert Jones."

"Monique Devareaux," she said shaking his hand.

"If you need anything, I'll be here on Tuesdays and Thursdays," he offered.

On the sixth day in the shelter Monique and Sonja boarded a bus that was taking a group of evacuees on a shopping excursion. It was taking them to an outlet mall in Grapevine, which was north of Dallas/Fort Worth International Airport. As they were walking through the mall, Sonja saw an outfit in a store that was denim with a tight top and small low riser shorts that would leave her midriff exposed.

"Do you like that outfit?" Monique asked.

"Well, some of my friends dress that way, but my momma would kick my butt if she saw me in something like that."

"You're eighteen and with the money we just got, we were going to get some clothes anyway," Monique said.

"Yeah, I know, but I'd better get some regular jeans. When my folks find me, I'd at least be able to wear them again. I even sneak around my momma to smoke a cigarette."

After Sonja bought some jeans they continued walking until Monique was transfixed by a gown in the window of a designer outlet store. They looked at it through the window. It was floor length with a combination of imported lace and silk. Thin straps were at the shoulders and the color was a muted red. Next to the gown was a pair of jeweled lace sandals.

"You would look good in that," Sonja said.

"You think so?"

"Let's, go in," Sonja said.

"I don't think so. I don't want to waste anybody's time."

Sonja grabbed Monique by the hand and pulled her into the store.

To her surprise the clerk took the gown off of the display and told her to try it on with the shoes.

Monique stepped out of the dressing room and looked into the floor length mirror and the image was incongruous. She fit the dress perfectly and her feet looked elegant in the shoes. She felt out of place without makeup, hairstyle or a manicure. She hurried back to the dressing room and put her clothes back on and cried a little but pulled herself back together before going back out. It was too emotional to see herself that way and feel that it was a fairy-tale to think she could wear such a gown and truly belong in that type of environment.

Soon afterward they made their way back to the parking lot, loaded onto the bus and went back to the shelter.

It was the tenth day at the shelter and Sonja came running up to Monique, "I found my family. They're in Houston with some of my cousins and coming to get me tomorrow!"

"That's great, Sonja," Monique said as she stood to embrace her.

"Come with us," Sonja said.

"Oh, no I couldn't, it's going to be hard enough with extra people in the house," Monique replied. "I'll be fine, give me a phone number so we can keep in touch."

"I'm going to miss you," Sonja said. "I don't know what I would have done without you looking after me. What are you going to do?"

"Everything will work out for me, I'm going to a couple of job fairs and with my money I bought some clothes, I'll be okay," Monique assured.

One thing she knew for sure is that she would soon be alone again. The next day Sonja's father and cousin showed up and they thanked her profusely for taking care of her. Sonja gave her one last embrace and then Monique watched as their car disappeared into the distance. About an hour later one of the volunteers came around and called her.

Monique went over to the administration station and the lady named Brenda said, "Miss. Devareaux a group of ladies want to take some mature women out for a day of beautification and you came to mind."

"What's a day of beautification?" Monique asked.

"Well, they're talking about taking you to getting your hair styled, makeup, nails done and maybe a spa treatment. They know in this environment you don't get to do the things you were able to do before the storm and it's their way of giving back. Are you interested?" Brenda asked.

"You bet I am. My hair is a mess. When are they coming?" she asked.

"Tomorrow, about nine in the morning, just meet me up here," Brenda instructed.

Now this was going to be something to look forward to. Monique always tried to look her best but given the circumstances it was good enough to try and remain clean and presentable. She could hardly sleep that night in anticipation of getting out of that shelter, seeing other parts of the city and meeting someone new.

The next morning she was at the station along with eight other women and a group of very beautiful women approached and introduced themselves. One of them named Prentice was a stunning black woman and she came over to Monique and shook her hand.

"Hi, I'm Prentice."

"Monique Devareaux."

"Nice to meet you Monique, I like that name. I guess it's you and me today, let's get out of here," Prentice said.

Monique followed Prentice out of the arena and they talked as they walked along. She had adjusted to the higher Dallas temperatures but the lower humidity was a good tradeoff.

"I can't begin to imagine how hard it's been given everything that has happened since Hurricane Katrina hit. I thought getting out of here and getting your hair and nails done and spending a day away would do some good for your spirit," Prentice said.

"It has been very tough being in a strange place and I really appreciate this, but I feel kind of strange having someone do this for me," Monique said.

"Don't even think about it, this is what Americans should do for each other and especially what women should do for other women," Prentice replied.

As they approached her BMW z4, Monique got the impression these women were not your run of the mill volunteer group. She couldn't help but think of her faithful Ford Mustang submerged underwater back home as she settled into the passenger seat. If it had been in better condition then she could have gotten out of harm's way and her grandmother would still be alive. The area they drove into was populated by small boutiques with designer names she knew but didn't use. She had a feeling she wasn't going to the corner beauty salon. A few minutes later they entered an exclusive spa and Prentice went to her stylists and told them to give Monique the full treatment. She sat in the chair next to Prentice and the process began.

Five hours later after a hair style, massage, wax, makeup, manicure and facial peel a full length mirror revealed a vision that she had not seen in years. Prentice was taken aback and just stared at her.

"Monique, you are stunning, look at yourself," Prentice said.

Monique blushed and smiled the widest smile and started to cry in buckets.

"Thank you ladies, I'll see you later," Prentice said to the staff at the spa as they left.

After getting in her car, "What's wrong, Monique?"

"I'm sorry, I just haven't seen myself like that in a long time and it reminded me of my mother. It was awful, I was dirty, hungry and smelled terrible from waiting for help for days and didn't think I would look this way again. I don't know what I'm going to do, I have nothing and no family here," she said.

"Don't worry, things have a way of working themselves out" Prentice said.

Prentice then took a leap of faith and drove over to her house and they entered. She made a call to the shelter and told them Monique was spending the night at her home. She didn't really know why she took this step with someone she knew nothing about. It could be a grievous error in judgment because this woman was a blank slate with her background information drowned in the water from the levee breach. One thing she did know was sometimes you had to take a chance on someone.

"Prentice, why are you doing this for me? I mean you don't know me at all and I don't want to be a burden on you…" Monique said before Prentice cut her off.

"You're right, I don't know you, but sometimes you have to have faith in something other than what you know as absolutes. Let's sit down and get to know each other. You don't seem to be someone that should be stuck in a shelter, not that anyone should, but being there was not your choice. I have been more than blessed in my life and if I can help someone, I will," Prentice declared.

Monique was stunned and just stared at her with her month open and said, "Thank you."

"Look, I know the first impression you have of me is of this socialite that is out keeping herself busy with various projects, but that's just on the surface. I grew up in Dallas and nowhere near here. The projects I grew up in were in a tough area and you had to be able to handle yourself pretty well to survive. I can slip back into that mode if I need to, just last week some woman cut in front of me at my favorite barbeque joint on Beckley Avenue. When I got through cursing her out, she went to the back of the line."

"Really, so you can bring out the claws if you have to?" Monique said.

"You got that right," Prentice replied.

But now she was feeling Monique out as to her potential and how worthy she was of a substantial investment of time and resources.

Monique then looked around at her surroundings and realized this was no ordinary home but a near palace. She started to wonder exactly who her benefactor really was in this city. The rich marble flooring, elaborate molding, ceiling treatment and fabric textured walls gave her thoughts of this room exceeding the worth of her old home. Massive chandeliers, granite countertops and other ornate furnishings were both fascinating and intimidating for someone in her newly reduced state of existence. Over the last two weeks Monique had noticed Dallas was a city where the rich and poor crossed paths, but didn't really interact with each other.

"Prentice, I don't mean to pry or seem nosy, but your home is like nothing I've ever seen, it's beautiful, what do you do for a living? I'm sorry that sounds so terrible, doesn't it?" Monique said.

"I know this is not exactly the cottage on the corner. My husband is Harry Grayson, CEO of Grayson Micro Technologies, and fortunately that affords us a very nice lifestyle," Prentice commented.

"The, Harry Grayson? I read about him in business school, and his company made some of the chips in the testing instruments I used to sell," Monique commented.

"So you were in high technology sales and did you complete your business degree?" Prentice inquired.

"Yes, I did. I have a Bachelor's of Science in Business Administration. I also worked for three years as a regional sales representative for Krovac Testing Systems, until I met my ex-boyfriend. He convinced me to give up my career and move in with him," Monique informed.

"You know I designed some custom chips for some of Kovacs products when I used to work at Tex Micro," Prentice recalled.

"You designed some chips, what did you use to do?" Monique asked.

"Well I have a Masters in Electrical Engineering and worked in multilayer substrate design before I married Harry. That's how we met as we were both at an industry conference in Las Vegas," Prentice informed.

"When I first saw you this morning, I didn't think there goes an Electrical Engineer," Monique said laughing for the first time since crawling through that roof.

"It's good to see a smile out of you, because I know there hasn't been much to laugh about lately," Prentice said. "Let me show you around and where you can sleep for the night."

During the tour Monique drank in the surroundings. She made mental notes of the things that really tickled her fancy for later reference in the event she could do the same thing if she ever got that opportunity. With the occupants both having their roots in technology, the house was awash in hidden electronics. The lights came off and on whenever you entered and exited a room. Her furnishings were contemporary with black marble table tops and soft leather surfaced couches with muted gold toned lamps. A huge crystal chandelier commanded the main entry and one wall opposite the foyer had been transformed into a massive floor to ceiling aquarium. A variety of colorful tropical fish populated the waters and a group of small yellow fish darted back and forth in unison. The hallways had small lights around the baseboards like in an airplane so you could follow the hallways in the dark without turning a light on. The stairs had similar lights along the steps. When the tour was over they were standing out by the pool house, which at eleven hundred square feet was larger than her house under water in New Orleans. She felt the distance between her and Prentice widen as the ultimate in have and have not. Yet this did seem to give her optimism she could reach new heights. Prentice told her of her humble beginnings in the West Dallas Housing Projects to where she was now. It was not too late to go beyond her imagination.

When they entered the house again the telephone rang and Prentice answered. She told a friend to come over for a visit because there was someone she wanted her to meet. About thirty minutes later the housekeeper announced her guest had arrived. An attractive oriental woman dressed in black leather pants and a red leather top trimmed in lace walked into the room. Monique could only gaze in amazement and she introduced herself as Kendra and reached out and shook her hand.

Kendra was a kindred spirit of Prentice as she grew up as the child of Chinese immigrants in the Chinatown section of San Francisco. She spent many of her young years in the back of restaurants her parents worked in until they managed to open their own place. Kendra developed an interest in ballet that eventually led her to Dallas and a spot with the local professional troupe. After hanging up her performance slippers she opened a studio and this is where she met her husband whose daughter was one of her students. Kendra also acted as a sounding board for Prentice to confirm or deny her instincts about certain issues and the issue of the day was Monique.

"Well, Monique it's good to meet you. I'm Kendra. You seem to have made quite an impression on Prentice and that's no small task," Kendra stated. "Well for one thing you are a beautiful woman and that can only help you out in the grand scheme of things."

"Thank you, you look very nice yourself," Monique replied.

"I know I dress a little different but it gets the point across," Kendra replied.

"Have a seat Kendra. Monique and I have been getting acquainted and it seems we have a connection through high technology. She used to sell products that had some of Grayson's chips in them," Prentice related. "She was in the hurricane. We spent the day together and are finding out a lot about each other."

"If she was in technology sales, then maybe you should talk to Harry about any open sales positions or training programs in the company. I'll bet he wouldn't mind having someone with brains and beauty representing the organization. I think Monique could get through doors of a lot of executives that would do business with the company."

In that moment Prentice had received a confirmation from her confidant to move forward with the time investment in Monique which could just as easily have gone the other way. This brief exchange would start her on a path as different from her past as she could find.

"You know Kendra, sometimes I forget how intelligent you are under that leather and lace, that's a good idea," Prentice said.

Kendra turned and looked at Monique and said sarcastically, "You know some bitches just can't give a complement without being a wise ass," she then looked at Prentice and they both burst into laughter.

Monique didn't know what kind of reaction to have being new to the dynamics between these two women.

"Don't worry about us, we're really close and might say anything to each other, don't let it bother you," Kendra said.

"What about it, Monique? Would you like for me to ask Harry about a job in sales?" Prentice asked.

"I wouldn't know how to thank you. I wouldn't let you down and it would mean so much to get an opportunity to get back on my feet and start over," Monique commented.

"It's settled, he'll be back in town in a couple of days and I'll get it set up," Prentice said.

"Oh thank you. I've got to get some clothes and I don't have a resume...," Monique said.

"Stand up for a minute," Kendra commanded.

Monique looked at Prentice and then stood as Kendra walked around her and said, "She looks to be about your size within an inch or two, don't you have some business clothes she could use since you've become a lady of leisure these days?"

"You know you're right, I think I have just the thing," and Prentice left and came back with a business suit with a skirt, jacket and top that was one of her favorites when she was working.

She gave it to Monique and said, "Go ahead and try it on."

Monique looked at it and went to the nearest bathroom and changed. She undressed, looked at herself in the mirror and noticed she looked better than she had in a long time with her hair styled and a fresh manicure. She tried on the clothes and was amazed at how well they fit. The top was a little too large as Prentice was better endowed than she was but for the most part the fit was perfect.

Monique stepped into the room where Kendra and Prentice were seated and said, "How does it look?"

"You look great," Prentice exclaimed.

"Shoes, let her put on your shoes," Kendra said to Prentice.

Prentice kicked off her heels and gave them to Monique and she slipped them on. Kendra raised an eyebrow and told Monique to have a seat and cross her legs like she was in the lobby area of the company waiting on an interview. The skirt was about an inch above the knee and the four inch heels accentuated the calf muscles in her legs.

Kendra pretended to walk in like she was the interviewer, looked over at Monique and said, "You're hired."

"Look I don't think getting hired is going to be the issue, keeping all of those men from trying to fuck you is going to be the problem," Kendra laughed.

"My god, Kendra, what won't you say?" Prentice remarked.

"Well it's true, you know how it is when a good looking woman is in the business world. My husband tried to get into my pants for five years and for four of those he was still married and picking his daughter up from ballet class," Kendra said. "Prentice you know they were after you too, so don't play dumb with me."

"Okay, I'll admit it, I had my fair share of propositions," Prentice said. "What about you Monique, were there any hounds after you?"

"Well my last boyfriend was a customer of mine and he just didn't stop until he got what he wanted and talked me into moving in with him. Everything was fine until he decided to go back to his wife and kids," Monique said.

"Ah, he was married," Kendra replied. "You have to know how to handle that kind. I wouldn't even give my husband the time of day while he was still married. After four years he came to me and said, 'I'm not married now, will you talk to me?' Only then would I say more than two words to him. I was not going to be a side dish, it's either the main course or stick to you're current diet. You've got potential in this town, but you need a little guidance."

"Monique, let me ask you something, when you were with your boyfriend, did you think about how his wife and children felt about the situation?" Prentice asked.

"Well, it did bother me for a while, but he was so persistent I thought it must have been mutual for him to leave his family for me and figured his wife had moved on. That why I was so shocked when he moved out and left me in the lurch in Chicago. That's when I moved back to New Orleans with my grandmother."

"You chose the wrong guy, that's all. That guy didn't have the ability to leave his family and move on without being destroyed financially. He came to a decision point. He could have lost both you and his wife and still would have been struggling. That's why a woman like you, with your assets, has to be more selective and could live like this," Kendra said while gesturing around the room. "Stop thinking with your heart and eyes and start thinking with your head, it's just as easy to be with a man of means as it is with a handsome face, and looks fade."

"What do you mean a woman like me? What do I have to offer that a wealthy man would want?" Monique inquired.

"Monique, look in the mirror, you are a very beautiful woman. You carry yourself well, you're educated and you have a quality about you men will gravitate to," Prentice said. "Don't put yourself in the discount section when you could be in luxury goods. It's all about attitude and who you associate with."

"Bring her to the museum tomorrow for the charity auction to benefit Hurricane Katrina survivors. Don't worry no one will know you are one of the evacuees," Kendra said. "Lend her that black strapless gown with the thigh high split and those silver backless heels."

"The one Harry told me not to put on again after that football player was putting the moves on me?" Prentice asked.

"Exactly, that's the one," Kendra replied.

"We may have to pry Saul Epstein off of her if she wears that," Prentice said.

"I'll handle that fat asshole, he only propositions Asian women. One day I'll get even with him for asking me to sneak off to the steam room, with my husband and his wife right around the corner," Kendra fumed. "Anyway, I've got to get out of here, my husband's back in town and I promised him a good fuck tonight. See you later."

Monique was speechless and said, "I've never known anyone like Kendra. Where did you meet her?"

"I met Kendra after I moved here with Harry at one of the charity balls and she made such an impact on me that we became fast friends. She is the only person I can say whatever I want and get a raw honest response," Prentice said. "She is pretty much a self made woman and plays by her own rules and doesn't let anyone determine what she does."

"How about it, you want to go to that auction?" Prentice inquired.

"Sure, I do, but I will feel strange knowing the benefit is for people in my situation without revealing who I am," Monique said. "I just remembered, I do have my resume' saved on one of those job search websites if I could get on the internet then I could print it off."

"No problem, come into my office and I'll log you on and you can pull it up and print it out," Prentice said as she led Monique into her office and logged her onto the internet.

Images of the horrors of the hurricane were the first thing Monique saw as the websites came up. The home pages of the internet service providers showed people being pulled from rooftops, wading in water, dying in the heat and begging for help from huge crowds. All of her raw emotions came flooding back and she was mentally up on the roof again waiting for rescue.

Prentice recognized the look on her face as the same one she had when she ran outside to her father when he was shot after getting off the bus when she was a young girl. She grabbed Monique and held her until she could pull herself back together. This was the first realization Monique had, that at any time, she could be transported back to that rooftop moment regardless of where she was in life.

Three

Monique opened her eyes in the luxuriously appointed room Prentice had her sleep in that night. Instead of a cot she slept on a pillow top mattress. The massive four poster king sized bed was so tall she almost had to jump onto it. While wrapped in silk sheets, it felt like this was the way she should be living. She knew this was a temporary arrangement and she needed to make the best of this opportunity. She had always heard luck happened to those that are prepared when opportunity came along. She had seen many posters stating that hanging on walls when she was in sales and it was going to be put to the test.

She got up, took a bath and put on her jeans she wore the day before.

Monique went into the kitchen and the housekeeper, Rose, said, "Mrs. Grayson is out by the pool having breakfast, do you want sausage or bacon with your eggs and pancakes?"

"I'll take bacon, thank you," Monique said feeling a little self conscious.

"I will bring some coffee out to you," Rose said.

Monique turned and went to the covered area by the pool and greeted Prentice. When she exited, the blazing Texas sun was already beating down on the parched Dallas area that had yet to receive relief from the drought. She needed to invest in a pair of sunglasses as a practical matter as September was still a very hot and sunny month in this part of the state.

"Good morning, Monique, how did you sleep last night?" Prentice asked.

"That was the best sleep I have had in weeks," Monique replied. "Is this your everyday life?"

"This is it," Prentice said.

"Wow, it's hard to explain how different this feels compared to what I've gone through or even my life before the storm. How long did it take you to adjust to this kind of lifestyle?" Monique asked.

"It took a while because I was accustomed to doing everything for myself, I mean washing clothes, shopping for food, cleaning, you name it. When my father was paralyzed after being shot and robbed, I outworked everyone, won a scholarship and got a dream job. I was very self-sufficient and it was hard to allow people to do things for me. This is a long way from where I came from, but now it's my new normal and I understand most people don't live this way. I know I'm fortunate and count my blessings," Prentice said.

"How can someone like me, get to a life approaching this, I mean until I met you and then Kendra, it never crossed my mind to even imagine living like this. I know both of your husbands are very accomplished. What attracted them to you or did you go after them?" Monique questioned.

"Well it's different for everyone. For Kendra and me, we were very independent and making our own way in the world. In fact I was debating with Harry about something when he asked me out to dinner. I think it was a combination of strength, intelligence and attractiveness that came together. The last thing on my mind was finding a husband. I was trying to put him in his place for a comment he made to me about how chip designers used technology as a crutch. In the middle of this debate he introduced himself and made a date with me," Prentice said.

"So, it's not about chasing anyone it's about being yourself and that was the attraction," Monique stated.

"That's part of it, but if you're not in the right place it may not matter how you are. Like we said yesterday, you need to be around the right people. You can't attract a thoroughbred at the glue factory. You will see tonight at the museum and after meeting some of my other friends, that being in the right environment can pay big dividends," Prentice said.

"What if someone asks me who I am, and what I do?" Monique asked.

"Just say, I am an associate of Harry and Prentice Grayson and I'm in town visiting for a while. If they ask what you do, then say you are exploring a business venture with Harry's firm. Everything you're telling them is true. You will also find that someone new and attractive on the scene will attract some attention from men and from some women trying to protect their turf," Prentice advised.

Monique started to develop an early case of nerves and Prentice told her not to worry, relax and just be herself. This event that wasn't even on the horizon twenty-four hours ago was now the debutante ball, prom and homecoming dance all rolled into one. She would be there in a borrowed gown hundreds of miles away from home.

"Hey, I'm going to drop by Kendra's before we get ready for the auction tonight. Do you want to come along? It not too far and it'll break up the day."

"Yeah, that way I can see a little more of the city."

Kendra lived about twenty minutes away in an area north of Dallas along Interstate 75. She wanted space and her husband sold his former home and had this place custom built around Kendra's exact tastes. She wanted some breathing room to create a near tropical garden environment with an oriental flair.

As they drove up to Kendra's home and walked to the dual black doors Monique thought about what was on the other side. The woodwork on the doors was very ornate and the massive handles were gold tone metal. This place was Kendra's expression of who she was, with a small bridge over a pond area leading to the front doors. Brightly colored tropical fish were swimming about with the entire area framed by lush green vegetation.

"Wow, look at this place. It's like going to another country," Monique remarked.

"This is her way of staying connected to her culture. Just wait until we go inside."

Prentice pressed the doorbell and soon the housekeeper opened the door.

"Mrs. Grayson, how are you?"

"I'm doing fine Cindy. This is Monique."

"It's nice to meet you. Just go to the parlor. She's waiting for you there."

"Thanks," Prentice said as they started walking inside.

They made their way down the hallway of the Feng Shui inspired interior to a sitting area. Outside was a vegetation lined walkway leading to a pond populated with waterfowl. This was a very quiet room and then Kendra came around a corner and gave Prentice a hug.

"Monique, I'm glad you came. Let me show you around," Kendra said.

Monique was thrilled because Kendra fascinated her with her boldness and she felt seeing her home would give her a better idea of who she was.

The house was magnificent but very minimalist in a way. There was not an abundance of furniture but what was there was original and very expensive. Her bathroom was hers alone because her husband had his own. The same went for closets as each had their own. Her closet was almost a living space with a sitting area, sound system and desk.

"I designed this closet this way because when I am getting dressed or need to escape, this is almost like an isolation chamber I can enter and shut out the rest of the world."

"Let me show you my favorite place."

Kendra led them outside to a pond connected to the water around the house and had small streams flowing throughout the property in a continuous fashion. At the edge of the water was a covered sitting area with lush vegetation all around. There were ducks, swans and geese in the water and a variety of local birds in the trees and shrubs around the edge. Green aquatic plants complimented bright tropical foliage with large red and yellow flowers.

"I can sit here for hours and read, meditate and sometimes I fall asleep because it's so peaceful. It's so hot in Texas that I added a misting system to keep it cooler in the summer."

"This is really something. You built all of this when you got married?" Monique asked.

"This was one of my conditions. I wasn't moving into a house built for some other woman. I have a unique arrangement with my husband. I get to do what I want, when I want, as long as it doesn't cause any issues for him or his business and as long as he is being taken care of. Let me tell you, he shouldn't have any complaints."

"Is this just an understanding between you and your husband?" Monique asked.

"It's written into my prenuptial agreement. He wanted me, so you have to give to get."

They proceeded back inside and Monique went to use the bathroom. She was on her way back to the parlor and overheard Prentice talking to Kendra.

"John ran into this actress while we were in Vegas and they hooked up. She told him she was in a network that paid her ten grand to meet men all over the country for encounters."

"No shit, did he try to find out if she knew who ran the operation?" Kendra inquired.

"He asked, and she only knew about her agent and that's it."

"This thing is making me nervous, these last few months can't go fast enough," Kendra commented.

Monique walked around the corner and entered the room.

"I guess we need to get back so we can be at our best for tonight," Prentice said.

"I really love your house," Monique said.

"Thank you. I'll see you guys tonight." Kendra said.

On the drive back to Prentice's home Monique tried to act natural, but she was wound as tight as a spring. Between what she heard these two women talking about and the upcoming auction, she couldn't have been more nervous. She didn't know what this network was about but wondered if she was being targeted in some way to be a part of this operation. She thought she would play it by ear, but if any conversations went in that direction, she would be out of there in an instant. From what she heard, it seemed they were anxious to end whatever they were involved in and that made her breath a little easier.

All too soon it was time for the charity auction and her hair was perfect and frankly she felt a little self conscious about the split of the dress than ran to mid thigh on her right side. This was a limousine event. It pulled up to the circular driveway and the driver opened the door, Prentice and then Monique slipped into the back seat and sat down for the trip to the arts district. Monique thought this must be how Cinderella felt; she only hoped at the end of the night there wouldn't be a pumpkin moment to spoil the experience. When they stepped into the museum and went to the floor for the pre-auction gathering Prentice stopped. Monique also paused.

Then to her surprise a voice rang out announcing, "Mrs. Prentice Grayson and Miss Monique Devareaux."

Clearly stunned by hearing her name announced Monique went forward following Prentice into the group of evening gowned women and tuxedoed men. A glass of Champaign was presented on a tray and she took one and had a sip. This was the first alcohol to touch her lips in months as her grandmother was a strict

Baptist and the house was an alcohol free zone. This reminded her of how many sensations she had to become reacquainted with after a prolonged time. She turned to her side and realized Prentice was on the other side of the room and a small sense of panic sat in. Dallas was full of the rich and those pretending to be rich. Tonight she was among the genuine articles.

The men were mostly white and in their fifties or older with a few young lions mixed in and there were plenty of creative combovers, hair implants and toupees in evidence among the more senior group. The women were a mix of original spouses with ages closely matched to their husbands and newer trade-up wives fifteen to twenty years younger than their husbands. Except for Prentice, Kendra and a younger Hispanic woman the profile of the women matched the men in ethnic makeup. The men were attired in tuxedos and the women were draped in designer gowns and adorned in jewels. An abundance of robust blond hair was the order of the day and Monique marveled at how they maintained their volume under the heat stress here in Dallas.

"Hello, I'm Doris Brickman and did they say your name was Monique?"

"Yes, I'm Monique Devareaux."

When she turned she noticed Doris was a very attractive woman in her fifties. She was an inch or so shorter than Monique but still fairly trim and fit. Her hair was of the larger volume blond variety. Monique could detect a slight hint of dark roots but the dye job was the best money could buy.

"What brings you to our city? I haven't seen you here before," Doris inquired.

"I'm an associate of Harry and Prentice Grayson and was visiting the area," Monique replied.

"Hello, Doris, nice to see you, I need to borrow Monique for a minute" Prentice said as she took Monique by the arm and said, "I have some friends I want you to meet."

Prentice then introduced Monique to her friends Randi, Jean, Barbara, Sandra, Ruth and Joyce. Kendra soon came over and joined them. Soon that group dispersed and other introductions were made.

Monique found herself looking over a couple pieces of art when a male voice slightly startled her, "Hello, I'm Stanley Brickman, welcome to Dallas."

"Monique Devareaux, how do you know I'm not from here?" she inquired.

"I asked around, and I know you are a friend of the Grayson's, and a lovely one at that," he said.

"Did you say your last name is Brickman, I met a Doris Brickman earlier are you related?" Monique asked.

"That would be my better half, my wife," Stanley replied.

It was then that Monique noticed even though Stanley Brickman was at least twenty years older than her twenty-eight years, he had quite an angular and athletic figure. He was about six feet tall with broad shoulders and a tapered waist. Remembering what Kendra had said she took a surprising route with her next statement.

"Your wife, I see, does she mind that you talk with strange women when she is not around?" she asked.

"Do you consider yourself strange, in what way?" Stanley remarked.

"Only in the sense that I am unfamiliar to you," Monique said. "Nice to meet you," she said as she walked away.

Somehow she remembered how her mother walked and arched her back and her leg would emerge from the deep split in her dress with every other step. She could feel his eyes on her ass as she walked away. Now another feeling she hadn't thought about in weeks was invading her thoughts and that was when would be the next time a man would touch her in a way that counted. It wasn't just when the storm hit that normal thinking ceased, but the week before was filled with constant anxiety as everyone watched endless reports of the projected landfall.

Later that evening the auction started and some displaced citizens from New Orleans were in the room and they were introduced to the assembled group.

There was one girl there Monique recognized from the shelter and she looked her straight in the eyes but given her appearance and the setting there was not a hint she knew she was an evacuee just like her. Monique stayed in character and sensed even though she had nothing to be ashamed of, it was best not to tip her hand as to her evacuee status yet. That time would come, but right now that information would be used to marginalize her as someone desperate to improve their lot in life.

As the event was starting to draw to a close she was again looking at a piece that caught her eye and heard two women chatting on the other side of the display where she was standing.

"Doris, earlier I saw that woman with Prentice Grayson walking back from down this way and a minute or so later your husband came back from the same direction."

"Well Alice, I'm sure it's just a coincidence. Can't two people walk in the same direction anymore?" Doris replied.

"Look Doris, you know how I am about this kind of thing. Saul tries to deny it but his tongue hangs out every time that Kendra walks by. I not a fool, I know he's been screwing around for years when he went on those trips to Asia. I'm just telling you to watch your ass. I can tell by the way she acts that she isn't used to being around our kind of people. Plus she's hanging around with Prentice, Miss Ghetto Queen," Alice said.

"Well she seems like a nice woman. She's white, not that it means anything," Doris said.

"You remember what happened to Marsha. That little slut Randi started showing up and next thing you know, she's out and Randi's in." Alice remarked.

"You might have a point. I'll keep an eye out for this Monique and see if she keeps hanging around our events. I guess that's how it starts."

"Now that's the most sense you've made all night."

Monique saw them walk by and went in the opposite direction, startled by what she had just overheard. Now she was wound up again and needed to somehow relieve this tension. She didn't ask to be here and now was being viewed like she was purposely crashing their private party.

Finally the auction was over and it was time to leave for the night. Instead of going home, Prentice told the driver to go by a jazz club she went to occasionally and when they arrived, Kendra was there also.

They settled at a table and ordered a couple of drinks.

"How did you like the auction?" Kendra asked.

"It was really nice, I had a good time," Monique said.

"You were a hit, the men couldn't stop talking about you," Prentice said.

"Really, who told you that?" Monique said.

"They did, I had three guys ask for your number and wanting to know if you were married," Prentice said. "Let me tell you, the wives had their antennas up for the new competition."

"You know, Stanley Brickman said something to me when I was alone and looking at a painting," Monique said.

"Stan Brickman said something to you, he doesn't talk much to anyone," Kendra said. "What did he say?"

"He introduced himself and said he had asked around and knew I was a friend of the Grayson's and a lovely one at that," Monique said.

"Oh shit, if Doris finds out then it's going to be hell to pay," Prentice said.

"I heard some woman named Alice telling Doris she saw me walking and then saw Stanley coming from the same direction a few minutes later," Monique said.

"Doris is about five years older than Stan and is very paranoid he is going to dump her for someone younger. That's why she was the first to grab you when I left, she wanted to see if you were a threat to her," Prentice said.

"Stanley made his money early, before the dot com crash, Doris was at the time his Director of Sales, and forty-five and he was forty. He sold his online company for close to a billion dollars and she was a very vibrant and sexy forty-five years old. The next thing you know they walked down the aisle. Now he's forty-eight and she's fifty-three and hasn't kept up with him in the fitness department and is feeling vulnerable. Someone like you shows up and her alarm bells go off like a siren. He is very private and the fact he came up to you is a big deal," Kendra said.

"Oh god, I don't feel like dealing with Doris. I think I have a lunch invitation coming and she is going to pump the hell out of me about Monique," Prentice said.

"Hey, I didn't mean to cause a problem by going to the auction," Monique said.

"That's not your fault, you can't help it that you got these guys' hormones all revved up. At least you know your stuff is still working, and working well," Kendra said.

"Miss, the gentleman over by the bar sent this drink over for you," the waiter said as he placed the drink in front of Monique.

All three of the women turned and there was a handsome mid thirties man sitting by the bar.

"What are we, chopped liver?" Kendra said.

"Maybe it's these gaudy wedding rings that are causing the problem," Prentice said.

"Oh yeah, that too," Kendra said laughing.

The next thing they knew the man was by their table and introduced himself as Barrett Austin.

"I don't want to be too forward, but could you join me for a moment at the bar, I would like to get to know you better," Barrett said.

Monique looked at Prentice and got a gesture to go ahead.

Kendra looked over and said, "She probably hasn't had any in weeks, look at those thighs, she could probably break him in two about right now. The first guy that gets hold of her, with all of that pent up energy had better be ready."

"Kendra, is that all you can think about?" Prentice said.

"No, it's not all I think about, but if you didn't have company, I could do more than just think about it." Kendra said.

"Well, you know we are keeping our thing low key, so hold your horses," Prentice said.

Monique came back to the table and said, "This guy is really nice, but I think he's hiding something, because he's kind of elusive about details. He wants me to take a ride with him, I don't know."

"If he's being mysterious, that may not be all bad," Kendra said.

"What do you mean?" Monique said.

"He wants to do you, how do you feel about that?" Kendra asked.

"I don't know him, he could be a nut or something," Monique said. "I'm in a city I know nothing about, this could be dangerous."

"How do you feel?" Prentice asked.

"I feel fine," Monique said.

"You're a healthy young woman and how long has it been since you've been with a man sexually," Prentice asked.

"About two months, I'm not used to talking about stuff like this so openly," Monique said.

"The key is to get him on your turf and that takes the danger away," Kendra said. "Take my limo and my driver will take you on a one hour tour of the city. The glass behind the driver is private, that way you're in your territory and see where it goes. There's a panic button in the ceiling above the back seat if things get out of hand and it will alert the driver if something is wrong."

Kendra pulled out her cell phone and called her driver to tell him someone was coming out to use the limo.

"We'll be here when you get back," Prentice said. "You sure you want to go with him?"

"I'm sure," Monique said.

With that Monique left with Barrett Austin and went out to Kendra's limo and got into the back seat

"How much did that guy cost?" Kendra said.

"I dropped a grand on him. He had some great reviews," Prentice said.

"With all of the extra money we're making from the network, that's nothing," Kendra remarked. "Yeah, you could tell she needs a good fuck, it wasn't that cold in the museum and her nipples were about to explode through that dress. No wonder the men's tongues were hanging out. I just hope she doesn't hit the panic button with the heels of her shoes or feet."

Prentice and Kendra both laughed and took more sips from their drinks.

As the limo drove off Barrett pulled Monique close to him and kissed her deeply. It had been a while since she felt a man's lips on hers. She certainly knew how to respond and kissed him back with all of her might. He slid his hands up the slit in her dress and slipped the other hand inside her top and pressed the bare flesh of her breasts.

"Barrett I'm not sure we should be doing this," she said feebly with her body betraying every word she spoke.

Barrett ignored the weak protest and continued his attention to her most sensitive areas and this sent electric shocks through her. She knew this was going to be the end of another drought and was determined to quench this thirst tonight. His hands expertly removed her underwear and slid the top of her dress down to her waist. She removed his pants and slid them down and helped him put on his protection, at least she maintained that amount of sanity as her head and heart raced against each other. Finally with one motion he went where no man had been in at least two months and now felt as if she had totally reentered life as a complete woman. This was urgent business she was catching up on and he had to be braced for her reclamation of something that had been missing for a while. Finally with sweat dripping from her torso, she moaned in a low tone that she had reached her destination and all manner of tensions were released at that moment. Sorrows, joy and pain flowed through her and were released. Then Monique collapsed onto his body and kissed him deeply. He laid her down on the leather of the seat and started again until she thirst no more.

About fifty minutes after leaving, Monique walked back into the club and went straight to the bathroom to freshen up and then returned to the table.

"What have you been up to?" Prentice asked.

Monique smiled and then laughed, "I hope I didn't mess your dress up, but that was quite a little ride."

"Hey, I understand if you don't want to talk about it," Prentice said.

"That's not it. I've never done anything like that before, but I think I needed it at this point. There were a lot of things held up inside of me that only something like that could release," Monique said.

"Was he any good?" Kendra inquired.

"Well, let's just say he knows his way around a woman without a map," Monique replied. "I don't think he's the relationship type, so this is probably the last time I'll see him, but he is good at some things. You know, it felt like I wasn't completely a woman again until tonight, after being shuttled around like livestock, you lose a sense of yourself. You don't think I'm some kind of slut do you for going off with that guy like that, do you?"

"Look you got what you wanted and he got what he wanted, sounds like a good deal to me," Kendra answered.

"I want to thank you both for being kind to me because you didn't have to. I know I will have to go back to the shelter or somewhere else. These two days have meant the world to me and I won't forget you for what you have done for me," Monique said.

"Well tomorrow, Harry will be back in town and I will ask him about setting up that interview for you next week. I will also ask him about you staying in the pool house. I can't promise anything but I will give it a shot," Prentice said.

"Look if you ask him at the right time he'll have to say yes," Kendra said.

"Kendra, good grief, what else are you going to come up with?" Prentice remarked.

"Well it's true, you know what I'm talking about," Kendra said and they all laughed.

"You can stay at my place tonight, but I've got to take you back to the shelter by noon, because Harry is coming in by two o'clock. How do I get in touch with you?" Prentice asked.

"Just call the administration desk and they will get hold of me," Monique said.

"Here's my cell phone number in case you need to reach me," Prentice said and handed her a card with her number on it. "Let's get out of here and go home."

That night was her last time to revel in sleeping on satin sheets and the pumpkin moment was fast approaching. She woke up around three in the morning and started to the kitchen to get a drink. She noticed how cold the black marble floor felt to her bare feet when she heard Prentice talking on the phone as she walked past the master bedroom. She paused for a minute and listened.

"Kendra you know when John started the network up the plan was to shut it down within two years. I know we're making a lot of money. Yeah, I've made over two million also. It's getting too risky, what if one of the providers slips up and we get exposed. It would be a disaster if we are caught running a high dollar internet prostitution ring. Can you imagine the headlines? The Trophy Wife Network gets exposed. Look I just want this thing to end so we can have our extra stash of money. Exactly, if you add that to our prenuptial payouts, we're golden. My payout is eight million and yours is seven, altogether that's nineteen million with our network money. Who cares what they think, they didn't want us crashing their little party to begin with. Look it's three in the morning and I'll talk to you later."

After hearing this Monique decided she wasn't thirsty after all and quietly went back to her room. She had to keep herself under control and act totally oblivious about what she had heard. There was more going with these people than she ever imagined and this was the second time this business they're in had come up. Obviously they were under a lot of stress from being involved. She could only deduce that their husbands didn't know about this thing at all.

The next day, all too soon she was back at the shelter and she found out they were moving her to another facility that used to be a jail and shutting down the arena site. That night as she slept in what amounted to a jail cell on a stiff cot with cotton sheets, it was hard to remember the two days spent in the lap of luxury. Another day passed by and there still was no word from Prentice about the job interview or pool house. When she was taking a shower on Sunday morning a female voice rang out in the shower.

"Hey, what's your name?" a woman asked.

Monique turned and looked and a stocky dark skinned woman was in the shower also, "I'm Monique, who are you?"

"My name is Melina, but they call me Mel," she said.

"Nice to meet you Mel," Monique said.

"It's not as nice as it could be; it looks like you have a nice little package going for you. There are a lot of things I could do for you to help you out," Mel said.

"I don't know what you're talking about," Monique said.

"A tender little thing like you needs protection, because everybody's gonna be after that sweet stuff," Mel said as she walked over to Monique.

Before she knew what was happening, Monique felt a hand on her right breast and another going between her legs and she jerked away.

"Get the hell away from me," Monique said.

"Come on baby, you know you want this just like I do," Mel said and tried to put her hands on her again.

Monique looked her in the eye and said, "I'm not telling you again to back off."

By now Mel had backed Monique up against the wall of the shower.

"Well what are you going to do, white bitch," Mel said as she approached Monique and pushed up to her and tried to plant a kiss on her lips.

Without saying a word, Monique pushed her back and planted her right knee firmly into Mel's stomach and she slipped and fell to the floor with a thud. Some years ago in Chicago, Monique took a self defense class, but this was the first time she had to use it in a live situation. She also knew she had to get out of this shelter, because Mel seemed like the type to come back on you in the middle of the night while you were sleeping. After getting dressed she saw Mel laid out on a cot pointing at her.

Monique made her way to a phone and dialed Prentice's phone number.

"Monique, is that you?" Prentice said.

"Yes it's me." Monique said.

"I tried to call you but the number is shut down," Prentice said.

"Yeah, they moved us to a new place that used to be a jail. It's across the freeway from the arena on Interstate 35," Monique said.

"I know where that is, look Harry said yes to both things, but he wants to meet you today before he goes out of town next week. How soon can you be ready with all of your stuff so you can move into the pool house?" Prentice asked.

"How soon can you get here, I don't have a lot to take. I'll be ready in an hour and waiting outside. Thanks," Monique said.

It felt like a weight had been lifted off of her shoulders.

"Don't you go to sleep bitch because I'm going to fuck you up," were the chilling words Mel said as she walked by and bumped up against her.

Monique was waiting outside when a silver Bentley pulled up and a distinguished man jumped out from the driver's side and hustled around and grabbed her cloth bag and placed it in the trunk.

"Hi, I'm Harry," he said as he shook her hand.

"I'm Monique," she replied as he held the back door open for her.

"How're you doing girl, it's good to see you again," Prentice said.

"Prentice says you used to be in high tech sales?" Harry asked.

"Yes, I used to sell testing instruments for Krovac out of Chicago," Monique replied.

"They are a good customer of mine, I knew Barry Krovac personally," Harry said, "You made quite an impression on Prentice and that's not easy to do. It took me a long time to have an impact with her and I'm still trying."

"Oh, Harry you know you're the most impressive man I know," Prentice said.

"Tell me anything," Harry replied. "I've got you set up with an interview Tuesday with the head of the custom board division sales and marketing department, I have everything written out at the house. I've told the manager to handle everything himself so it will be held in confidence. That's the division that contracts to manufacture to customer specifications complete assemblies like personal computer motherboards or cell phone main boards. His name is Frank Roberts, he's a good guy and we have a great training program. You can stay in the pool house. I'm having the staff get it ready for you and it'll be good for Prentice to have someone around because I'm constantly traveling and she really likes you a lot."

"I don't know what to say, except thanks for the opportunity," Monique said.

As Harry started to drive off, Monique looked over to the right and saw Mel glaring at her, she waved goodbye and Mel threw her a middle finger salute and yelled a few choice words that couldn't be heard inside the confines of the car.

Monique marveled at her good fortune to meet people like Prentice and Harry and she knew her life was just taken off pause and the play button had been pushed. It was going to be up to her as to what kind of music was going to come out.

Four

"Let me show you the pool house," Prentice said to Monique as she led her around to the back.

When she entered, she saw there were drapes, a kitchen, bedroom area, a full living area, a sound system, flat screen television with satellite hookup and surround sound and a full music system. She literally fell to the floor and cried because she was so taken by the idea that tonight she could actually sleep alone, shower in private and watch television on any channel she chose. Prentice opened the refrigerator and it was stocked with food and drinks, juices, fruit and everything she could think of.

"Oh my god, Prentice where did you come from, I can't imagine anyone doing this for me, I have no words," Monique said.

Just then Harry came by and said, "How do you like it?"

"It's great, thank you. Can I give him a hug?" she asked Prentice.

"Well Harry, can she give you a hug?" Prentice asked Harry.

"My goodness is life this complicated?" he remarked as both Prentice and Monique hugged him.

"Gee, I knew animal magnetism would get me in trouble one of these days," he said as both women released him and started laughing. "I'm going to the golf course and I'll be back a little later."

"Prentice, he is a funny guy with a great sense of humor," Monique commented.

"Well, after a few years, I've heard all of the one-liners, believe me," Prentice said. "I'm going to leave you alone to get settled in and I'm just over there, okay."

After Prentice left, Monique felt a sense of loss and didn't quite know what to do next. One thing she had decided was not to mention to anyone the conversations she overheard Prentice having with Kendra because the less she knew about that the better. She decided to fix a snack and sit down and watch television to catch up on the news and current events. What she found was a never ending cascade of news stories about the aftermath of the disaster along the Louisiana and Mississippi coast and the ruined lives it left behind. How this twist of fate allowed her to be where she was now couldn't have been an accident.

Harry even had a computer system and desk installed so she could get on the internet. She decided to make good use of it to refresh herself on technology and learn about Grayson Micro before she went on her interview two days from now. She also noticed a telephone in the room but realized she really had no one to call. Then she saw a story on television about a satellite viewing program that would allow you to zoom into a specific address. She went to the website and put in the address of her grandmother's house and what she saw was gut wrenching. There was the roof with the hole she had cut her way to freedom through sitting there in plain sight. Every fiber in her body told Monique her grandmother was still under the rubble and one of the nameless legion lost when nature's fury was unleashed in those terrible days. Looking at the house on the screen had a physical effect and she used the bathroom the first time as she vomited from a reaction to seeing the image of her old home. What a whirlwind the last few months had been. She moved back home, was rescued from her rooftop and had a tryst in the back of a limo with a complete stranger. Now it was time to move forward with her new life.

Monique pulled out the purse she had purchased at the discount store and took stock of her remaining resources from the two thousand dollars she got through FEMA. She had a total of fourteen hundred dollars left and wanted to get some things tomorrow to get ready for her interview. She had spent the initial money on a couple of changes of clothes, shoes, personal items and meals when they were taken on shopping excursions from the shelter. Maybe Prentice could take her shopping or she guessed she could take the bus. Right then she was ready to get a good night's sleep.

Bright and early Monday morning she got up and showered before making breakfast and decided to eat outside by the pool. When she walked out of the door she was greeted by Prentice who was having a cup of coffee there as well.

"Good morning, did you sleep well?" Prentice asked.

"Yes I did. I feel great.

"I thought that I would go shopping and pick up a few things before my interview tomorrow, but I have no idea where anything is right now," Monique replied.

"Do you drive?" Prentice asked.

"Yeah, I drive and I've managed to get my license from Louisiana replaced over the last two weeks," Monique replied.

"You can take my Jaguar, I don't drive it much anymore," Prentice said.

"Are you sure? I mean, I'm not used to driving someone else's car," Monique said.

"Cars are one thing we have plenty of as Harry is a bit of a collector. You see that building by the trees. That's his garage for his collection of favorite wheels, as he calls them," Prentice said.

Prentice then told her that going down the street and a few miles down the south toll road was all of the shopping she would ever need. She said she would go with her, but she had a meeting with her group about a project they were involved in.

A couple of hours later, Monique was driving through the gated driveway in her friend's 2003 Jaguar S Type and literally headed into uncharted territory. She decided to stay on the street that ran alongside the toll road to avoid using any more of her money than was necessary. Soon she spotted what she was looking for as the sight of a discount store loomed two streets up. She pulled into the parking lot and found a spot after dodging a few shopping carts. She decided to park near the edge of the lot to reduce the likelihood of anyone dinging the side of the car.

She entered the store and realized for the first time in a while she was completely on her own without a curfew, chaperon, or schedule to keep. It's hard for most people to imagine always being under the control of others. For the last three weeks from the time she was rescued, Monique had been under some form of structured supervision that controlled where she went, when she ate, slept and showered. This shopping trip was her first taste of unstructured freedom since before the storm hit. It must have been somewhat akin to the feeling a newly released prisoner has after exiting the gates after a long incarceration.

Monique bought a few personal items and a new pair of jeans. She wanted something really nice for her interview that would go with the outfit Prentice was lending her for the meeting. She then went to the upscale mall that was a few exits down. She noticed the patrons of this shopping Mecca were decidedly more upscale than the discount store she had just left. The contrast was startling for places to be within two miles of each other they were worlds apart. These shoppers on the whole were crisp, starched and polished. If the women wore jeans they did so fabulously with heels and sandals. These people were refined and manicured which caused her to take stock of her own attire. She had on a pair of her newer jeans, red top and new white athletic shoes. She figured she could fit in well enough to get by for today.

She soon found what she wanted at a leather shop. It was a beautiful portfolio with elegant stitching. She ran her hands over it and noticed the price and winched. One hundred dollars was a lot of money for her to spend on something like this but she took a deep breath and thought this could be her good luck charm. She turned and went to the counter and paid for the portfolio and started to leave when a male voice called to her.

"Is it, Miss Devareaux?" a man said.

"Do, I know you?" Monique inquired.

"Stanley Brickman, we met at the auction," he said.

"Oh yes, Mr. Brickman, I didn't recognize you without your tuxedo," Monique said.

"Please, call me Stan, and I'd recognize you in anything."

"Are you here with your wife shopping?"

"No, my wife is out of town visiting her mother this week, so I decided to shop for some new golf clubs," he replied. "What brings you out today since you're just visiting some friends?"

"I decided to pick up a few things while I was in town, is that okay with you?" Monique replied.

"I'm sorry, look it's almost lunchtime, would you join me, my treat?" Stan asked.

"I don't know, I've really got to get back…," Monique said quite half heartedly.

"I'm just asking since we're both here alone and I thought we could keep each other company, and get to know each other," he said cutting her short.

Monique found herself in a quandary, because her last foray with another woman's husband is one of the reasons she was in her current predicament. She was feeling some powerful vibrations towards this man and decided to get an idea of what his intentions were. She pondered a response. After looking at him in his version of casual with pleated dress pants, brown leather shoes and a short sleeved golf shirt than showcased his toned arm definition her decision was reached.

"Okay, we can go to lunch, but it's just lunch," she said.

"Great, I know just the place, it's on the top floor," he said as they went to the escalator.

They entered a Chinese restaurant on the top level and were shown to a private booth. Monique was surprised at how personable Stan was given how private Prentice and Kendra said he could be. She was careful not to let her guard down with him about her past and true reason for being in town. He was very formal in his mannerisms and speech and it took her a while to become comfortable with his conversational style.

"How long are you going to be in Dallas, Monique?" Stan asked.

"I don't really know, a lot of my trips are open ended until I figure I have all the information I need to make a proper decision," Monique replied.

"You are a very intriguing woman and I would like to get to know you better," Stan said.

"I think you are getting to know me as well as a married man can. Why do you think it should go any farther than that?"

"I didn't mean to imply it should go any farther than something platonic. That would make a presumption about you that is inappropriate and I didn't mean to infer that at all."

"Well what did you mean to infer. How much better could we get to know each other under these circumstances?"

Stan was speechless for a moment and then said, "You know you are one of the most interesting women I have met in a long time. I have a business mixer Wednesday night at the Broadnax hotel in the Crescent room at eight pm, here's an invitation. If you can fit it into your schedule I think you would meet some interesting people there."

Monique took the invitation and placed it in her purse and continued to eat her meal. She felt she had played a card that left it up to her to tip her hand as to the level of interest she had in seeing him again. This could be a game that could blow up in her face if her facade unraveled at the wrong time.

After lunch Monique made her way back to Prentice's house and upon entering the code for the gate she drove up and parked behind the main house. She felt a pang of guilt and wondered if the years of watching her mother seek fulfillment from the promises of men was manifesting itself in learned behavior from her. If it was, she hoped to avoid the negative consequences. For the time being, she had managed to bluff her way out of the situation at the mall. Now she was getting in even deeper with the invitation to the mixer.

"Hello, Miss Devareaux, did you have a good day out?" the housekeeper said.

"Yes I did, thank you."

She went into the pool house and sat down to rub her tired feet because that was the most walking she had done in a long time. After dozing off for a few minutes she heard a knock on the door and got up to look outside and it was Prentice and Kendra.

She opened the door and invited them in and they sat on the love seat across from the couch.

"How was your day?" Prentice asked.

"It was great, I found my way around and managed to end up where I started," Monique replied.

"Did anything exciting happen?" Kendra asked.

"You know of all people, I ran into Stan Brickman at the mall," Monique said.

"Did he recognize you or say something?" Prentice asked.

"Yes, he recognized me, but I didn't remember him until he reminded me we had met before. Then he talked me into having lunch with him at this Chinese restaurant on the top floor of the mall."

"He took you to Jon Chins for lunch? No shit," Kendra remarked. "That place is impossible to get into on short notice."

"Where was Doris?" Prentice inquired.

"He said she was out of town visiting her mother," Monique answered. "Then he invited me to some business mixer at the Broadnax hotel Wednesday night."

"There are people that would kill to go one of those, they're legendary," Prentice said. "Nothing but movers and shakers and a few select outside invited guests."

"What have you done to this guy, Monique? He is like a dog in heat behind you," Kendra said.

"I've only met the man twice, I don't get it, besides I don't know if I'll even go to this mixer thing anyway," she replied.

"On no, you're going. I want to know what goes on in those meetings anyway," Prentice said.

"It looks like Doris had better watch her ass. Stan has somebody we know in his sights," Kendra commented. "Just remember, don't let him off cheaply, he has to work for what you have, after all he's after you and not the other way around."

"Do you think I'm trying to take him from his wife?" Monique questioned.

"That's not the question, the question is, does he want to replace his wife with you," Prentice said.

Monique looked at them in a quizzical manner and was not accustomed to the topic of this conversation taking place so boldly.

"Okay, let's cut the bullshit. Monique, you just went through hell during the last month. Here's a guy worth a billion dollars with his tongue hanging out behind you after only two meetings. He just invited you to an exclusive event. He's trying to see if you can be a possibility in his world, this world we live in, okay. I'm not saying you should throw yourself at him, but play along and see where this goes. You could end up living in the main house instead of the pool house," Kendra said.

"But what about his wife?" Monique asked.

"Fuck her, okay, what I mean is, if he is thinking about moving on, it will happen with you or someone else," Kendra said. "This could be a once in a life-time opportunity and you need to look at it that way."

"But he thinks I'm someone I'm not. If he really knew I was an evacuee with nothing..." Monique exclaimed.

"Look, you are yourself. If things progress, there will be a time you can tell him everything, and it won't matter," Prentice said.

"How do you feel so comfortable talking about a married man as if he was unattached and available, I'm not used to that," Monique said. "I thought I was in love when I met David, but now my eyes are wide open and this feels risky and a little dirty."

"I know what you're feeling and it's natural, but in the social circles we run in, this is par for the course. These are very wealthy people that are used to getting what they want. Sometimes they want something or someone that makes them feel younger than they really are. Doris Brickman knows she is in the danger zone, she's five years older than her husband and he is still a youthful forty-eight years old. That story about her visiting her mother is a load of crap; I hear she is getting a major tune up all over. She went out west for a facelift, and some other nips, tucks and enhancements. If she gets thrown aside she will be sitting pretty with millions from a settlement, and with her upgrades, then she can be a great Cougar," Kendra remarked.

"A Cougar, what the hell is a Cougar?" Monique inquired.

"Monique, a Cougar is an older woman that goes after young men to have a good time," Prentice said. "You know a woman in her forties or fifties snagging some twenty and thirty year old beef for a good roll in the sack, and then move on."

"I must be way out of touch, this is the first time I've heard Cougar used with that meaning," Monique said.

"Well why the hell should the men have all of the fun going after young women, we want something young and firm just like they do, if you get my drift. Women like something young and hard, just like they like something young and tight, fair is fair," Kendra said.

The three women looked at each other and burst out in laughter and rolled on the floor. Just then Harry knocked on the door and came in.

"You three seem to be having a good time. Honey, I'm heading to the airport and I'll see you this weekend," Harry said and Prentice got up and gave him a kiss goodbye. "Monique, good luck on your interview tomorrow, I'm sure you'll do just fine."

Monique covered her mouth and said, "I hope he didn't hear us."

"Don't worry about that, he has a slight hearing problem and wouldn't care anyway," Prentice said.

"Look, I kind of noticed at the auction that quite a few of your husbands are quite a bit older than you are, am I missing something?" Monique asked.

"I wondered when you would point out the obvious. For the lack of a better term, I guess you could say we're trophy wives, not that anything's bad about that, it's just the way it is," Prentice said. "These men are successful and felt like they wanted to show their success in every aspect of life, including having a young woman on their arm. That tells the world when you're rich enough, you can get whatever you want. They can be old, bald, out of shape, in poor health or whatever, but they have a wife that could be on the cover of a fashion magazine. It's the ultimate "in your face" move for a successful man and now some women are getting in on the act."

"That's what we're telling you about Stan Brickman. He may be at that stage when he's looking at the women in the room. There's Doris standing next to one of his associate's thirty-three year old eye candy wife and the wheels start turning," Kendra commented. "Some of our friends, like Randi, she just took the old wife out like it was nothing. She started showing up at the balls and events and when Mike bit on that bait it was over. In less than a year the old wife was out and she was in."

"That's kind of ruthless, isn't it?" Monique asked.

"It is what it is, because there is strictly hardball played behind all of these gated driveways. If Stan's radar is up and you're on it, then you had better make your move before some other gold digging bitch shows up, and they are coming up in droves. Your advantage is you have something they don't and that's intelligence, class and just the right amount of sass and ass to get you where you need to go," Kendra commented as they laughed.

"Well it's true, most of these new women have been tattooed and using all sorts of stuff before they try to come clean. I've talked with some of them and from ecstasy, meth, weed, cocaine, you name it and they've tried it. Then they try to throw on an evening gown and show up at the opera and blend in, give me a break," Kendra remarked.

"Look, I've got to run, good luck tomorrow," Kendra said and then she planted a kiss right on Prentice's lips and left.

"She is so refreshing, and I guess she's right about Stan, but I have to get used to the idea of having a married man pursuing me that way," Monique said.

"Just act natural and you will be fine," Prentice said. "So, are you ready for tomorrow?"

"Yeah, I think so; I've studied the company and brushed up on the industry jargon. I have the directions and other information Harry printed out for me. I'll be there at nine thirty for my ten o'clock appointment," Monique said. "I even splurged and got one of those prepaid cell phones so I can be reached easily. In fact here's the number in case you need to get in touch with me," she said as she wrote it on a notepad and gave it to Prentice.

"You need to get a good night's sleep so you will be sharp in the morning. Take the Jag and the traffic shouldn't be too bad that time of day. It should be full of gas because Joe makes sure all of those kinds of things are taken care of as well as looking after other details around the place. He is kind of our chief of staff around here," Prentice said.

The next day Monique was up bright and early getting ready for her big interview, her hair, makeup, clothes were all in place. With a little help from some tissue paper padding she even filled out the top of Prentice's outfit just right. The drive out to Grayson Micro showed her another side of this metropolitan area. She went from the exclusive confines of Grayson manor to the considerably more blue color location of the company's main plant and corporate offices in Garland, Texas, a nearby suburb of Dallas.

The streets were lined with auto repair shops and the pawn shop trade must be a staple in this area because there were plenty of outlets. There was also a fair complement of coin laundries or washerterias as they were called back in the Lower Nine. Independent corner convenience stores were prominent as well. In some ways it reminded her of her old neighborhood. Some of the people she saw reminded her of the dock and refinery workers back home and had a toughened look about them from years of hard work. It was ironic to see how such a pedestrian location could allow such a lavish lifestyle as the profits flowed upstream. However the design of business is for those that make the big investments to reap the big rewards.

Monique parked and went into the reception area.

"May I help you?" a bleached blond receptionist asked.

"I'm Monique Devareaux. I have a ten o'clock interview with Frank Roberts."

"Here hun. Take this application and fill it out. I'll call him and let him know you're here. Hey, I like those shoes."

Monique was a bundle of nerves as she waited on her interview. She didn't realize an endorsement from Harry Grayson behind someone to fill an open position was no small matter. By the time she emerged from the session, she had been given a tour of the plant and felt like more of a visiting dignitary than a job candidate.

On the way back home, yes, she could the word home again; her new cell phone rang for the first time. She answered and was told pending a background check she could start in two weeks on her new job. She couldn't wait to tell someone. The only person she could think of was Prentice. She decided to burn a few prepaid minutes and called her cell phone.

"That's fantastic Monique," Prentice said. "We need to go out and celebrate tonight, my treat."

There was no way to describe the feeling that coursed through her veins as she drove down the freeway. She didn't feel invisible anymore and soon she would be in the flow of traffic with everyone else that fought the bumper to bumper war each morning. Most of all, in a few weeks she could buy lunch for Prentice or someone else for a change and not feel dependent on the charity of others. Once she started getting a paycheck she could relax and not feel a sinking feeling every time she made a purchase with her limited funds.

This was another piece of her soul that was being reclaimed on her journey back to being a complete member of society again.

That night Prentice took her to a club that was pulsing with reggae and hip hop beats and a lively young professional crowd. Kendra and another one of Prentice's friends, Ruth, joined them. They were having a great time talking, dancing and drinking.

"Monique, I hear you may have one of the older wives frantic about her husband's interest in you," Ruth remarked.

"How do you know about that?" Monique asked

"This is a very small circle and people talk, something like that is not going to go unnoticed," Ruth said. "Don't let her intimidate you, because I've been through this before. Prentice and Kendra are close friends of mine. I know you're from New Orleans and ended up in a shelter here. I understand your predicament and you're playing this the right way. Don't worry I won't say anything, if I'm good at anything, it's keeping secrets. Well, my husband's ex wife cornered me one day and told me if I knew what was good for me, then I'd better go back to bum fuck Tennessee where I came from. She called me an inbred slut. I mean she had run a background check, criminal check, it was unbelievable."

"What did you do?" Monique asked. "I told her if she was having trouble with her husband, then she should take it up with him. She stood there like someone had just shoved a stick up her butt, turned beet red and stormed off."

"What if Doris Brickman does something like that. She could find out I was pulled out of New Orleans by the Coast Guard and ended up in a shelter?" Monique said.

"So what, you don't owe her anything, or Stan for that matter," Prentice said. "He's married, and that entitles you to tell him what you want. Suppose he says, I found out you're really an evacuee from Hurricane Katrina, so what? You look the same, and you're the same person he went after. I would think he would be fascinated at how you have bounced back after such an experience. Enough about him, his overhauled wife will be back home next week. It'll probably be a month or so before we see her in public until she heals up enough to look presentable."

Kendra grabbed Prentice by the hand and they hit the dance floor and disappeared into the crowd of bodies.

"You'll do fine here, Monique, you're smart, attractive. Just stick with Prentice and Kendra. Those two know the ropes and won't steer you wrong," Ruth said.

"How do you like it here compared to where you came from?" Monique asked.

"Look, my folks were dirt poor and lived in the hills. I fought my way out of there, went to college and moved to Dallas after graduating. I got a good job in retail management. That's where I met my husband. He was buying some high end custom suits and I came out to meet him and he let me know he was interested in more than just our clothing. I took my cues from him and here I am today."

"So I take it, you like this life better," Monique said.

"It's not a matter of better, because this is not paradise. He's gone a lot, is much older and you know it's not perfect. I want for nothing, but I'm in my thirties and oh well never mind," Ruth said.

"No, go ahead," Monique asked. "I need to know, just in case."

"Frankly, at your age and mine, a woman is hitting her stride sexually. If your husband is ten to twenty years older, you may not be getting everything you need in that department on a regular basis. That's about the only way I can put it," Ruth said as she took a drag from a cigarette.

"Well, how do you handle that?" Monique asked.

"I supplement," Ruth said. "You can read between the lines on that one."

"Enough said," Monique replied.

Just then Prentice and Kendra came back to the table. They gathered up their belongings and headed for the exit. Monique then remembered the function Stan had invited her to tomorrow night and she still hadn't decided if she was going or not.

Monique was sound asleep, then woke up and thought she heard something outside. She glanced at the clock by her bed and it was two o'clock in the morning. Then she heard another sound. She got out of bed and pulled the edge of the curtain aside and saw the spa was running. Someone was in it and moving around. The moon was bright and she went into the bathroom of the pool house. This area had a clear view of the spa which was elevated above the pool with rocks around it and a waterfall in front that ran into the pool. With the design of the spa, the rocks in the corners could completely conceal someone sitting there. Monique hadn't mustered the courage to get in the pool. Being in water deep enough to cover her head conjured up certain images she didn't want to recall.

Now she had made her way to the bathroom window and pulled the curtain back slightly and saw two people in the corner of the whirlpool. She almost gasped when she recognized it was Prentice and Kendra and they were in an intimate embrace. Their swimwear was lying on the edge of the pool deck. Monique watched in silence as the two women that befriended her gave pleasure to each other in what they thought was a private setting. She watched for a few minutes and then quietly went back to bed and tried to sleep but couldn't get the images she had just witnessed out of her head. How would she react the next time she saw them without tipping off she knew what was going on? She decided as soon as possible, she needed to get her own place. These people practiced a lifestyle that was beyond what she could handle. She was also risking offending them by slipping up and saying the wrong thing. Then she heard some muffled gasps and moans from the pool area as someone was hitting all of the right pleasure spots.

The next day went by uneventfully and Prentice behaved as if nothing out of the ordinary had occurred. Monique decided being discrete about what she saw that night was the best course of action. She had also chosen to take Stan up on his offer and attend the mixer at the hotel.

As the time for the event approached, Monique realized she was looking forward to seeing Stan again. It made her feel somewhat strange to know tonight the man with the most interest in her, was another woman's husband. She also had another task to take care of today and that was to go by the shelter to check her mail. She had reapplied for several items to be reissued to her. One of those was a credit card that surely was still buried in New Orleans somewhere. It wasn't an unlimited credit limit by any means, but at this point she was down to her last five hundred dollars. Monique hoped it had come in so she could survive until her paychecks started. She had bought some clothes to get ready to reenter the workforce and it put a dent in her finances. Certainly the last thing she wanted was to be forced to go to Prentice and ask for more help after all she had done for her.

As she took the exit to the shelter, everything came rushing back fresh to her. This time she knew she didn't have to stay and would drive away after getting her mail. She could see the cracks in the ground from lack of rain as she went into the building and of course the constant heat was present as well.

When she approached the administration station, the volunteer named Brenda that introduced her to Prentice was there and looked at her and said, "Miss Devareaux, is that you?"

"Yes it is, it's me," Monique answered.

"You look fantastic. Where are you staying?" Brenda answered.

"The lady that took me out for the day for the hair, face and spa treatment is letting me stay at her place and I'm getting a job soon," Monique beamed.

"I'm so happy for you," Brenda said. "You know they can get reimbursed for living expenses since you're staying there, here's a form for that. Your employer can also get credits for hiring you, tell them to contact FEMA."

"Okay, I'll do that. I was here to get any mail I might have," Monique said.

"Sure," Brenda said as she left to check on the mail.

"I see your ass is back down here," a voice rang out.

Monique turned and there was her nemesis Mel whose pride obviously was still smarting from having her ass kicked by what she thought was a lightweight.

"I guess that old man that took you out of here got tired of fucking you and dumped your skinny ass back at the shelter," Mel surmised.

"Why don't you mind your own business? I never would have hit you if you hadn't touched me," Monique explained.

"I know your type. You think you can get what you want by showing your ass to every man that comes around. You're going to get yours bitch since you're back in here with me," Mel said. "So you got a choice, you can give me what I want or you may not make it out of here a second time."

Just then Brenda came back with a bundle of mail wrapped in a rubber band and glared at Mel who walked off when she approached.

"Here you go. Was she bothering you? We've had a few complaints about her," Brenda said.

"We had an incident in the shower that didn't end very well for her. She's had it in for me every since."

"It's a good thing you're out of here. She's leaving tomorrow. It seems she has some relatives in Dallas that are taking her in."

As Monique flipped through the envelopes she spotted one from the credit card company and felt the hard outline of a plastic card inside. At least one prayer had been answered. She said goodbye to Brenda and turned to leave.

After walking out of the door, she saw Mel glaring at her as she went to her car to drive off.

"You're going to get yours bitch. You may have fucked your way out of here, but don't let me catch your skinny white ass off somewhere by yourself," Mel said.

This time as Monique drove off she gave Mel a middle finger salute out of the driver's side window and shouted back at her, "Kiss my ass."

This enraged Mel and she grabbed a rock and hurled it at the car as it drove off, but Monique was long gone. The rock fell harmlessly to the pavement.

Five

After leaving the shelter, Monique decided she would use most of the day to find her way around the city because it seemed Dallas was going to be her new home. She noticed the flat lay of the land, the endless parade of cars and stretches of freeways. Every other vehicle on the road seemed to be a pickup truck and the bigger the better. She had to dial up her driving aggression a few notches because the notion of moving over a lane to let you onto the freeway was a foreign concept. Learning to aim for gap in traffic that was traveling at seventy miles per hour was a required skill. The eighteen wheelers were the most intimidating and Interstate 35 was a main freight conduit as it was the primary route northward from Mexico to Canada. Monique tried to keep some distance between herself and the barreling monsters.

Most of all she missed the ever present Mississippi River and rich culture of New Orleans that you could almost taste. Dallas was a city of chain restaurants and sameness with a few pockets of authenticity, but it would take awhile to get to that level of local familiarity. Instead of gumbo and seafood, here barbeque and steaks was king. The central business areas cleared out at night. A parade of vehicles carried people to their suburban homes by night and back again in the mornings. New Orleans had a jazz trumpet melody and Dallas was a driving synthesizer rhythm that never stopped. A pang of homesickness set in but it would soon pass.

She stopped and had a quick bite to eat at a local landmark eatery on Inwood Road named Sonny Bryan's. There was this little white building with cars parked all around. Once inside the smell of hickory smoked barbeque was everywhere. She got in line and ordered a rib sandwich. She wondered how you would eat ribs in that manner, but it ended up being ribs with bread and not a true sandwich. Two rows of small one piece school desks comprised the inside seating and all manner of people were shoehorned in while eating elbow to elbow. She decided to eat outside on one of the picnic tables. The food was fantastic and she made a note to come by here again when she was in this part of town.

Monique decided it was time to go home and get ready for the event tonight at the hotel. Soon she began getting ready for a debut of a different type. She now felt almost complete as her social security card, credit card and driver's license were all now safely in her purse. She went through a period of time being devoid of any documents that could identify her. In fact a few weeks ago if she had been hit by a bus, a Jane Doe toe tag would have been attached to her body. It felt good to have an identity she could actually prove again with government issued documents and to be able to say that most American of phrases, "charge it."

After looking in the mirror for ten minutes to make sure everything was in place, Prentice came to the door and Monique let her in and posed to get a reaction. She was dressed in a classic little black dress that hugged her trim figure. The hemline ended two inches above her knees, her shoes were black backless sandals with four inch heels and a smart black jacket with silver sequins finished the ensemble. Her hair was a dark brunette color. It hung straight down and was cut right at the length of her shoulders. She thought a sharp red lipstick would set her full lips off perfectly against her light natural makeup that accentuated her slightly tanned skin tone. The slightest red tint brought out her high cheekbones and her eyelashes were long and luxurious. Her long curvy five foot eight inch frame now extended to six feet tall with the heels accounted for.

"Girl, you look like your ready for whatever comes your way," Prentice said. "Don't be surprised if you draw a crowd tonight. You look slightly exotic, a bit of a French flavor, but with a name like Devareaux, it's perfect. I know what it is. It's the look of a runway model, a little international flair. Now all you have to do tonight is work the room."

"So I look okay?"

"Monique you're like a kid with a fast car. You know how to drive it, but you don't know how to drive it to the limit. Listen to me. You can be whoever you want to be and can get people to do whatever you want. You are driving a really fast car. Learn how to shift the gears. I was like you, totally oblivious, until I saw the effect I had on Harry. It took me a while to get a clue when he said he was attracted to me and it wasn't just my mind. A few months later he slipped this on my finger," she held up the five carat diamond ring set in platinum that Harry gave her as an engagement ring. "Maybe my mind got me one of these carats, but the other four, well you know."

My god, Monique thought, these women go for the jugular and she thought she needed to channel some of her mother's spirit to survive in this environment. She grabbed the small black clutch purse and placed the invitation inside and headed out of the door to her next adventure.

Monique pulled in front of the hotel, parked and started walking towards the front entrance. She felt a little unsure of how to handle tonight but figured she would take her cues from others in the room. She checked with the front desk and was directed to the Crescent room where the meeting was taking place. The door attendant took her invitation and ushered her into the room. Stan spotted her immediately and started in her direction.

"Monique, I'm glad you decided to make it out to my little event," Stan said.

"From what I hear, this is a very coveted ticket. It seems your mixers have quite a reputation among those in the business community."

"Well, there are some very well connected people that attend. You'll meet some of them tonight and we try to have a little fun also. Help yourself, we have an open bar and a few goodies set up in the corner and the servers will get whatever you desire," Stan said. "By the way you look stunning tonight, I've got to get ready to kick this thing off," he said as he left.

She made her way around the room, took a glass of Cristal champagne, a cracker and scooped a bit of caviar on the edge. This was another new experience of the palette variety because she had never had the pricey delicacy. This collection of drinks, cheeses and other delicacies were not a part of her diet in the lower ninth ward of New Orleans.

"Hello, I'm Robin Summers," a mid fifty year old woman said introducing herself.

"Monique Devareaux," she said shaking her hand.

"We seem to be outnumbered in here with all of these men around," Robin said. "I'm standing in for my CEO tonight. He is out of town but passed his invitation on to me, he says he always makes at least one good business contact here. I'm with Colbert Network Devices, I'm the COO."

"I was invited by Stanley Brickman. I'm in town working on an association with Grayson Micro."

"Oh that's a great company, we use some of their chips in our routers and switches," Robin said. "I would like to do more business with them but I'm not real pleased with the sales support we're getting."

Just then Stan called the event to order.

"Welcome to our monthly mixer and tonight we want to focus on getting an early start on how we can become involved in business opportunities related to rebuilding the Louisiana and Mississippi Gulf Coast. I believe in getting ahead of the curve on these things while everyone else is still trying to figure out if there is any opportunity to be had. One of the glaring things that occurred was the destruction of the communications infrastructure from land lines to cell towers. I feel this will bring opportunity to rebuild and replace old networks, but also will open the eyes of planners for other areas located in danger zones worldwide. Backup systems, redundancy, satellite based failsafe networks and other ways to safeguard communications and data so a localized event does not cripple any recovery. I'm saying locating offsite data storage and backup in the heartland away from the danger zones will be a burgeoning need as recovery planning and future contingency preparation for other areas goes forward. That's why I'm staging my reentry into active business operations with the announcement of Brickman Communications and Data Systems which will offer information and network redundancy in addition to on-demand capacity. The operations center will be in an underground bunker in the Midwest and corporate headquarters will be in Dallas, Texas. I plan to launch this venture in four months," Stan said.

He then went through a multimedia presentation on the concept for the next thirty minutes. Monique was mesmerized by Stan's presentation as well as his presence and command of the audience and material. Soon the lights came up and he told everyone to mingle and have a good time. Then Monique heard the sound of a live ensemble playing jazz standards in the background.

"Are you having a good time?" Stan said to Monique.

"I was very impressed by your presentation. It's fascinating to hear your motivation for resuming an active business career?"

"After seeing what happened in New Orleans after the hurricane hit, my juices started flowing again. A lot of the problems were caused by communications and data problems. I mean the local officials were in total blackout, locally based companies lost their data because it was all in one place and I think this is a needed service that could speed recovery in future catastrophes."

"I think you've hit the nail on the head with this venture, I don't see any reason why it wouldn't be a success."

"Monique I was hoping you would show up tonight because I want to get better acquainted with you, I mean as a person."

"Look, I don't want to beat around the bush, why are you interested in me, you don't know me and you're married."

"I would like a chance to explain, I have a suite here for the night, would you join me for a nightcap after this is over so we can talk?" Stan asked. "Just talk," he assured again.

Monique looked him in the eyes and had all manner of alarm bells going off in her head then she said, "Okay, we can talk."

The meeting wrapped up around ten o'clock. Monique waited in the lobby until Stan came by and they went to the suite on the top floor. Stan poured both of them a glass of wine and they sat facing the window that overlooked downtown Dallas.

"Monique, I know I am a married man and this may sound strange to you, but my wife and I have not been very close for a long time. We are moving towards a separation and afterwards a divorce. Our marriage was one of two people with a long relationship that evolved into marriage. Doris was older than I was when I first got into business. She used her experience to introduce me to a relationship based a lot on physical contact of a sexual nature. As I matured and that part of our life cooled off, we began to drift apart a bit."

"I don't like to hear about anyone's marriage ending and I'm sorry about that. I'm puzzled about why I interest you?"

"From the first time I saw you, I was intrigued. Do you know how beautiful you are? You're intelligent and there's a toughness I can't put my finger on. I want to see you in more than a platonic fashion."

"I don't know what to say."

At that moment Stan stood up and took Monique's hand and pulled her up from the sofa and kissed her at first gently and then forcefully on the lips. She responded by kissing him back and felt a rush of blood to her face as she felt hot and lightheaded by his sudden move.

Then she felt his hand cup her buttocks and pull her torso in close to him and she was getting heated in other areas at this point.

"Stan, I don't know if we should be doing this," she gasped.

Her resolve was weakening by the minute as his strong arms circled her waist and his hands and fingers caressed her. He could feel the excitement stored in her body. As his lips went down the length of her neck, Monique knew she was close to a tipping point and placed her hand on his as it started to slide under the top elastic band of her bikini panties. She kissed him deeply but said she had to go right now and pulled away. She gave him her cell phone number and readjusted her clothes and turned to leave. He embraced her from behind, kissed the back of her neck and she could feel his manhood against her ass. She pressed back into him and then pulled away and left.

Monique made her way home, took a shower and stretched out on the bed without a stitch of clothing on reflecting on the night. Then her cell phone rang and it was Stan checking to see if she made it home safely. After hanging up, she gave herself some relief by using her hands as a poor substitute for what could have happened tonight with this strong virile man. She thought in the long run this was a better alternative.

The next day Monique got a call from the personnel department at Grayson Micro telling her the background check came back clear. She needed to take a drug screen at one of the local labs and then would get her formal offer letter with a start date. After she passed the drug screen her offer letter arrived by email. She signed it and faxed it back and of course a copy went into her new scrapbook.

The letter read as follows:

Grayson Micro Technologies, Inc. is pleased to extend an offer of employment to Monique Devareaux in the capacity of Southern Region Sales Manager, custom products division. Salary will be at an annual rate of $75,000 salary paid biweekly, there will also be an automobile allowance of $500 monthly paid on the first biweekly pay period per month.

A commission based upon reaching targets to be determined at a later date will be paid on the second biweekly pay period if any are earned in the previous monthly period. Upon reaching 100 percent commission attainment the annual salary and commission compensation will be approximately $115,000 annually.

You will also be eligible to be enrolled in the company matched 401k retirement plan and health, dental and vision care.

Your signature below confirms your acceptance of this offer of employment with Grayson Micro Technologies, Inc.

Monique read this letter over and over after she faxed it back. Her start date was in one week and this was more money than she had ever made in her life. She told Prentice and said she was never more excited about getting back in the flow of things and getting her career back on track.

Prentice also asked about the mixer.

"Well things took a bit of a left turn and I ended up in a suite with Stan."

"Did anything happen?"

"There was some heavy petting but it could have gone further very easily, he told me he was separating from his wife."

"He was testing you," Prentice said. "If you had slept with him last night, I think it would have been over."

"You're probably right. He really pressed me, but I still left.

"This guy is rich and he can find a woman ready to spread her legs any day of the week if they think they can become the next Mrs. Brickman. He told you about his marriage to see if you were an opportunist ready to jump in on the off chance of being able to live in the lap of luxury. Even when he pressed you, you didn't give in, and that still means something to a man. All men like the thrill of a chase and they can't chase a woman who's on her back."

Six

Knowing she was going to work and having more structure to her days was a comforting thought. She knew the life Prentice and her friends led was something she had a sample of but was far from what she could do on a daily basis. Her brief exposure to this lifestyle did give her a glimpse into something she only thought she knew about.

While she was watching the news the Mayor of New Orleans talked about when residents could come back and take stock of the condition their homes and possessions. Monique wanted to go back if only to get a sense of closure and try to find out what happened to her grandmother. Now she thought about her father, a man she had only seen once to know who he was, and someone she hadn't laid eyes on since she was eighteen. She knew he lived in a part of town that didn't flood and probably left the city long before the storm hit. She searched for his office phone number on the internet and it came up, she stared at it for a long time and then picked up the phone and dialed.

After three rings a male voice answered the phone, "Dr. Morgan's office."

"Is this Dr. John Morgan?"

"Yes it is. May I help you?"

"This is your daughter, Monique,"

"Oh my god, are you alright? I've been trying to find you. I didn't know if you made it out alive."

"They had to pull me off of the roof of my grandmother's house. I was up there for three days," she said as she started sobbing to a man she hardly knew but this was her first time to really pour out her emotions to a relative.

"Monique, I'm so happy to hear from you, I've been worried sick." After the hurricane hit, I told my wife about you. She said she knew already and just never brought it up."

"She knew? I'm really surprised about that."

"She wants to meet you, and so do your sisters and brother."

"I have sisters and a brother?"

"Yes, Meagan is twenty-one, Jenny is twenty-three and John Jr. is twenty-five. They were excited to find out they had an older sister. Someone here wants to talk to you."

"Monique, this is June, I'm John's wife, and I guess I'm your stepmother. I want you to know I'm looking forward to meeting you and you're welcome in our home anytime."

"I thought you would hate me, you know because of who I am," Monique said.

"You didn't have any part in that, it shouldn't have happened, your mother was too young to know better, but someone else knew better and wasn't responsible. Believe you me, he knows it was wrong. Where are you?"

"I'm in Dallas, it was horrible, but I'm doing better now."

"What about your family?"

"My grandmother didn't make it. The water came in too fast. I don't even know if they found her body."

"Give me her name and we'll see if we can find something out for you."

Monique gave her the information and her phone number so she could call with any updates.

"I'm helping John at the office now and we're taking care of a lot of the workers that have come into town. The staff and receptionist have all left because their homes were destroyed. When can you come see us?"

"I'm starting a new job soon. Thanksgiving will be the first time I will have some days off."

"Will you come if we get you a plane ticket, we can pick you up and you can spend Thanksgiving with us and meet everybody?"

"You would really do that for me?"

"If you want to come, we would love to see you."

"I think I would like that. Could I speak with Dr…I mean my father again? It was nice talking with you?"

"Sure, here he is."

Monique talked with her father for an hour as if she was trying to establish a bond that had been missing for twenty-eight years.

Monique then sat down and reflected about the ramifications of that conversation. Instantly her family tree had gone from being nearly barren and sprouted limbs, branches and leaves. There was one other contact she needed to make. She did have an uncle, her mother's brother that she hadn't laid eyes on or spoken to in thirteen years. Monique last recollection was he had moved to California and that's where she started her search.

Her uncle Albert was a Baptist minister. He had distanced himself from her mother because of her lifestyle and didn't pass up a chance to tell her to change her ways. California was a big state but she knew the last name of Devareaux would narrow the list considerably. She entered the name and got a few hits but they didn't seem to match up. The she decided to put the word Reverend in front and one listing came up in Los Angeles, Rev. Albert Devareaux, this had to be him, she dialed the number.

"Hello," a female voice answered.

"Is this Aunt Gracie?"

"This is Sister Gracie, who is this?"

"This is Monique Devareaux, your niece."

"My god child, how are you doing, are you alright, this is a miracle," she said as she called in the background, "Albert, pick up the phone."

"Hello."

"Uncle Albert, it's Monique."

"Praise the lord, child I didn't know what happened to you, where are you?"

"I'm in Dallas, Texas and I'm doing fine."

"What about momma?" he asked.

"I'm sorry, she didn't make it. The water came in too fast and I had to cut my way through the roof. Before I knew what was happening it was up to my neck, I called for her and there was no answer, I'm sorry."

"Listen to me child, momma lived a good life, she was eighty years old and we can't question the wisdom of God, he knows best. He saw fit to take her then and spare her the suffering some of those old folks went through at the convention center and the Superdome. I would have rather she went the way she did instead of dying of thirst on the sidewalk. Don't blame yourself one bit for this because at least you got out alive. Do you want to come out here, we can come get you?"

"No, Uncle Albert, I'm staying with some very nice people and I'm about to start a real good job next week."

"You were always a very smart girl," Aunt Gracie said. "You'll do just fine. Give us your phone number so we can keep up with you."

"Monique, you know me and your mother had our differences. I just had to get out of there because it was not where I could spread my wings and become a man without being called boy all the time. Momma told us all about how proud she was of you when you were in school and got your job."

"She did? I had no idea."

"We were all proud of you."

Monique then told him about the conversation she had with her father and his wife.

"Look, age can sometimes bring about wisdom. You didn't know this but I had a visit with your father after your mother's funeral. I told him I might be a preacher but he had a responsibility for your future and he had better take care of that obligation if he knew what was good for him. I checked to make sure it was done," Uncle Albert said.

Monique was stunned by this revelation because it seemed she had a guardian angel she didn't even know about.

"Thank you Uncle Albert, I had no idea. Listen I'll talk to you guys again soon," Monique said as she hung up the phone.

What a surprise, Monique thought no one cared and she was all alone. The whole time there were forces put in motion that allowed her to achieve more in life than her mother ever had a chance to accomplish. Her Uncle who she hadn't said a word to in over a decade had changed her life in ways she couldn't imagine. Maybe she was loved after all and not a forgotten child.

Something new was causing Monique to have terrible flashbacks of the horrors of Katrina. A monster Hurricane named Rita was advancing on the Texas Gulf Coast and the reports of its approach were sending shivers up and down her spine. She couldn't take her gaze off the news reports of the projected landfall and it felt as if the storm was going to hit her location instead of three hundred miles to the south. All of her nerve endings were on edge sharpened with the knowledge of what a killer could do as it came ashore. She slept in fits and had nightmares as replays of her ordeal were on a continual loop playback heightened by the images from this new emergency.

When Rita turned and hit the area between the Texas and Louisiana border Monique cried in empathy for those newly devastated by nature's latest nightmare and she could physically feel their pain.

Rita hit on a Saturday. The next day Monique went to church with Harry and Prentice. This was a church in the loosest sense of the word as it seemed to be about the size of the arena she stayed in when she first came to town. Seating in the sanctuary was arranged in a stadium fashion and the size of the congregation seemed to rival that of a major sporting event. There were prayers for the people of the gulf coast as Rita had made landfall but the extent of damage wasn't yet known.

Seven

This was the first day of work on her new job. She now had a desk with a nameplate, a box of business cards, a new laptop computer and people shaking her hand and welcoming her to the company.

"Hi, Monique I'm Dorothy, I'm the administrative assistant for the sales department and if you need anything, just let me know," Dorothy said.

The desk next to hers was occupied by another female sales representative that covered another territory and her name was Brandy Monroe. She wasn't in the office, but her desk was adorned with numerous plaques and awards that indicated a certain degree of success. There was a picture of her with Harry and Prentice on what appeared to be a cruise ship and she was quite attractive. She appeared to be about thirty years old, with long blond hair and a great figure.

Around ten o'clock Brandy came in and put her laptop bag on her desk and Dorothy said, "Brandy, here's your proposal and five duplicate sets with electronic copies burned on CDs."

"Thanks, Dorothy, you're the best as always," Brandy said.

"Hello. You must be Monique. I'm Brandy."

"Yes, Monique Devareaux, nice to meet you."

"It looks like we are going to be neighbors. It's good to have another girl in the sales pit. Hey, you want to do lunch around eleven-thirty, so we can get acquainted?" Brandy asked.

"Sure, just let me know, I'll be at my desk going through some of this computer based sales training."

"Great, and this afternoon I have a sales call they wanted me to take you out on for your first field ride," Brandy said. "We'll leave around two o'clock for that."

"That sounds great," Monique said as she poured herself into her online class.

Brandy must have taken the employee manual and checked off every item on the dress code and made sure she challenged it. Her dress was a couple of inches two high, her neckline plunged low and her clothes had precious little space between her and the fabric. Forget about the closed toe shoes as she wore dress sandals sporting four inch heels. All of this was topped off by semi big Texas blond hair and red lipstick. At five feet nine inches tall she made quite an impression.

Before she knew it Brandy said, "Let's get out of here before you fall into that computer screen. Grab your notepad and purse because we can go from lunch to the appointment."

In the parking garage Brandy was parked in the salesman of the month slot. They got into her victory red Corvette Z06 and when she turned the key a smile went across her face. She engaged reverse and pulled out of the parking garage. Once on Interstate 635 she ran through the gears and slammed Monique's back up against the passenger seat with a rush of power and speed she obviously enjoyed.

"Wow," Monique said, "This is some car. I can't believe you can drive it like that."

Brandy was utterly giddy, "I love it. I bought it as kind of a freedom present. I just got divorced and my ex-husband was trying to screw me over on the settlement and had put a bunch of stocks and mutual funds in his mother's name. Well my lawyer busted him and made him pay out the ass. This is my little gift to myself to say goodbye to that bastard. Turns out, he was screwing his little twenty-two year old bimbo secretary. Well, I hope the pussy's good because I've got the house and the money. Get outta my way you asshole," she yelled as she whipped around a pickup truck laughing as they exited and parked in front of an Italian restaurant and went in.

They both ordered lunch and Brandy ordered a glass of wine also while Monique ordered iced tea.

"Don't you have a call after we leave here?" Monique said.

"Look it's no big deal, its just a glass of wine, I'll suck on a couple of mints and it'll be fine. As long as I'm bringing in the numbers, nobody gives a shit anyway. Hey, I overheard a couple of guys in the break room talking about you."

"About me, what were they saying," Monique asked.

"They're guys, what do you think. They were making bets on who could get into your pants first," Brandy replied.

"You're kidding, I don't even remember anybody's name yet," Monique said.

"They're men, they don't care if you remember their names, as long as they can get some," Brandy said as both of them laughed.

"I saw a lot of awards on your desk, it looks like your doing well," Monique said.

"This is a good job and I'm having some great years. I've been here four years and have made the Summit Club three out of the four," Brandy said.

"I saw a picture of you with Harry Grayson and his wife, when was that?" Monique asked.

"That was last year, my best yet. I really busted my ass last year and ended up two hundred percent of plan. I was working a lot and on the road all the time. I guess that's when that little secretary bitch made her move on my ex-husband. It was her black and blond hair strands in my bed that got his ass busted. Can you believe it, he brought that little trailer tramp to my home and to our bed. I was furious," Brandy said.

"Look, I'm sorry that happened to you," Monique said. "What were Mr. and Mrs. Grayson like? Are they nice?" Monique asked.

"Oh yes, they're great people. I've even been to their home for a company party, what a place," Brandy said. "She is so lucky. I was just really shocked to find out his wife was black. I guess there's nothing wrong with that. It's just the way I was raised. My daddy would have beaten my ass if I went with a black guy. I guess times are changing."

"Would you go with a black guy now, since you're an adult?"

"I don't know. I have a lot of things to unlearn. If he was nice and liked me for me, I might be open to that. Do you have someone in mind? Are you into black guys?"

"No, it was just a question. I really just look at everyone as an individual."

Soon their food arrived. They ate and talked until about one o'clock. Then they left to head up to a defense contractor for Brandy's two o'clock appointment.

Once on the property and clearing endless security checks, they finally went in to the procurement office to meet the buyer. Brandy certainly knew her business and products. She enhanced the presentation with a very strategic positioning of her shapely crossed legs. She pointed out the fine points of her proposal from the same side of the desk as her customer with her top open to the third button.

By the time they left she had the promise of a purchase order by Friday and a broad smile across the face of the buyer.

"Well what did you think?" Brandy asked.

"Well, you sure know your product and all of the benefits of doing business with the company. That buyer seemed a little friendly and touchy feely."

"Well, Tom is a harmless good old boy. If my visit gets him through the rest of the week, then I'll just call it added value. After all, I could just email him the spec. sheets and a boilerplate proposal, but it's the personal touch that keeps the competition out," Brandy said as she smiled.

Once they were in the car she pinned Monique back into the seat again and ran through all six gears and didn't miss a beat on the clutch in her four inch heeled sandals.

It was near four o'clock when they got back to the office and noticed the sales area was a ghost town. Brandy said salespeople have a little more latitude than other employees. The measure of success in sales was not how many hours they put in, but how much revenue they brought to the table.

"If I hit my quota on the first day of the month, they don't really care what I do the rest of the time. That's why I love sales, you get to write your own ticket," Brandy said. "I'm going to be out most of the week but I'll be in Friday, maybe we can go out one Friday night after work and check out one of the hot spots."

"Yeah, that might be fun," Monique replied.

"Grab one of my business cards off my desk, my cell phone number is on there. Ok, I'll see you later, welcome aboard," Brandy said as she left.

"Well how was your first day?" Dorothy asked.

"My head is spinning, but it was fun," she replied.

"How was Brandy?"

"She is something else, is she always so wound up? She has a lot of energy, and the way she drives that car."

Dorothy looked around and said, "She scares the shit out of me with her driving. One day I was with her, I told Brandy to slow down or just let me out of the damned thing and I would get a taxi back to the office. Brandy is a great girl, but she really got screwed over by her husband. I think she's having a harder time getting over it than she wants to admit. Hey it's five o'clock, let's get out of here," Dorothy said.

They both packed up and walked out. As they left two guys were checking Monique out as they watched her walk to the elevator.

"Watch out for those two, they're hot shots from emerging markets, nothing but walking hormones," Dorothy said.

By the time she fought the traffic home Monique was ready to just lay on the couch for thirty minutes to decompress. She nodded off to sleep and woke up about an hour later with an appetite. She needed to get something to eat and went to the refrigerator. Monique decided to make a turkey sandwich, a salad, grab a diet coke and sit by the pool. Maybe she would even hit the whirlpool spa later on, if it wasn't otherwise occupied. Right as she was taking the last bite of her sandwich her cell phone rang and it was Stan Brickman.

"Hello."

"Monique, this is Stan, how are you doing?"

"I'm doing fine, how are you?"

"I have been thinking about you since last week and I want to see you again, can we meet somewhere for dinner. I'm going to be out of town so how about two weeks from now on Friday night."

"Stan, I can't just meet you in a public restaurant like that, it's too risky."

"Come to the Flagstone hotel, I have a suite on the top floor and we will eat there. Wear the dress I first saw you in at the museum. Will you join me?"

"Yes, what time?"

"Eight o'clock."

"I'll see you then."

For some reason she knew after this date she may never have a normal life again. She called Prentice and asked her if she wanted to join her in the whirlpool to talk and relax. Later the two women that had become friends met at the pool and climbed into the steaming waters of the spa. This was a real luxury as Dallas was in the middle of a prolonged drought and the earth was dry and cracked. It wasn't uncommon to hear about wildfires or smell the scent of burned grass in the air. Many of the lakes had boating bans due to record low water levels. To have your own personal oasis like this was a true luxury.

"How was your first day on the new job? Prentice asked.

"My head is swimming with names and faces right now and they all run together," Monique answered. "I met someone you know, Brandy one of the saleswomen, she sits next to me."

"I've met her a couple of times, she's nice," Prentice said.

"I was invited to a private dinner by Stan Brickman in two weeks on a Friday night and he asked me to wear the dress I had on at the auction. I don't know what to think about this."

"Be yourself, he's trying to see if you remain the same person each time he's with you," Prentice said. "You might want to think about how you will respond if things get heated in a sexual direction."

"I know. I'm extremely attracted to him, but I don't want to be used by a married man and hung out to dry."

"Let me ask you something, who has the most to lose if it got out he is having an affair with you? If Stan is willing to risk what he has for you, then what are you risking for him. He is a powerful man, respected in the community and by all reports he doesn't do a lot of dipping on the side. He told you last week his marriage is over and this is his first step to move on. What you did with the guy in the limo is no different than what you would do with Stan but the payoff may be more than just getting your rocks off."

With that said they laid their heads back and soaked up the relaxation from the swirling waters and talked about other topics such as how Monique had reconnected with her family. After soaking in the warm waters of the spa they cooled their legs by sitting on the edge of the pool.

Eight

With Brandy gone the rest of the week at work was fairly uneventful. One of the emerging markets guys made his presence know and asked Monique to lunch but she found a suitable excuse and went with Dorothy to her new favorite restaurant, Pappadeaux's. Their seafood was New Orleans inspired and it cured some of her homesickness.

The next week Monique decided to really pour herself into her training and chose to forego much of the office social activity. She felt this was the best way to settle down and get past her rush of emotions rekindled by all of the turmoil cause by the arrival and aftermath of Hurricane Rita along the gulf coast.

Soon it was Friday again and time to go home and get ready for Stanley Brickman and whatever the night may bring. When she turned her television on she heard the following report:

"Saul Epstein, CEO of H.R. Weinstein International Clothiers, was found dead this morning in his Houston hotel room. When he did not show up at his display at the convention center, his employees became concerned and placed repeated calls to his hotel room. After getting no response from Mr. Epstein, hotel security entered the room and found him dead in his bed. It seems he died of natural causes and had a history of heart disease. Left to mourn his death is his wife Alice and three adult children. Saul Epstein was sixty-four years old."

Monique thought that name sounded familiar. Then she remembered Prentice and Kendra mentioned his name before she went to the charity auction with them at the museum. She thought maybe she would ask Prentice about it when she saw her again.

She didn't have to wait long as Prentice stopped by about thirty minutes later.

"Oh, I meant to ask you, I heard on the news, this guy you and Kendra mentioned, Saul Epstein, the report said he died in Houston of a heart attack in his hotel room. What's the story with him?"

"Well we are all in shock, he and his wife Alice are bedrocks on the society scene in Dallas and this was very sudden," Prentice said.

"Kendra didn't seem to care for him very much" Monique said.

"Well you know about the indecent proposal he made to her at the country club when he asked her to go to the steam room and do him. What's worse was his wife and her husband were only a few feet away. You know Kendra, Saul has been on her shit list every since. I'll go so you can get ready for your dinner date."

She decided to be as radiant as she could and gave extra attention to her hair and lips. The lack of humidity in the air made the use of skin moisturizers a must. The expected rain from Hurricane Rita went east of Dallas and the drought persisted. It required extra attention to keep body in her hair and avoid a dried out frazzled appearance. This was a tough environment to keep your appearance at it best and also an expensive proposition to say the least. When there was nothing else she thought she could do to enhance her look, it was time to head out for this meeting with destiny.

When she arrived at the hotel, there was no need to stop at the front desk. She went straight to the elevator and headed to the top floor. She approached the door and knocked. There Stan opened the door and his eyes lit up and he escorted her inside. She tried not to seem too overwhelmed by the surroundings as a trio was filling the room with music. The table was set with silver. Stan picked up a decanter filled with Remy Martin Louis XIII Cognac that cost over eighteen hundred dollars a bottle and poured both of them a drink.

"To your beauty," Stan said as he toasted Monique and they took a drink.

"Come let's sit while the food is being prepared," Stan said.

"Stan, everything is just perfect tonight," Monique said.

"I asked you here tonight because I wanted show you some of my world to see how you like it. I also wanted to see if it is a world you might have an interest in becoming involved in on a full time basis," Stan said.

"That sounds suspiciously like an invitation to go steady," Monique said.

"You know your right, it would have been much simpler to just say would you be my girlfriend, I thought it wouldn't sound grand enough in this setting, I suppose," he said laughing.

"Okay then, will you be my girlfriend?" he asked.

"Yes, yes I will," Monique said and she kissed him deeply.

"I see dinner has arrived, shall we," Stan said.

They went to the table and began a four course meal of the highest nature and Monique finally relaxed and enjoyed the company of this man without reservation. After a couple of hours the servants cleared the table and they shared a dance before the trio left them in private.

Stan then kissed Monique as deeply as he could and told her he had something else to show her and they headed for the elevator. Monique had no idea what this was about but Stan was very excited and pressed a button to go to the first floor of the parking garage. When they went out there was something Monique could not identify, it was a car but she could not figure out what kind.

"What is that?"

"This is a Bugatti Veyron 16.4. It's very rare like you and it's near priceless, it's the fastest production car in the world, let's go for a ride," Monique literally stepped down into the seat and felt like she was molded into the vehicle instead of sitting in it.

Stan started the engine and the left the parking garage, and he asked, "Do you have any pressing plans for the rest of the weekend?"

"Well no, why do you ask?"

"I want to show you my boat, it's in Galveston."

"What, are you out of your mind?"

"Yes, I am."

"Ok, I'm game."

Stan was soon on Interstate 45 headed south. When he cleared the city he gave Monique a thrill and briefly hit one hundred and seventy miles per hour before slowing to a more pedestrian ninety.

"What did this thing cost?"

"About a million three, I think."

Monique almost choked to think this was the world she was flirting with given where she was a few months back. Their mood was tempered by lingering signs of the aftermath of Hurricane Rita with stranded vehicles still strewn along Interstate 45 as they traveled southward. With the roads jammed during the evacuation, some vehicles broke or simply ran out of fuel and their owners have not been able to reclaim them over two weeks later. Still they pushed onward.

There was a swarm whenever they stopped for fuel and it was as if Bigfoot had showed up to pose for photographs. People were taking pictures with camera phones and not even leaving until they pulled off and continued down the freeway. A few hours later they literally drove the vehicle onto the bottom level of a boat which was a boat only in the loosest of terms as it was about one hundred and eighty feet long. The captain greeted them and they retired to the master suite.

By this time Monique was overwhelmed by the entire experience of being in Dallas a few hours earlier and now ensconced in the opulent master's quarters of this vessel.

Stan came towards her, scooped her up in his arms and placed her on the king sized bed and began to slowly remove her clothing piece by piece starting with her shoes. There was no resistance this time and Monique's senses were heightened by the environment. Slowly Stan removed her dress and let it fall in a heap on the floor, her bra was next and he placed tiny bites on her burning flesh before pulling her thong panties down with his teeth. Monique then helped Stan remove his clothing and once he was naked before her she reached for him and pulled him down. She wrapped herself around him like she was trying somehow to get to the other side of his body without going around, but through him.

Monique was a strong woman and she exercised that strength and flexibility with a smooth rhythm like the sultry music of her birthplace. For Stan this was even more than he imagined and he was caught in a web that could have been made of the most decadent chocolate. He was nearing sugar overload as she poured herself into him over and over until they both convulsed with a release that had built up since they first laid eyes on each other.

He looked at her and said, "Monique you are what I have needed for years to bring me back to my vibrant center I've been missing. I had no idea it would be this way, but I knew when I saw you, if I could ever gain your trust and get you to let go, it would be extraordinary. It was more than I ever imagined. I could be with you forever and never tire of this kind of love."

"Stan, who do you think I am?" Monique asked.

"What kind of question is that, you're a very intelligent woman and know what you want out of life," he replied.

"What if I was someone that was pulled off a rooftop in New Orleans after the hurricane and came to Dallas with a bus full of evacuees and ended up in a shelter," she said. "What if not for the kindness of strangers, I could still be in that shelter or god knows where by now. Would you still feel the same way about me?"

The response she received was not what she expected. Stan grabbed her and pulled her down on top of him and they proceeded to exhaust themselves until they fell asleep.

They woke up around eleven o'clock the next day and Stan said, "I wondered when you would tell me everything. I've known for a while. Doris tried to make a big deal out of you coming to the auction with Prentice Grayson. I don't care where you came from, I care that you are here now, the way you are. Money is something people have and something they lose. The heart is what counts and you have the heart I want. Because you told me this now means everything to me."

"Really Stan, I was thinking you would think I was somehow not worthy of being with you and my background would be an embarrassment."

"Look, I started my business in a trailer park. It was my ideas and drive that got me where I am today, not some blueblood pedigree. If I looked down on you then I would be looking down on myself," Stan said.

Monique hugged him and asked, "What happened between you and Doris, why are you getting divorced?"

"That's a fair question. Doris was more of a teacher to me in ways of the world and used that to lead me into marriage. It worked well for a while but as I became more mature there were different things I wanted out of life. She was becoming this society person and separated herself more from events that affected people at large. After the disaster of Hurricane Katrina, I mentioned I wanted to do something to help prevent something like that from happening again and her attitude was shocking. She blamed the victims for not doing better with their lives and expecting the government to bail them out. When I confronted her about this she said I needed to remember we were different from those at the bottom. There was a reason we lived the way we did and they lived in their condition. That was the last straw. It let me know if she met me now and I was in that trailer park trying to start my business like I did in the beginning, she would just as soon spit on me as to help me."

"Do you still love her?" Monique asked.

"I don't think you ever stop loving someone or at least loving that part of them that first attracted you, even if they're not the same person anymore," Stan said.

"Does she know how you feel about me?" Monique asked.

"She knows I'm interested in you, but she doesn't know how interested," Stan answered. "She thinks anyone that isn't already in our circle is an outsider or some kind of gold digger. The unusual thing about our circle is most of us are first generation wealth, it's not like some dynasty passed down through generations. I have heard us called nouveau-riche trash by others whose money came from trusts and inheritance so you see there's snobbery among snobs."

"You know that is the strangest of social commentaries, because from what I know of history, some of those old money fortunes were built on illegal activities. Now it has been washed by the passage of time into being legitimate," Monique said.

"Let's take it a little further, how about on the back of slavery or in league with dictators and war criminals, you know about glass houses," Stan said.

He grabbed Monique by the hand and said, "Let's hit the shower. I packed some clothes in the car."

He called up to the captain and told him to head out to sea about thirty miles as they entered the shower.

Once out of the shower Stan wrapped himself in a towel and went up to the car and came back with a bag with a few clothes in it. He gave Monique what could be loosely called a swim suit. It amounted to a thong bottom with a small triangle patch to cover her front and a matching small spaghetti string top. The top had small strips of cloth that would cover only small parts of her breasts.

"You expect me to put this on. This is not covering up much of anything?"

"Well, we've just seen each other naked."

"Yeah, but the captain of the boat hasn't."

"Rick, he's pretty cool about stuff like that," Stan said. "But if you insist, here's a wrap you can put on," he said as he pulled out a sheer blue wraparound with ties.

"You were just going to see if I would go up there with my ass hanging out first, weren't you?"

"That's the first rule of sales. See if they will say yes to the first offer."

"Well my grandmother always told me not to go out of the house with my butt hanging out and I listened to that advice," Monique said as they went to the top deck.

When she emerged into the sunlight she was awestruck by the site of the end-less stretches of water in the Gulf of Mexico and the sound of the diesel engine pushing them further out to sea. Sea gulls flew around the vessel as they stood by the bow railing and peered into the horizon. Stan wrapped his arms around her and she felt like the queen of all she surveyed at that moment. Soon another crewman or crew woman to be precise brought cold margaritas and announced lunch was waiting on the upper deck.

Every experience was fresh and new. She wondered how someone could get used to this as a normal part of everyday life. Was she leading the life her mother envisioned in her mind? Monday morning she would be back in reality and would this ever happen again?

"Stan, where are we going with this relationship? This is not something I'm used to and I don't want to set myself up for a big letdown by reading something into this that isn't there."

"Monique, I'm a cautious man. Let's see, I drove you three hundred miles in the middle of the night in my new million dollar toy and pulled right onto the deck of my yacht. Didn't you have guys doing stupid stunts when you were in school to try to get a pretty girl's attention? Last night was my way of getting a pretty girl's attention and to get some time alone with you."

"That was to get my attention? Well you have my attention. I just don't want to lose myself with you."

"What do you mean?"

"Stan, I have a very small life right now, and its being put together brick by brick. Your life is so large it could swallow me whole just like the hurricane did when it came through, it scares me."

"That's the most honest thing I've heard in years and I understand it perfectly."

"Let's take it slow at your pace, the last thing I want to do is overwhelm you with a wave of new experiences, places and things. You really surprise me, not to be smug, but a lot of women would be so focused on the obvious. You know, the lifestyle and so on, they wouldn't have the courage to tell me what they really felt."

"Well, I have to look out for myself and there is only so much change a person can absorb in a short period of time. I hoped you would understand."

"I do understand. It took years for me to get where I am now, if it had happened overnight, I wouldn't have been ready for it. Let's enjoy ourselves today and tomorrow we will get back to Dallas in plenty of time for you to get home and blend right back into your regular life. Think of me as the amusement park that allows you to escape from reality, but don't be surprised if one day I don't want to let you leave."

"Okay," Monique said as they shared a kiss as the boat stopped and dropped anchor.

The rest of the day was spent sunning, eating and drinking and that night they made love in the whirlpool spa, under the stars with the waves gently lapping against the side of the boat. Monique marveled at how something this peaceful could also spawn something as terrible as the hurricane that ultimately caused her to be here. The irony weighed on her that if her old life hadn't been shattered she would never had been at the museum in a borrowed dress to meet this man she was entwined with right now. Life is bittersweet and she knew others didn't fare as well as she did and their suffering continued.

Sunday morning they left the dream world of life on the high seas and headed back to Dallas in a car from another world. When they pulled into the hotel parking lot, Stan told her he would drive a normal vehicle next time like a Mercedes and they both had a laugh about that.

"But if you see me pull up to get you in this thing again then it's going to be a special time," Stan said.

Monique kissed him, said goodbye and went back to her borrowed car to drive home.

Nine

Monique was met by Prentice when she arrived home and they went into the pool house to talk.

"I couldn't believe it when you called and said you were on Stan's yacht out in the gulf," Prentice said.

"I had no idea where I would end up when I left here Friday night, I mean he gets me in this Bugatti car he had just bought and drives down to the coast in the middle of the night. Then he drives right onto his boat and we go out into the middle of the ocean," Monique says.

"Was that all that happened?"

"Well, we got real close."

"Look, did you give him some or not?"

"Yeah, he got some."

"Well, well Miss Devareaux, it looks like the games have begun."

"I told him we needed to slow down."

"That's how you need to do it, if you did your thing right, he'll be calling. But he needs to work for that second go round."

"No it's not that. I just have so many new things going at once. I need time to absorb some of this before I lose control. Now, how was your weekend?"

"Not as exciting as yours, I went to Saul Epstein's funeral," Prentice said.

"I'm going back to the house, Harry is here all week and I get a chance to actually spend some time with him for a change. By the way with that tan, you might be mistaken for a sister."

"Well, I do have a little coffee in my cream."

Prentice looked at her and said, "I think we need to talk about that later."

Prentice left and Monique felt drained from her busy weekend and decided to turn in early so she would be ready for work the next day.

Monique was starting to get into a rhythm at work. The daily grind was good therapy because she knew what to expect every day and the longer that regular pattern persisted the better. Five weeks into her training period Brandy suggested they go out after work and let their hair down. Monique agreed to meet her at ten pm at a club off of Interstate 35 called Culture Clash.

When she arrived and entered she saw Brandy sitting at the bar with a barely there dress on and silver backless sandals that sparkled in the lights from the ceiling.

"Hey, now that's something you can't wear to work," Monique said.

"If, I wore this to work, I'd be giving guys heart attacks," Brandy commented.

Monique ordered a drink and Brandy proposed a toast, "To independent women."

"I'll drink to that," Monique said.

They were talking and having a great time when a guy came up to them, "Hello ladies my name's Darius and I wondered if you would do me the pleasure of joining my friend and I at our table?"

"Why exactly would we join you at your table?" Brandy replied.

"Well we like the company of intelligent, beautiful women and from what I see, no one else here holds a candle to the two of you."

"We'll be over in a minute, after they bring our drink refills," Brandy said.

With that said, Darius went back to the table to wait on them. Brandy watched him as he walked off.

"Damn, he has a nice ass at least," Brandy observed.

"Why did you say we would go over there?" Monique asked.

"They're kind of cute, and Darius may make me give that black guy thing a try, it's been a while since, you know," Brandy said as their drinks came and they walked across the club.

They went to the table and made introductions after sitting down.

"Brandy, Monique nice to meet you, I'm Matt," the other man said.

"I don't recall seeing you ladies here before. Is this your first visit?" Darius asked.

"Yes it is, I heard about this place and decided to check it out," Brandy said.

"I glad you came, there's always an interesting mix of people here," Darius replied as he had definitely zeroed in on Brandy.

"Monique, you seem kind of quite tonight," Matt said.

"Oh, I was just getting adjusted, I don't go to a lot of clubs," Monique said.

"It's funny you mentioned that, because a noisy club is not the greatest place to have a good conversation. That's why I sometimes rent a suite at the Capstone hotel because I live way out in the suburbs. Like tonight I have one reserved and we could go there so we can have a civilized conversation, if you like," Darius offered as he placed his car keys on the table with the Mercedes emblem showing.

"Well I'm not sure about that, we just met, you know," Brandy said. "It is getting late, so maybe we'll follow you for a nightcap."

"Excuse me. I need to visit the ladies room. Brandy would you come with me?" Monique said as she got up and grabbed Brandy's hand.

After they crossed to the other side of the bar Monique said, "I don't think this is a good idea. We shouldn't go to a hotel room with these guys."

"Come on, it'll be fun, we'll have a couple of drinks and leave," Brandy said. "I can't go there alone, plus we'll be driving our own cars and can leave when we get ready."

Monique sighed and said, "All right, just this one time and that's it."

They went back to the table and Brandy said, "Ready when you are."

Soon they were outside and waiting to leave and they trailed Matt in his BMW and Darius in his Mercedes. After arriving at the suite, it was obvious Darius had stocked the place with liquor of every kind and they started talking and having a surprisingly good time. Then out of nowhere Brandy pulled what looked like a makeup compact out of her purse and opened it. It turned out it was not makeup in the small case but a white substance of a different type. She scooped a tiny amount on the end of the fingernail of her pinky finger, raised it to her nose and inhaled.

She looked around and said, "Anyone else what some?"

Monique looked on in stunned silence and knew she would soon be making her exit from this group. Brandy continued to revel in the moment as the cocaine and alcohol were having their effects upon her judgment.

"Your friend seems to like to have a good time," Matt said to Monique as they sat on a sofa watching a music video station.

"This is the first time we've gone out together, I really only know her from work," Monique offered.

"You're more of a reserved type aren't you?" Matt observed.

"I just like to know someone a little better before I let my guard down," Monique said. "You can't be too careful these days because there are a lot of strange things going on."

"You're smart to take that attitude, actually I was surprised you came up here," Matt said. "This is kind of Darius's way of meeting women and he talked me into going out with him tonight."

"Shit, I'm horny, come here," they heard Brandy say and turned around to see her drag Darius into the bedroom.

"Should I go get her?" Monique said to Matt.

"Look, she's an adult and works with you," Matt said. "This could make for an awkward day at the office at the worst of it, but if you try to stop her, in her condition, it could get ugly. You know this is probably not the first time she's pulled this. It looks like she has something she's trying to hide or forget. Using drugs and drinking must be her way of dealing with it."

"Come on, let's fuck," they heard Brandy say from the bedroom.

After a couple of minutes the bedroom door opened and Darius came out with Brandy barely able to stand. She had no clothes on and he sat her down in the seat across from the sofa.

"Could you put her clothes on? I'll make some coffee. Nothing happened," Darius said. "She's too wound up on all of this stuff, mixing that junk with alcohol. We need to get her in shape to go home or let her sleep it off."

Monique put Brandy's clothes on, and she promptly ruined them by throwing up all over her top.

"I'm sorry, guys," Monique said. "I had no idea she got this way."

Darius went and brought a wet towel so Monique could clean Brandy up the best way she could.

"Do you think you should put her in the shower?" Matt asked.

"I think since she threw up most of the alcohol, she'll be okay after a couple of cups of coffee and a little rest," Monique said.

"You know I've been doing this same little routine for a long time and I think it's about time I hung it up, this could have ended badly," Darius said.

"You had no idea she was like this and neither did I," Monique said.

"I know but most of the women that fall for the keys on the table bit aren't like you two. They're usually on the prowl for someone they think is a good catch and will take care of them. I could tell you didn't fit that profile," Darius said.

"How could you determine that?" Monique asked as she poured coffee down Brandy's throat.

"Both of you had looks of confidence about you and you weren't scanning around the club looking for targets," Darius said. "But your friend here needs to get some help before she hurts herself or has someone really take advantage of her. She's lucky to have a friend like you."

"Oh shit, my head is killing me," Brandy said as she opened her eyes and held her head in her hands. "What the fuck happened?"

"You had a little too much fun," Monique said.

"Please don't say a word to anybody at work," Brandy pleaded.

"Don't worry about that, are you going to be able to drive home?" Monique asked.

"Just give me a few minutes and I'll be ok," Brandy said.

"Are you alright?" Darius asked.

Brandy looked as if the realization of where she was had just hit her and said, "What did I do?"

Darius knelt down to her and said, "Nothing happened,"

Brandy put her head in her hands and started sobbing. Monique placed her arms around her, hugged her tight and contemplated that everyone had their own brand of pain. Sometimes they employed unhealthy ways of coping.

After an hour Brandy felt sober enough to drive and Monique followed her until she took the exit near her house. Then she continued towards home herself to find the comfort of her own bed after this trying night.

Monique had made a couple of decisions on her own and one was it was time for her to get her own car. The other was to find somewhere else to live. Things had been tense around Grayson manor and she didn't quite know what was going on, but last week Prentice took a sudden trip out of town for a few days. She went somewhere in East Texas and seemed to be preoccupied about something but didn't bother to share what was on her mind. Monique wondered if it had anything to do with this network she overheard Prentice and Kendra talking about.

Her relationship with Stan was in a holding pattern as his divorce from Doris was hitting critical mass and he didn't want to make any moves to make the fires any hotter. He was sure she had hired a private detective to keep tabs on him. He felt his prenuptial agreement was ironclad, but didn't want to take any unnecessary chances.

Monique decided to upgrade her wardrobe and was browsing through the racks at an upscale clothing boutique when she heard a voice behind her.

"That's her over there. That's the little Katrina evacuee whore that's fucking Stanley."

Monique turned and Doris Brickman was headed straight for her with a scowl on her face. She was being trailed by another woman Monique recalled from the auction.

"Doris," the other woman called after her.

Monique was facing her with no more than two feet separating them.

"Look you little piece of refugee trash, I know all about you. You're nothing more than a ghetto slut from the lower ninth ward. What makes you think you can walk in where you don't belong and latch onto someone else's husband?

"I really don't know what you're talking about".

"Don't play dumb with me. I'm going to expose you for the fraud you are. A man like Stanley won't tolerate being linked to a low class mutt."

Monique was having every button pushed but calmly replied, "If you're having a problem with your husband I suggest you take it up with him. Good day Mrs. Brickman, isn't it?"

Monique left the store and got in her car and drove away. She then noticed her hands were shaking on the steering wheel. She pulled into a parking lot and started crying and tried to regain her composure. After a few minutes she continued towards home.

Determined not to let her run in with Doris throw her off track, Monique had settled on a car and decided to get one of the new Toyota Camry Hybrid vehicles. It made sense to her to get somewhat of an anti-Brandy mobile. She felt with where she came from and with tight gasoline supplies, this was a good choice to express her views about the state of things. She could always take a ride with Brandy or Stan if she wanted to feel the ultimate rush of power.

There was an upscale apartment community nearby that she planned to look into also this weekend because it was time to move on and let Harry and Prentice reclaim their pool house. By the end of the weekend she was driving her new car and had put in an application for a new apartment. Miss Devareaux was becoming fully self-sufficient and it was a great feeling.

She showed her new car to Prentice and she congratulated her and asked for a ride. While they were out, Prentice directed her to a modest house on a street in an unfamiliar part of town. When they parked, Prentice announced this was her parent's house. She introduced Monique and her mother insisted they eat something because in her opinion they both needed a few extra pounds on them.

Prentice's father came around the corner in his powered wheelchair.

"Prentice, come give your old man a hug."

"You're not old Daddy."

"Well I guess not, I'm old enough to be your husband," he laughed.

"No, you didn't say that, did you," Prentice laughed.

"I'm the same age as her husband Harry," he said to Monique.

"Dad, this is my friend Monique,"

"It's nice to meet you. Are you one of her country club friends too?"

"No Daddy, she's new in town. All of my friends aren't country club people."

"It's nice to meet you Mr. Davis."

"Have you talked to your brothers and sister recently?" he asked.

"You know they don't call me. They think I'm uppity or some kind of snob."

"They'll come around. You didn't do anything to them. If you were doing badly in life then I guess they would be happy."

"Are those sweet potatoes I smell?" Monique asked.

"Sweet potatoes, I thought you white girls called them yams," Prentices mother said.

"Momma," Prentice said.

"I grew up around a lot of black people," Monique said.

"Anyway, you two get in here and eat something. Both of you look like you could pass out from hunger."

After eating way too much, Prentice and Monique left and drove back to the north side of the city. When they got back they sat in the pool house talking.

"Your folks are so nice. It must be great to be able to visit them whenever you want to."

"I wanted to ask you about your comment about having a little coffee in your cream, what did you mean?"

"Well, my mother in the old days would have been considered some form of Mulatto or one of those other terms they used to describe someone with a mixed race background. She was very fair and was called redbone, hi yellow and all of that kind of stuff. When she was sixteen she became pregnant with me by a respected doctor in town who happened to be white. For years I didn't know who my father was until my grandmother told me at my mother's deathbed. So I hung between worlds letting people assume whatever they wished about my race. Of course at home most people knew who I was and I lived in a mostly black area in the lower ninth ward. When I went to school in Chicago, it occurred to me, white people felt free to use the n word in my presence because they thought I was one of them," Monique said.

"How did that feel to know someone would say that, but wouldn't if they knew your heritage?" Prentice asked.

"It's like being the invisible man, you know, people said whatever they really feel around me, but when they were around other blacks their whole conversation would change. My complexion has allowed me to get a feel for people as they really are, probably except for black people," Monique said.

"Why do you say that?" Prentice asked.

"Black people think I'm white so they don't say what they really feel about white people around me. It is a very strange situation to be in, to say the least. Let me ask you, is something going on, you've seemed distracted the last week or so?" Monique asked.

"I wish I could tell you about everything that is going but you're better off not knowing. It's just someone I care about is going through a rough time right now and I'm trying to help them through it. So, you said you found an apartment and put in an application?" Prentice said.

"Yes I did, it's off of Preston Road and is gated. It's really nice."

"I think I know where you're talking about. You know you can continue to stay at the pool house as long as you want."

"I know, but it's time I got my own place and get out of your hair. Then you and Harry can go skinny dipping again without worrying about me seeing you."

"Oh please, if Harry decides to go skinny dipping I'll call you so you can witness it first hand. I'm going to miss you for those instant therapy sessions. You've become one of my best friends. I'm so proud of what you've accomplished for yourself, I feel like an older sister, but not much older," Prentice said as they burst out in laughter.

Then Prentice's mood changed and she said, "I didn't want to bring this up, but you need to know what's going on. Come here."

They moved over in front of the computer in the pool house and Prentice brought up her email and opened a message. An e-Newsletter came up called "In The Know" and the headline read "Imposter Poses As Society Member".

Monique read the article:

It has been brought to the editor's attention that at the Hurricane Katrina Charity Auction held in September, all was not as it seemed. One of the guests of a prominent couple was posing as a well heeled aristocrat when in fact she was a Hurricane Katrina Evacuee fresh out of one of the local shelters. Monique Devareaux, pictured above may have pulled off the prank of the year and the joke was on us. Just above the article was a picture with a circle around Monique's face.

"What is this?"

"It's an e-Newsletter a lot of society members in Dallas receive. Country club types can sign up as part of their membership in various organizations. This looks like Doris' handy work. She's going down swinging."

"How many people get this?"

"I think about three thousand. My group has run ads in it for some of our charity projects and that's the circulation number they mentioned."

"I ran into her at a store and she really came after me, but I guess that was just part one. It doesn't matter anyway. I don't owe any of these people anything."

Monique put up a brave front but she was clearly shaken that Doris was capable of such a brazen act. This really fueled her desire to get on her own and lessen the chance of running into any of these people anytime soon.

The next day at work Brandy met Monique at her desk and asked her to come outside with her to talk.

"Monique I want to apologize for last Friday, I'm so embarrassed about how I behaved. That was my first night out in a long time and I went overboard. I'm really not that way, my divorce has knocked me for a loop, and I guess how I'm coping with it is not exactly the best way to handle things."

"Brandy, what if those guy's weren't as nice as they were, you could have been in trouble, we both could have been raped or worse," Monique said.

They approached Brandy's car and she said, "Get in for a minute."

She started sobbing, "I'm such a mess. I act tough around the office to try to fool everybody, but this has got to stop. After my divorce I met some guy five years younger than I am and started partying with him. He started me off using cocaine to get high before we would have sex. Then one day I was with him and got so loaded that when I woke up there was some other guy with me and he was having sex with another girl. I just lost it after that and didn't care, so whenever I'm with someone, I feel like I have to get high to get in the mood."

"Why don't you call the Employee Assistance Program on our insurance plan? They can get you someone to talk to. You've got too much ahead of you to keep going this way."

"Thank you for listening to me. I think I will call and try to get some help. All right, how do I look?" Brandy said after wiping her tears away with a tissue.

"Like a million bucks," Monique said as they went back inside the building.

Brandy followed through on her thought and called the assistance line from her cell phone while she was out making calls and set an appointment to visit a counselor.

Within two weeks Monique was moving into her new apartment and as a surprise house warming gift, Harry had everything that was in the pool house delivered and installed at her new place so she would feel at home. When she called to thank him he made a joke about it saved him from having a garage sale. She thought how fortunate she was to have friends like these. He also told her not to worry about that newsletter because everyone started from somewhere. The editor was assailed for running that story and a retraction was coming in the next issue.

After getting settled in her new home she got a call from New Orleans. Her new found stepmother asked if she still wanted to come visit them for Thanksgiving which was a couple of weeks away. She agreed to go back to New Orleans for the first time since being pulled out of there on a cable hanging on for dear life.

Time passed all too fast as the holidays approached. She knew this would be a trying time because she thought of the thousands of people that were in strange surroundings instead of their homes with loved ones. Families were scattered across the country and some were living with strangers. Some like her had lost loved ones forever and that stark reality would hit home especially hard during a traditional time of togetherness and sharing. Monique knew it would be difficult for some to refrain from cursing God instead of praising him during this season.

Ten

Monique sat at the boarding gate for the flight to New Orleans to meet her new family and return to a place she wondered if she would ever see again. Soon she was seated by a window and felt the thrust of the jet engines push them down the runway and the plane rose into the air over Bachman Lake as it left Love Field and headed for the place she used to call home. As they flew over Dallas she looked down upon the dry parched landscape and blackened areas where wildfires had raged and realized the toll taken by the prolonged drought.

The flight from Dallas to New Orleans was a short one and it didn't take long before they were making the approach into the recently reopened airport. As the wheels touched the runway, she looked out and it was hard to tell if the city was any different from this vantage point.

Once she was in the terminal and beyond the secured area she looked at a man she vaguely recognized and he said tentatively, "Monique, is that you?"

"Dad?" Monique said.

They stood and looked at each other and he grabbed and embraced her for the first time in his life and she hugged him back.

"I'm sorry," he proclaimed through tears.

She wiped away a tear also and noticed an attractive woman in her fifties behind him and she approached and said, "I'm June, your stepmother."

She also embraced Monique and her father took her bag and they proceeded to the car and headed to a sibling meeting she never imagined would happen. The trip to the house revealed the scars and brutal beating the city had absorbed, as some homes looked as if the hurricane had struck yesterday instead of three months ago. She could taste the scent in her mouth and the images sent chills down her spine, truthfully she had doubts about being able to withstand the emotions of being here again.

When they arrived at her father's home she recalled her mother driving her by this very spot on numerous occasions with no idea of who lived there. Once inside she met her two younger sisters and her brother. Looking at her sisters was a surreal experience, particularly Jenny as she had the same cheekbone structure and long flowing legs as she did and was about the same height.

That night they all sat on the screened porch and talked until it was late and time for bed. She would sleep in the room with Jenny and there were two beds there as she and her sister used to share a room. They added another room to the house when they both reached their teens and wanted privacy.

"Did you have any idea you had another sister?" Monique asked.

"No, it was a complete surprise to me until dad set up a conference call and informed us after the hurricane hit. Meagan and I were in college and John Jr. was at home in Florida. He had told mother and apparently she already knew. That threw all of us for a loop. He was worried sick and tried to locate you but it was amazing how difficult it was to get any good information. Then when you called him that day, you should have heard the relief in his voice," Jenny said.

"I didn't have a clue either, I didn't even know he was my father until I was fifteen and my mother was dying when I found out," Monique said.

"Look he's my dad and your dad. What he did wasn't right, your mother was too young," Jenny said. "Let's be honest here, that's statutory rape and I'm making no excuses for him on that front, but we can't undue the past. I'm just glad I found my new sister."

"So am I," Monique said. "Goodnight, Jenny."

"Goodnight Monique."

The next day was Thanksgiving and Monique surprised June by coming to the kitchen and asking if she had an apron she could borrow.

"You know your way around a kitchen?" June asked.

"Well my grandmother told me the way to a man's heart is through his stomach," Monique said.

"That helps," June said as she looked around for prying ears. "There's another room you need to know how to cook in also, after his stomach is full."

Monique looked at her with her mouth open, "I can't believe you said that, we're going to have some fun in this kitchen."

"Look I can't talk like that to my girls, I mean, I'm mom, you know, asexual. You'd think I found them in the cabbage patch. To you I'm step mom and step moms are spicier than moms. I don't know who made those rules but I like them. So thank you for making me a spicy step mom," June said.

"You're welcome," Monique answered. "You could have been bitter about me and the way you've welcomed me into your home means a lot to me."

"My outlook on life changed when that storm came through here. I saw people suffer like I thought I'd never see in my lifetime. Before John could even tell me about you, I asked him had he heard from his daughter Monique and if he knew if you were okay."

"But I thought he told you about me," Monique said.

"I let him off the hook because I could see he was being eaten up inside from guilt, about you and your mother. What was happening was far more important than the past and my children had a sister out in the world we couldn't find. When you called the missing piece of the puzzle was found and it's time for this family to be complete."

"I have to go to my home before I leave, just to lay eyes on it, did you find out any information about my grandmother?" Monique asked as she chopped up celery and onion.

"We tried, but the agencies are a nightmare to get information from and we couldn't find out anything," June said.

The two women continued to talk and moved in unison like they had shared a kitchen together for years. The food was prepared and finally it was time to sit down for a traditional Thanksgiving meal. John Sr. surveyed his newly assembled family for the first time around a holiday setting, said a prayer of thanks, praise and asked for forgiveness from any past transgressions.

After the meal was over her father came to her and said, "Monique do you want to go see your house?"

They all looked and waited for her answer.

"Yes, yes I would," Monique answered.

Soon they left and John Jr. and Jenny went with them. They could only drive to within three blocks and got out and walked the rest of the way. The area resembled a war zone with cars tossed into trees and the waterlines clearly visible up to roof level. Then they rounded a corner and there it was, the home Monique grew up in, saw her mother die in and she cut her way to freedom through the roof.

The hole in the roof was still there, her car, the trusty Mustang that brought her out of Chicago was upside down against the side of the house. They approached the house and the stench in the area was thick enough to feel in the pits of their stomachs. Monique went to the front door and pushed at it and it slowly came open. After stepping inside she let out a blood curdling scream.

The rest of them ran to her and she fell back out of the front door into their arms. Her father went inside and on the floor was a decayed body lying alongside a rusted wheelchair. It could only be her grandmother and why was she still here, with all of the searches, why did Monique have to find her? Jenny flagged down a soldier on patrol and told him her sister just found her grandmother's body inside. He got on the radio and contacted the officials with the morgue to come and take care of the issue. As it turned out many returning residents found the remains of loved ones when they entered their homes again.

Jenny went and helped Monique off of the ground and she said she needed to go in to look for something.

"Are you sure?" her father said.

She nodded yes and covered her nose and walked past the decayed body, climbed on a dresser and reached into the crawl space above the ceiling and felt around until her hands touched a metal object. She got a grip on it and pulled it down and quickly left the building, clutching her prize to her chest. Once outside she brushed it off and looked at it. It was a picture of her mother she had taken into the attic with her but dropped it before she climbed onto the roof. Amazingly it was in remarkable condition and instantly became her most treasured possession.

Her father looked at the image and his mind flashed back to the young girl he remembered and a tear came to his eye and all he could do was say, "Let's get out of here."

"Not yet," Monique said. "This was my block, I grew up here, my mother, uncle and grandmother all lived here. My grandfather paid for this place working on the docks. The corner store, Mr. Jones house next door, my friend Vicky's place over there, everything's destroyed."

"I know it's hard to see everything you knew just wiped out. There has to be a way to put it back together, but it's going to take a long time," her father said.

"Why didn't they just fix the goddamned levees?" Monique said as she walked away towards the car and the others followed.

As they drove back the scars and open wounds of the city were in plain view. Cars littered the street in the same location they were in when the storm hit months ago. The scarred roof of the Superdome seemed to shout out to the world that this city was still bleeding.

Once they were home Monique asked her father and stepmother when it was just the three of them on the porch, "How do you stay here, with all of this chaos around?"

"This is our home and if we left then who would stay," June replied.

"I thought about leaving, but what would I do," her father said. "Sure I could go to some small town that is begging for doctors, but I'm needed here more. You see the hospitals over there. Some people I have known a long time went through hell in those places after Katrina passed through. They were in there for days with patients dying all around them, and no one came to help until it was much too late. Some of those people have left and won't come back because they're damaged by what they went through. I know you'll never get completely over what happened to you. How do you feel about it?"

"It is the strangest thing I've ever had to deal with. I could be fine for days and then it's with me like it happened yesterday. The grocery store, a movie or just sitting at my desk and then I can feel the rough shingles of that rooftop on my legs burning me from being heated up by the sun. Even getting thirsty will trigger a feeling of how dry my mouth and throat became until someone rescued me," Monique recalled.

"Have you thought about seeing a therapist about the way you feel?" June asked.

"I might do that, my job has it as part of our benefit program, do you think it would help?" Monique asked.

"You went through a traumatic event. It was like a war zone and normal people aren't equipped to cope with something like that," her father said.

"Okay, I'll call and get some assistance, maybe it'll help me move on from all of this," Monique replied.

"Monique, we were thinking about going to The French Quarter to lighten the mood a little, how about it?" Meagan asked as she came to the door with Jenny and John Jr.

"Is there anyone there?" Monique asked.

"Oh it's pretty busy with workers that have come in, plus most of that area was barely touched because it's one of the higher points in the city," John Sr. said. "Just be careful if you go, there's a midnight curfew, and the police are on edge, some of those guys are working nonstop, and their homes were destroyed like everyone else. John, you need to go and look after you sisters."

"Sure, I'll drive them," John Jr. said.

"Dad, do you think we're ten years old and need big brother to protect us?" Jenny said.

"Well you can't be too careful, there're a lot of strangers in town," he replied.

"If things get out of hand, I'll give little brother a hand, I've had a little self defense training," Monique said.

"Really, that's so kick ass," Jenny said as they left.

Once they arrived on Bourbon Street, the crowds of people, jazz music and smell of food filled the air like a soothing potion to Monique. Some of the good memories of her home town came flooding back. She even did a little dirty dancing with a strapping soldier to one of her favorite jazz tunes.

"Damn he's cute, you sure you don't want to talk to him," Meagan said.

"I'm leaving here in two days, I might not ever see this guy again," Monique said.

"That's the idea, hit it and forget it," both Meagan and Jenny said in unison and burst out laughing.

"Are my little sisters a couple of wild little bitches?" Monique said.

"Not totally wild, but a girl has to have a little fun," Jenny said.

"Look how John Jr. is pushing up on that woman by the bar," Monique said.

"That guy is a hound," Jenny said. "In school, all of my girlfriends were after him. Later on, I found out he let quite a few of them catch him."

"Hey guys I'll be right back," John said when he came back to the table.

"Who is that?" Meagan asked.

"She a reporter from out of town," John answered.

"Isn't she a little older than you are?" Jenny said.

"She wants an exclusive story, so we're going where we can talk," he said.

"Look, you can tell that bullshit to someone else, go on and tame that Cougar, big brother," Jenny said.

"I'll be back by eleven," he said.

"You know, that's the second time I've heard the word cougar to know what it means in that context," Monique said.

"Let me tell you something about that from personal experience, you can't go to a bar now without seeing these older women all over the young guys," Jenny said. "I was talking with a guy and this woman about forty comes up and practically shoves her tits in his face. She sits on the other side of him and made it so obvious she was interested that he just blew me off. About thirty minutes later he left with her."

"You're shitting me, look at you, and he left with her," Monique said.

"That's not all, a couple of hours later he came back in and came over to my table where I was talking with some friends and tried to carry on a conversation. I told him to fuck off. He went for the easy lay. These guys know these women don't want a serious relationship, but a quick fuck and suck and move on. Then they go back to the kids or whatever," Jenny said.

"They're just trying to catch up with what men have been doing all along, I run into this in Dallas with older guys, especially wealthy ones, snagging these younger women as trophy wives. So these women that have gained some independence are doing the same thing," Monique said.

"Well I'm taking the state bar exam next month. Then I can help liberate some of these cougars from their husbands, for a hefty fee of course, and then negotiate the prenuptial agreement for the new gold digging young wife, cha ching," Jenny said as they all clinked their glasses together.

Soon John returned and Jenny started right in on him, "Oh the great white hunter returns," she said laughing as he pushed the side of her head.

"Shut up," he said.

"Did you put granny to sleep," Meagan said.

"Let's get out of here," he said. "You see what I had to put up with."

That night prior to getting in bed she asked her sisters, "If I get married one day, would you be in my wedding, I know we're sisters, but you don't really know me?"

"Of course we'll be in your wedding, plus I want to come and visit you and for you to come and visit me so we can really get to know each other," Jenny said.

"The same goes for me, also," Meagan said. "Especially since miss know it all here is not the oldest girl anymore."

"Why you little bitch, you couldn't wait to throw that in my face could you?" Jenny said as Meagan pranced out of the room.

Sunday came too soon and they all went to the airport to say goodbye to Monique and she had a much different feeling in her heart than when she arrived. She found a kind woman she could call on for advice and siblings to call her own. Monique also found a man that had grown through tragedy to be what he failed at in better times, a father. Most importantly she reclaimed a piece of her life with her mother's picture. She could finally let her grandmother's memory rest with the other souls freed by the flood waters.

She waved goodbye as she cleared the security checkpoint and headed to her departure gate. This visit was both a traumatic and healing event she knew would have to happen, but she was thrilled she was not alone during the worst moments.

Eleven

It was time for Monique to spread her wings at work and today was her first day solo in the field making sales calls. She was a little anxious about venturing out on her own. She discovered there was nothing to be concerned about after having three great meetings with prospects. Two of those appeared to be solid sales opportunities.

Later in the week she had stopped by a furniture store to pick up a pedestal to place her mother's picture on after she had it framed and restored. Once at the apartment she started to remove the pedestal from the trunk of the car and realized it was a lot heavier than she thought. Carrying it up to her second floor apartment was going to be a chore. After getting it to the ground and closing the trunk she got a firm grip on it and started to try to get it to her shoulder. Monique succeeded when suddenly it was lifted from her and she turned around find her face was about chest level with a very large man.

"Can I give you a hand?" he said. "I'm Moses, I live across from you."

"I'm Monique, sure I was trying to get this upstairs," Monique said.

"After you," he offered.

Monique went up the stairs and opened her door and showed him where she wanted the pedestal. She watched and noticed broad shoulders and toned muscles rippled under his crisply starched white business shirt. His bronzed skin left no doubt he was a black man.

"Thank you Moses. Would you like a soda or something else to drink?" she asked.

"No, that's okay. I've got to change and hit the exercise room for my workout. Have you used it yet since you moved in?" he asked.

"I would almost ask if it looks like I need some exercise, but no I have not used it yet."

"Oh no, you look fine, I mean you seem to be fit, never mine. Would you like to join me in an hour for a light session?"

"Sure. I'll meet you there, in an hour, okay."

She watched as he walked off and thought how did she miss seeing this guy across the courtyard?

When she toured the property they showed her the fitness center and she noticed it had a heavy punching bag. Monique had bought some new training shoes and a uniform. She could workout on the heavy bag for a while. An hour after changing clothes she went to the exercise room. Moses was already there wearing a tight two piece spandex training suit that left his arms, midriff and lower legs bare.

"I see you made it," he said as he was doing squats with about two hundred pounds across his back on barbells.

"I'm going to work out on the heavy bag," Monique informed as she started stretching and sneaking peeks at Moses as he made the rounds on the weight machines.

The last self defense move she had made was when her knee contacted Mel's stomach. Although a little rusty, she started pounding the bag and soon was in the flow and throwing multiple punches. After an hour it became apparent she needed to ease into this kind of routine as she was perspiring heavily.

Then Moses said, "So this is your thing, boxing?"

"It's been a while, what about you, any self defense or do you just bulk up?" Monique asked.

"I do a little boxing for agility and flexibility," he said.

"Want to do a little sparring?" she asked.

"I don't think so," Moses said.

"Open hands just to test the reflexes," Monique said. "I won't hurt you."

"All right, just a little," he agreed.

Moses was about six feet two and two hundred and twenty pounds of muscle contrasted to Monique's five foot eight one hundred and thirty pounds. They began to bounce around the room back and forth. She lunged at him with an open hand swing and he bobbed backwards and she missed. Again she swung and he put up his arm and blocked that shot. Monique was starting to get competitive about this and went in with a right fake and tagged him on the jaw with an open hand inside left. His eyes widened with surprise and he became a little more focused. She swung again with a right and he countered with a left open hand and lightly tapped her on the jaw and she was surprised. Then she threw a left he ducked and scooped her up in his arms before she knew what was happening and sat her down.

"I give," he said. "I'm hitting the whirlpool, want to join me? It keeps me from getting sore."

"Ok, but I was kicking your butt," she said. "Hey, I'm going to get something to drink, and come back, soda, wine or sports drink?"

"Wine and water," he said.

"I'll bring a bottle of both," she said.

She came back with a bottle of wine, a couple of plastic cups and some bottled water. When she took off her uniform she had on the bikini Stan had given her in Galveston and quickly slid into the water even though Moses took quick notes on what he saw. It was now about ten pm and they had the whirlpool to themselves and sat back and relaxed.

"Where did you get the name Moses? That's not one you hear everyday." she asked.

"My grandmother, that's her favorite figure in the bible, so there you go," he said.

They chatted and she found out he was an architect and she told him what she did in order to make a living. This was the first extended conversation she was having with a man since being with Stan. The wine and hot water were like twin conspirators in their soothing effects. She was on the other side of the whirlpool kicking her feet slowly when he caught the heel of her right foot. Moses then proceeded to massage it from her toes individually to the ball and ending at her heel.

She leaned her head back and moaned, "What are you doing to me? That feels so good?"

Then he proceeded to massage her calf muscle. Monique offered up her other foot to him and he repeated the process. This time the feel of his hands on her were causing her to have sensations in other parts of her body. He took her hand and pulled her across the water and turned her around so she was facing away from him, and started to massage her shoulders. The water supported her weight and she leaned back into him. As he massaged her shoulders his hands were slipping down and under the small material of her top and kneading the delicate flesh there as well. She could feel a growing interest from his body pressing against the small of her back. Consciously she pushed backwards to let him know she was aware of his state of arousal. Monique then did something she would not have imagined as she reached back and slid her right hand under the elastic waistband of his spandex shorts and caressed him tightly.

Moses spun her around and with his hands around her waist, he lifted her onto his lap and they shared a deep probing kiss. Monique pushed down the top of his tight briefs and pulled aside the small covering of her thong bikini bottoms and slowly let the water control the rate of her descent until she was sitting with her strong legs wrapped firmly around his waist. He gasped as she let the rhythm in her head direct the movement of her body. This was a meeting that happened by chance and neither of them knew if there would be a repeat performance. This one act play was building to a great ending. The small patches that covered the most sensitive areas of her breasts had been pushed aside by his hands and mouth. She was at a fever pitch and muffled a scream as she tensed every muscle in her body before falling relaxed onto his heaving chest. He also had nothing else left to give this night. She kissed him on his lips and wiped the sweat from his brow and slowly moved to the other side of the whirlpool. Monique readjusted her swimsuit and he pulled his bottoms back up. Just then a couple in their forties entered the room and she got out and dried off just before they entered the whirlpool. Moses got out also and the man couldn't take his eyes off of Monique and the woman drank in more than an eyeful of Moses' muscular form.

They exited the area without speaking to each other. The new couple in the whirlpool had no idea of what had transpired just prior to them coming in, but were destined to repeat the same scene with different actors.

The next day Monique woke up to a wonderful soreness from the activity the prior night. The smile on her face reflected thoughts in her head about what happened just hours earlier. She would blame it on the hot water and wine in addition to the obvious fact that a smoldering hot man was rubbing all of the right places. Would something come of it, who knows? At this point she wasn't committed to anyone. Stan was preoccupied with his divorce and she had an itch and he was the perfect man to scratch it at the time. When she left to get into her car, of all times to run into someone, there was Moses in the garage about to leave for work also.

"Hey Monique, about last night, that's not something I usually do," Moses said.

"Look, I was there also, let's chalk it up to two people, wine and hot water," Monique said. "I don't usually do that either, but it happened, I just don't want it to be awkward with us living in the same building. We're both adults and don't really know each other, except in the biblical sense. I won't get upset if I see you with someone else and you should feel the same way about me."

"Well actually that was what I was leading up to, I'm engaged and last night kind of happened before I knew what was going on," Moses explained.

"You're engaged, congratulations, consider that a wedding gift, and you need to watch inviting strange women to exercise with you, it could lead to something happening," she said.

"I know, that's what I mean, I don't want you to think that's why I invited you to workout, things went too far," he explained.

"Let me let you off the hook, here. I expect nothing beyond that hot tub last night. It was good, don't get me wrong, but it ended when we left. Now don't compare your fiancé to what happened last night with me. I wouldn't want the poor girl to get a complex," Monique said as she got in her car and drove off with Moses standing there with his mouth open.

The amazing aspect of this situation was she didn't feel anything in particular about what happened, but it did bring something else into focus and that was Stan. He was going to have to make a decision on where she fit on his list of priorities. Being put on hold while he worked out other issues was not going to be an acceptable way for her to proceed with her life because she was either the main course or off the menu completely.

Twelve

On this day Monique had an appointment in downtown Dallas late around four o'clock. She probably wouldn't get out of there until about six and needed all day to prepare for it. Brandy greeted her upon her arrival at work and was dressed a little more conservatively and had cut back on the heavy makeup since she started her therapy sessions. Monique was going to some sessions herself for survivors of the hurricane disasters. It was really helping her to talk with people that had gone through similar experiences.

"Monique, I want you meet someone I met a few weeks ago and I owe it all to you," Brandy said.

"How do you owe it to me, I didn't introduce you to anyone," Monique said.

"I know but it is something you said to me that made it possible. Meet me at Culture Clash tonight at eight."

The rest of the day flew by and Monique was heading to her downtown appointment and it was on the southeast edge of downtown and not in the best of areas. On weekends and at night this area was a haven for the homeless. Not far away on Interstate 75 there was a large homeless camp that occasionally was dismantled by the city when high profile events came to town. After parking in a lot behind the building she was going into, she made her way up the steps to get to her meeting.

"What the fuck, that looks like that skinny white bitch from the shelter," Mel said from the bus stop across the street.

"What are you talking about?" another woman said that was standing with her. "Where are you going, the bus is coming?" she said as Mel ran across the street to go into the building Monique went into.

"You tell that motherfuckin bus driver he'd better not leave until I get back," Mel yelled as she ran.

Monique had already gone into her appointment when Mel entered the lobby.

"May I help you?" the security guard asked as Mel approached.

"Are you hiring?" Mel asked as she looked down at the sign-in register and saw the name Monique Devareaux written on the log.

The guard turned to get an employment application. Mel saw a business card Monique had left up front, quickly grabbed it and ran out across the street to get on the bus.

"Hey," the guard called after her, because she had left without the application.

Mel pounded on the door of the Dart bus as it was about to leave, it opened and she hopped on.

"Janice, I told you not to let this fucking bus leave without me," Mel said.

"What was I gonna do, jump in front of the motherfucker?" Janice said. "You shouldn't have been taking your ass across the street. What did you go in there for anyway?"

"For this," she showed Monique's business card. "You remember that skinny white bitch I told you about from the shelter. That was her ass that went in there. Now I know where that bitch works and that's all I need."

"You need to let that shit go," Janice said.

"I ain't letting a goddamned thing go. I told that bitch I was gonna get her ass and I meant what I said. If you don't want to help me then I'll do it by my damned self," Mel said as the bus drove off.

Monique's appointment went great and she left without having any idea Mel had been on her trail. She decided to let the traffic die down a bit by going to the West End and getting a bite to eat as it had been a long day and she was starving. By the time she parked, ate and made her way to meet Brandy and her mystery man it would be about eight o'clock. Finding a park was the first problem. By the time she ate and paid it was seven-thirty. She needed to hit the road if she had any chance of being at the club by eight.

She pulled into the parking lot, saw her Corvette and went in. Brandy saw Monique and waved her over to her table.

"Okay where's superman," Monique said.

"He went to the bathroom and will be right back. There he is behind you."

Monique turned around and Brandy said, "Monique, I want you to meet Moses!"

"Pleased to meet you," Monique said.

"Likewise," Moses said as he shook her hand.

"Look at this," Brandy said as she turned her hand around and showed off a ring. "We're engaged."

"Wow that seems fast, congratulations, how long have you two known each other?" Monique asked.

"About two months," Brandy said. "I've decided to sell my house, you know to start over fresh and found a house plan I really liked. I was looking at some models, but wanted some changes. Well Moses is the architect for the builder and drew up some ideas. He made an appointment for me to come by, go over some options and we kind of clicked."

"I'll go refresh our drinks. What will you have Monique?" Moses asked.

"I'll have a red wine," she said as he walked away.

"How could you be engaged after just a couple of months?" Monique said.

"Well when we met at the model home everyone else had left and he broke out some wine so we could relax and talk about options. The next ting I know after a few glasses we're laughing and talking. We ended up on the floor and shit, it was so hot. I would have never considered being with a black man until you asked me that question at lunch and he's wonderful. It's just been nonstop every since, and last week he gave me this ring, asked me to marry him and I said yes. Now he's designing the house for both of us as our love nest."

"Are you sure?" Monique said feeling sick to her stomach.

"Positive, I was with my ex for three years before we got married and he still screwed me over. Moses says he loves me and I am crazy about him," Brandy said.

Moses returned to the table and Monique put up a brave front and made polite chit chat. The next time she would see him there would be nothing polite about her or the conversation. When she left the club her cell phone rang and it was Stan on the line.

"Monique, it's Stan, I want to see you. Can we get together tomorrow night for dinner at my house?" he asked.

"Your house, that's a first."

"Doris has moved out and I want to show the place to you and really talk about us. How about seven o'clock?"

"I'll see you at seven."

"Just come comfortable, no need to dress up," he said.

Monique felt a little blasé about seeing Stan at this point. She felt a little set aside by being put on ice because of his divorce. This incident with Moses and Brandy had really put her in a bad mood. She waited with her curtains cracked to watch for him to return to his apartment. She saw him around twelve midnight and she stepped out of her door and gestured for him to come over. He dropped his head and made his way to her door and she pulled him inside.

"What the fuck was that display tonight?"

"Monique, I had no idea you knew Brandy."

"So you don't do that type of thing often. Does taking advantage of a business client on the floor of a model home qualify? What kind of man are you? That woman is in a fragile emotional state and you used it to get what you wanted. By the way what do you want? Money, what is it?"

"Hold on. I see where you're coming from and it's an unfortunate circumstance that you know Brandy, but I'm sincere in the way I feel about her?"

"That sincerity didn't stop you from fucking me two nights ago on our first meeting. I'm going to be watching your ass like a hawk. If I have too, I'll lose my friendship with Brandy rather than see her hook up with a sleaze trying to clean her out."

"What do you mean?"

"I'll tell her you screwed me after you were engaged to her, but before you knew who I was."

"You wouldn't do that, you're bluffing."

"I've stared down the barrel of a hurricane and sat on a rooftop for three days, just try me."

"Ok, I get the point."

"Piece of shit," she said as she slammed the door.

The next day she gave Brandy the number of her sister Jenny and told her to call her about a prenuptial agreement because this time she should protect herself. Brandy thought that was a good idea.

If her life settled down, then it wouldn't be as much fun she thought as she got ready to go over to Stan's home for the first time. She pulled up and an attendant opened her door like she was at a five star resort. The architecture there did indeed rival and surpass some of the finest resort properties. In the past two months of living in her small apartment, she had become unaccustomed to the almost decadent level of luxury Stan and his circle enjoyed on a daily basis. Once inside, Stan was there dressed in a crisp pair of jeans and somehow seemed out of place in his own home. His décor was reminiscent of an old English castle with claw footed furniture, rich dark walnut wood wainscoting and high arched door-ways.

He walked up to Monique, hugged her tightly and kissed her. She gave him a somewhat lukewarm response and he led her by the hand to a sitting area.

"Monique I want to apologize for not being more attentive over the last couple of months, but this has been very difficult. Doris and I have been together since I was twenty years old and the last eight of those we were married. I felt I owed her the respect of not publicly parading around with another woman while we were still living under the same roof. It was more about respect for her as a person and as my legal spouse and not a slight against you. I hope you understand," Stan explained. "I also feel terrible about that e-Newsletter stunt she pulled on you. That was below the belt."

That explanation wiped away the hurt feelings and in fact made her feel somewhat childish and selfish for the way she felt. She would want the same treatment if she was in Doris's shoes.

"I understand and it was noble of you to show that kind of respect to someone you have spent over half your life with," Monique said. "I must admit I was feeling sorry for myself and now it makes perfect sense. I feel a little selfish."

Monique then kissed him to make up for the half heated effort she gave upon her arrival.

"Now that we're back on track, I have a dinner invitation and I want you to be my date. Harry and Prentice Grayson invited me and a guest to dinner Saturday night at their humble abode. Would you like to join me?" Stan asked.

Monique looked at him in awe, "Wait, this has to be a setup."

"Well, they did say something about how some people never visit, but I have no idea what they're talking about."

"Sure, I'll go with you. Here's my new address."

"You mean the place on Preston Rd. apartment 206."

"I'm going to kill Prentice, she told you, didn't she."

"I will be there to pick you up at seven. Let me show you around the place," he said and took her by the hand and gave her a grand tour.

By the time they made it back to the main house it was time to eat and a sumptuous seafood spread was laid out for their enjoyment. Tonight after they ate Stan took her to the theater room and they watched a romantic movie and then they expressed how much they had missed each other by retiring to the master suite.

Stan had a surprise for Monique. He waited until she was nude and laying out on the silk sheets of the custom bed. Once she was looking up at the ceiling he pressed a button on a remote. The ceiling and roof began to retract. Slowly the stars and moon came into view. Monique thought she had witnessed everything but this expressed extravagance at a new level. Being outside while still in the bedroom was a powerful aphrodisiac. She went to him and started to remind him of that night at sea. This time there was no sleeping involved as she only stopped when she had just enough time to get home and get ready for church. Stan didn't rise for hours. He felt he had found someone special enough to let his guard down and invite into his private world.

Monique was now wondering what to wear to dinner Saturday night. Delightfully this presented an opportunity to go shopping. She had just had her first big commission check deposit so she went to one of the designer outlets stores at the mall and saw just the thing. It was still there, the dress she saw in the mall when she was there with Sonja. The finishing touch was a pair of fashion sandals with a barely there look and red sparkles that reflected the light brilliantly. The price tag made her gasp a little but for her first visit to the Grayson home as a dinner guest, she wanted to be appropriately attired.

That Saturday was spent getting prepared all day with hair, facial, nails and a wax just in case. Back at home she was putting on the finishing touches and looking in the mirror when the speaker in her apartment came on. She pressed the button and a voice replied saying it was Stan. She buzzed him in and he came up to retrieve her. She let him in and he was obviously pleased with what he saw. As he turned to leave he spotted the picture sitting on the pedestal.

"Who is this?" he said.

"That's my mother."

"Really, she's black?"

"Yes, she was. Is that a problem?"

"No, not for me," Stan replied. But it could cause a problem in the trailer park when I tell my mother I'm dating someone that had a black mother."

She looked at him and said, "Your mother doesn't live in a trailer park, does she?"

"Well, she doesn't, I was just pulling your leg."

"But really, is my black heritage an issue with you?"

"Why should it be? I see a beautiful woman when I look at you on the outside and who you are inside is who I'm falling in love with. The beautiful outside parts certainly make things more pleasant," he said laughing.

"You know you're a pretty funny guy, sometimes," Monique said.

Across the courtyard, Moses was taking in the whole scene and went down to the parking garage to see what Stan was driving. When he saw Monique slip into the passenger seat of the Bugatti, he almost wet his pants. This was pure visceral testosterone flexing of cubic dollars of the highest order. His biggest question was how could someone he was having sex with in an apartment hot tub a few days ago drive off in a one point three million dollar car and work with his newly minted fiancé. His curiosity was eating at him to no end because maybe he had selected the wrong target in Brandy but after what happened, that was an opportunity lost.

When Stan and Monique arrived at the Grayson home they were introduced by the butler, "Mr. Stanley Brickman and Miss Monique Devareaux have arrived."

They entered and Prentice and Harry greeted them with handshakes and hugs.

"Stan the buzz around the club is you're driving a new toy," Harry said.

"Yes, come out here and I'll show it to you," Stan said as he and Harry went outside.

"Men," Prentice said. "So how have you been Miss Independent? You look fantastic."

"I'm doing great, my life hasn't felt so good in a long time," Monique said. "How about you?"

"Things are fine. I'm very busy with my projects."

"How's Kendra doing, I haven't seen her in a long time?"

"Kendra's not doing so well, she getting a divorce."

"I'm sorry to hear that. I hope she comes out of it in good shape."

"I think Kendra will be fine, she's a pretty strong woman."

Just then Harry and Stan came in and they sat down to eat and after dining the group adjourned to the parlor area to talk.

"Stan here is getting back in the business game and we've been having some discussions on joint ventures between his new company and Grayson Micro. Some of the technology that is going to be required can be supplied by us and now is the time to get the early design phase going," Harry said. "I need someone to be the relationship manager and liaison between Grayson and Brickman Communications. That person is in this room, Miss Devareaux."

"What, me, are you serious, I just started a few months ago?" Monique said.

"Look I spoke with your manager and you're doing a great job, and for some reason the head of Brickman Communications requested you personally," Harry said.

Monique jumped up and gave Harry a big hug, "Thank you. I can't believe it."

"Stan, is it appropriate for the CEO to get a big hug from a female salesperson? I'd better check the employee manual," Harry said.

Monique then leaned over and gave Stan a big kiss.

"There has to be something in there about running your tongue down the throat of a client," Harry said and burst into laughter. "With this new title I suppose we will have to pay you more money, get you a company car and a bigger expense account. Your new package will be ready at personnel on Monday. Well what else is happening. Are the Cowboys still playing football?" Harry asked.

"I'm just teasing you Monique, congratulations," Harry said. "Dear would you pass her a tissue?"

"Won't the other people with more experience be upset?" Monique asked.

"Look, don't worry about them, you know the big boss and you know the main man at the customer. It helps to have friends in high places," Harry said. "You don't owe anyone any apologies. You deserve it. It'll take a couple of weeks to go into effect but by the end of the year you can leave your old territory and start the new job. I think with that company car program you can get an E class Mercedes or a five series BMW. We had to stop somewhere."

"Congratulations, darling," Stan said.

"Can he call his salesperson darling?" Harry said jokingly. "Stan come out back, I've got a stash of Cuban cigars, lets go fire up a couple."

Harry and Stan left and Prentice said, "I had no idea this was coming, I think those two were in on this together."

"I didn't even know they talked," Monique said.

"They speak a universal language, money," Prentice said.

"I'm so happy for you," Prentice said.

They talked the rest of the night away and that night Monique stayed over at Stan's house. Monique woke up with the realization their relationship had moved into a new realm. She didn't even go home that weekend and quietly became the new lady of the house.

Thirteen

Monique was a few days from ending her time in her old territory and starting her new position working strictly to develop business with Brickman Communications. As she was pulling into the company parking lot in her new company issued Mercedes, she had no idea about being watched from across the street.

"That's her Janice. She got out of that white Benz. Let's come back around five and follow her ass home," Mel said.

"Look, I need to get my mother's car back home. She's going to kill me," Janice said.

"Look you are either with me or you're not. I don't need you to punk out when this is ready to go down," Mel said.

"All I'm gonna to do is drive. I ain't going back to jail behind your bullshit. What did she do to you anyway, besides turn you down?" Janice asked.

"Fuck you. That bitch got lucky and landed a punch on me. She ain't nothing but a ho anyway. She was in the same motherfuckin shelter I was and she's driving a goddamn Benz. The first time somebody picked her up it was an old man in a Bentley. Then she shows up in a Jag. Now this skank ho is driving a Benz. That some bullshit. She from the same place I'm from. Just because she's white and is spreading pussy around, she's on top and I'm riding the Dart bus. I'm gonna change that shit up tonight. Let's go to the mall and come back here about four-thirty."

Janice started the Buick and it took several turns to get the engine fired.

"It's cold out here and this car don't want to start good in the cold," Janice said as she drove off.

Around four thirty the green Buick pulled across from the Grayson parking lot and watched as the cars started to leave. After thirty minutes Monique went to her car and left the lot. Janice and Mel pulled out behind her with about four cars between them and had to hustle to keep up with her in the traffic. Then the freeway came to a standstill because of a disabled vehicle up ahead. Finally they inched past the bottleneck and had to floor it to catch up to Monique. She exited on Preston and made her way to her apartment building. Mel watched as she went in and surveyed the area which was gated and fenced all around. But she saw one vulnerable area and that was where the limbs of a tree had grown over the fence near a hill. She felt she could climb in over the fence by going up the side of the hill and use the tree limb as her way in.

"Back the car up, so I can see which door she's going in," Mel said. "All right it's the third door from this end on the second floor."

"Look let's get out of here now," Mel said. "There're too many people around, but I know what I need to do. I'm coming back tomorrow and I'll be waiting for her ass when she gets home."

"I'm not driving you back up here tomorrow," Janice said.

"Then I'll take the bus, there's a stop right down the street," Mel said. "If you gonna punk out, then fuck you."

The next day was fairly normal and Monique went to work as usual and nothing out of the ordinary was taking place, but back at her apartment an activity of a different sort was going on. Mel had taken the bus from the south side of town to north Dallas and was determined to finish what she had started months ago in the shelter. The bitterness that brewed inside of her was fueled by her belief she had been dealt an unfair hand in life. Seeing how Monique had moved far beyond where she was, when in her mind they started at square one together only a short time ago. How did it happen, they were both homeless and broke when they first arrived in Dallas on buses from the broken city of New Orleans. The only things Mel could attribute the difference in their positions in life was skin color and her using sex as a way to get ahead. The fact that Monique rejected her advances and struck her was just an exclamation point to inflame her hatred.

Melina was her given name, and she grew up in the lower ninth ward of New Orleans along with two brothers and one sister. Her father never stayed with the family and ended up in and out of prisons. Her mother had to work day and night to provide for her children and keep them from being hungry and homeless. With a general lack of adult supervision Melina was introduced to a rough crowd at an early age and the streets became the main classroom where she gained her education in life. The lesson she learned there was survival of the fittest and as she matured she applied those lessons well. Dropping out of school in the tenth grade allowed her to get into more trouble than her mother could bail her out of and she ended up in juvenile detention for carjacking and possession of a controlled substance. While incarcerated another side of her personality came out and she started calling herself Mel, cut her hair short and dressed in a masculine manner. She was released after two years and continued to delve into criminal enterprise. She rose to the top of one of the local female gangs and held that position both in and out of jail.

The storm hit while she was on one of her stints in jail. In the ensuing chaos she walked out with several other inmates and disappeared into the madness that occurred over the following days. When the buses rolled out of New Orleans she just blended in with the people getting on board and rode out of town with everyone else. Now she has remained underground in case her criminal record resurfaces to haunt her in this new city while she was trying to get a new foothold. This mission was about retribution and revenge. It would also release months of frustration brought on by her sudden loss of status due to being shipped out to a new place without her former organization to support her. For Mel the hurricane destroyed everything she valued most in life and frankly she didn't see much of a future. Monique had unknowingly become the symbol of everything Mel thought kept her down, race, class, appearance and sexual preference.

After a couple of route changes Mel exited the bus at the stop about one hundred yards from Monique's apartment building. When she approached the building she caught a lucky break when a delivery truck entered the security gate. She quickly went in and headed for the covered parking area. Entering locked doors was no problem. Her extensive list of illicit skills included breaking and entering and she could pick any lock on the market. There was one point when she invested in a collection of locks of various types from the local hardware supply and practiced how to pick each one within one minute's time.

Once inside the garage she took out her tools and looked around the corner to a first floor apartment door to size up what kind of locks the building had. She knew generally all of the doors should have the same brand of lock because the management office would keep a spare key for each unit. She recognized the type of lock and figured it would take thirty seconds for the door knob and thirty seconds for the deadbolt. She scanned for any security guard or maintenance person and the area seemed to be clear. She knew if she went up and did her job right it would look like she was using a key and it's not unusual for someone else to have a key to an apartment. In today's society it's rare for people to be very familiar with their neighbor's extended friends or family members and this worked to Mel's advantage.

It was about two in the afternoon and quiet. The management office was in another building and she made her move up the stairs and counted the doors until she got to the one she saw Monique go into the prior day. Once in front of the door she nonchalantly pulled out her pick tool that looked like a gun and she had already inserted the right blade. Thirty seconds later the bottom knob was unlocked, within a minute total the deadbolt slid back. She calmly entered the living area of the apartment and closed the door behind her.

Mel looked around and only became more upset by looking at the furnishings, entertainment system and decorations that adorned the inside of Monique's home. A pang of hunger hit her. She went to the kitchen, opened the refrigerator and scanned for something to eat.

"I should have known this bitch wouldn't have nothing good to eat in here," she said. "I'll be damned; this looks like some gumbo and cornbread."

Mel looked through the cabinets and saw Tabasco, Louisiana Hot Sauce, filé powder, corn meal and other seasonings. In another cabinet she found a bowl, took the pot of gumbo from the refrigerator, poured some into the bowl and placed it in the microwave. After heating it, Mel sat down at the table and ate. This was as brazen as it gets. If this wasn't enough, she took it beyond this absurd point by turning on the television and watched as she waited for her victim to return.

When four o'clock came Mel decided to clean up her mess. She chose to wait in the bathroom and sat on the toilet seat so she wouldn't be seen when Monique entered the door. She had a knife on her but figured she wouldn't need it, but a small chain that was wrapped around her hand and the element of surprise were the main weapons. This was turning into a long wait but around six o'clock she heard the click of high heels walking towards the front door. Then she heard the distinctive rattle that only keys on a chain made. Each click of the locks acceler-ated Mel's heart rate up a notch and she was coiled to spring when the time was right. Then she heard the door open and close again. Soon the sound of the tele-vision filled the apartment. Lights came on in the bedroom and there she was, facing away from her. She sprang from the bathroom and took one swing and her fist with the chain wrapped around it made contact and Monique went sprawling across the bed face first. The blow was solid, but Monique lowered her head down just before she was hit as she was bending to remove one of her shoes and that lessened the impact.

Because of that slight head movement Monique was coherent enough to turn over on the bed as Mel pounced on top of her and she sunk her manicured nails into the side of Mel's face. She dug in with all her strength and chunks of skin and flesh became lodged under their edge. Blood streamed down Mel's face as the two women struggled in silence. Mel had a grip around Monique's throat and she couldn't speak and Mel wouldn't utter a word to avoid being discovered. This was not a gentile cat fight between to ladies, but a struggle for survival as two women fought with every fiber of their being, one for domination and the other for existence itself. Minutes passed and perspiration flowed from the strain of muscles and sinew against each other. Mel had the upper hand due to her initial advantage of surprise and her position allowed her weight to work for her as she pressed down upon Monique's body.

Soon the deprivation of oxygen combined with the damage from the blow to her head started to cause Monique to feel lightheaded and her grip on Mel's face started to loosen. Ten minutes into this fight for life, Monique's arms fell to her side and she slipped into semi consciousness. She could hear and feel but couldn't speak. Mel loosened her grip from Monique's neck and took out her knife and cut her dress open from the bottom to the top and ripped a strip of it off and tied it around her mouth so she couldn't make any noise. Then she tied Monique's hands together, pulled her arms over her head and tied the other end to the headboard. She then proceeded to tie each of her ankles to the legs of the footboard and had Monique's legs spread eagle on the bed. Mel then delivered a slap across Monique's face with enough force to start a trickle of blood from the right corner of her mouth.

"That's for what you did to me in that shower, slut," Mel said.

Monique's eyelids were fluttering between being open and closed as her head rolled from side to side. Mel then used her knife to cut every piece of clothing from Monique's body and when she was completely naked she climbed onto the bed and straddled Monique's torso and started to talk to her.

"You remember me bitch. Yeah that's right it's Mel from the shelter. I told you to watch out for me and if I ever caught you alone, I was gonna get your ass. Look at you now, what you gonna do, kick me?" she said as she stood up and scanned Monique's body from top to bottom.

"So this is what been gettin you over? Mel said as she ran her hand the length of Monique's frame. "Not bad, no wonder those old men are giving you what you want after you give them a piece of this."

Mel began to undress. When she was naked she looked at Monique who seemed to be coming out of her stupor a little more and proceeded to squeeze her breasts roughly and pinched her hard. She laughed afterwards.

Since you wouldn't give me what I wanted, I guess I'll have to take it," Mel said.

Mel then crawled over Monique and turned facing her feet and she lowered her head between Monique's legs and proceeded to violate her with her mouth.

She took every liberty while she was in total control. Mel at the same time was roughly smothering Monique's face with her body as she used her to satisfy her own carnal desires. This was not enough for Mel because after she satiated her desires she then wanted to take from Monique the one thing she thought was getting her ahead in life, her appeal to and desire for men.

"I know you liked that didn't you bitch? If you thought that was good then you're gonna love what I've got for you now," Mel said.

Mel reached into her bag and pulled out various devices she had with her. She then proceeded to violate Monique with them and did so in a manner as brutal as any man could if he was forcing himself on a woman. It is said rape is not a crime of passion but of violence and it was never more evident than it was at this moment. Mel reveled in this side of her dark personality. She was a dominator and liked to take her conquests forcefully and would never be mistaken for trying to mask her preference for the fairer sex. She was on the outer edge and too extreme for most women in the lesbian community. Her aggression had driven her into a subculture when it came to intimate relationships. Mel had some of the tools of her brand of pleasure with her and was utilizing them now to inflict pain and humiliation.

Monique had regained a lot of her clarity of thought and cold see Mel's face as she brutalized her body while taunting her, "You like that, huh white bitch, is that how those old rich bastards fuck you."

Tears streamed down her face as the assault continued and when she couldn't stand the pain anymore, Monique passed out. When she felt she had made her point, Mel cleaned herself in her victim's bathroom, doctored her wounds and started to leave. Prior to leaving she looked up and saw Monique's college degree hanging on the wall. Then she picked up the picture of her mother and the frame was engraved "Margaret Lacroix Devareaux" and the bottom read "Mother".

"Well I'll be damned, her mama's black," Mel whispered as she pulled the hood of her coat over her head to hide the fresh wounds to her face and went back and left one more insult and spat on Monique's battered body.

"Trash," she uttered and turned to leave.

When she went out of the door and closed it, she glanced across the courtyard. Moses looked her in her eyes and then went into his apartment. He thought it was just a guest leaving although it was rather warm to be wearing such a thick coat.

Monique lay across her bed bleeding from the abuse Mel had inflicted upon her and she was still out from the combination of shock and pain. It's amazing how time can slow down when you are in desperate need. She regained consciousness and initially was numb as her body had shut down as a defense mechanism against going past her pain threshold. Slowly her nerve endings and sensory relays started to send signals to her brain again and she was on fire. Her pain level from raw flesh and tears were more than words could describe. There was nothing she could do to ease her condition as her hands and legs ached from their bonds. Minutes melted into hours and she wondered if she would ever be found as the first light of day came through the window above her bed.

The next day Moses went to his car and thought it strange that both Monique's company car and personal car were still there as she always left for work ahead of him. For some reason his radar was up and he went to her apartment and knocked on the door and there was no answer. He really became concerned and went to the manager's office. The manager, whose name was Rose, went to her door with him, called in from her cell phone and no one answered. She used her extra key and entered.

"Miss Devareaux, are you here?" Rose asked.

Then they heard moans from the bedroom and cautiously walked in. The sight of Monique's battered body and bloodied bed shocked Rose and she turned away and screamed. Moses grabbed her and then rushed to Monique and removed the gag from around her mouth and held her.

"Call 911!" he yelled to Rose and she picked up the phone and dialed.

He looked in the bathroom pantry and found a sheet and wrapped it around her body.

"Just take it easy, help is on the way," Moses assured.

"Water," Monique whispered.

"She wants some water," he told Rose who rushed into the kitchen and poured some into a glass and brought it to Monique and held it to her lips.

She took a drink and then another. Then she started to sob and shake.

"Who did this?" Moses asked.

"Mel," Monique managed to say. "From New Orleans."

"You're saying Mel and he's from New Orleans?" he repeated.

"Mel is a woman," Monique said weakly.

He looked at Rose and both of their faces expressed shock at her revelation of her assailant being a female. Just then there was the wail of sirens. The ambulance and police showed up about the same time. He moved back and the paramedics attended to Monique. After a few minutes they placed her on a stretcher and rolled her out to the ambulance.

"Where are you taking her," Moses asked.

"Medical City," the paramedic shouted.

The police took statements from both Rose and Moses. They both told them Monique said someone named Mel from New Orleans did this and she said Mel was a woman. Rose went to the office and the files had Prentice written down as her emergency contact. She made the call to inform her of what had happened.

Prentice was frantic and rushed to the hospital and she called Harry who was at the office to inform him also. Moses got in touch with Brandy and told her what had happened. Brandy knew he lived in the same apartment building with Monique. They had laughed about the coincidence that they didn't already know each other until Brandy introduced them at the club.

Harry made the call to Stan and told him the woman in his life was headed to the emergency room from a brutal sexual assault that happened in her home.

There was a group about to converge at the hospital emergency room out of concern for someone they all cared deeply about, even though six months ago they never knew she existed.

Fourteen

Monique lay in the examination room and the doctors, nurses and police sex crime scene investigators all poured over her. They collected samples from her private areas and scraped the skin and flesh from under her fingernails. She required stitches to her head and multiple sutures to her genital area to close tears. The deepest wounds were internal, to her psyche.

Since Prentice was her emergency contact, the doctors told her about Monique's medical condition.

"Mrs. Grayson, I'm Dr. Franklin."

"How is she?" Prentice asked.

"Miss Devareaux suffered a brutal sexual assault. She has a moderate concussion from a blow to the head and we closed the laceration there with three stitches, but those are hidden by her hair so they won't show after that area heals. She also has vaginal and anal tears that required a total of seven stitches. Luckily we didn't find any evidence of internal bleeding or damage to her uterus, but there is a lot of deep bruising to her legs and pelvic area. There are some minor scratches to her neck and face. Also her ankles and wrist have burns where she was tied.

"This is bad but it could have been worse," Dr. Franklin said.

"How is she behaving?" Prentice asked.

"She is very quiet and isn't talking very much," Dr. Franklin replied. "We have great counselors on staff and they will speak with her in a day or so."

"Can I see her?" Prentice asked.

"Sure, but don't stay too long," he said. "She's this way."

Prentice went into the small room and Monique looked at her and held up her arms and Prentice went over and embraced her. Monique held onto her tighter than anyone ever had.

"Why did this happen to me?" Monique asked through tears. "I'll never get away from all of this misery following me. I came all the way here and it's like I'm marked by a curse that followed me from New Orleans."

"You didn't deserve this and it's not your fault."

"She hurt me bad, Prentice. Really bad," Monique said. "Nobody will want me now and I don't know if I want anyone to ever touch me again."

"I know. It'll get better."

"Could you call my father and tell him? My purse is over there in that chair."

"Sure, I'll call him."

"My Uncle Albert, his number is in there also. What am I going to do, look at me? I should have known better, my life couldn't be this good, it couldn't last."

"Don't say that, this is not your fault, we're going to find out who did this to you," Prentice said.

"I know who it was, but I don't know where she lives or any details about her at all. I ran into her at the shelter and she tried something with me then and I fought her off. I guess she's had it out for me since that happened. For some reason she resents me for what I represent in her mind. I didn't do anything to her, I don't even know her."

"How could a woman do this to another woman?" Prentice said with her own special understanding.

Soon they moved Monique to a private room and the police came in and took a statement.

Harry, Brandy, Moses and Stan came by to visit her although she was very reluctant for Stan to touch her and felt ashamed to look into his face. He comforted her and assured all of his resources would be used to bring whoever did this to justice. Then he did something she didn't anticipate, he told Monique he was in love with her. Monique felt she was a long way from loving someone else right now because at this moment she felt no love for herself and didn't know if she ever could again. Then someone she didn't expect to see came to visit her.

Kendra walked in and sat by her bedside and just held her hand, "You don't have to talk if you don't want to."

"No, It's good to see you and thanks for coming by," Monique said. "I'm surprised and I haven't seen you in a while."

"The person that did this to you doesn't like herself and you point out to her what she could have been. I have met that type myself, instead of improving themselves; there is a voice inside telling them it's easier to tear others down to their level and feel good about it," Kendra said.

"Could that be it, this person wanted to strip me down to feel better about her life and doesn't she feel any emotions when pain is being inflicted on another person?" Monique asked.

"You can't measure this type of person by normal societal standards because they have been twisted by circumstances and their mental makeup to be predators. The rest of us look just like a mouse does to a cat. To them we are prey to be exploited," Kendra said. "You get some rest and remember this was not about you."

Kendra left the room and Monique had another point of view to ponder while she lay in her hospital bed amidst a near garden of flower arrangements. Soon the morphine drip meant to ease her pain allowed her to drift off into a deep sleep that would last the rest of the night.

In another part of town a television was tuned to a local news program that was recounting a brutal sexual assault that took place in a North Dallas upscale apartment complex. Then the station displayed a picture of the prime suspect.

"Dallas police are searching for this person. Twenty-four year old Melina Hawkins also known as Mel Hawkins is believed to be in the Dallas area. It has been confirmed Hawkins is a fugitive from New Orleans who escaped during the aftermath of Hurricane Katrina and blended into the regular population. Apparently she came to Dallas with other evacuees and at one time was housed in one of the temporary shelters set up to assist the hurricane victims. According to authorities it is believed Hawkins may have several deep scratches on her face. There is a reward for twenty thousand dollars set up for information leading to Melina or Mel Hawkins capture and arrest. At this time it is not known if she is armed," the news reporter said.

"Janice did you see that?" an older black woman said.

"Yeah, momma I saw it," Janice said. "I don't know anything about it. I ain't seen her in almost two days."

"I don't care if she is your first cousin or not, I don't want her in my house anymore," her mother said. "I don't want you to hang around her either. She's nothing but trouble, fooling with women and now she's attacked one. Lord help me."

Janice's eyes were as big as saucers because she knew if Mel was busted she would go down also for helping her find out where Monique lived and driving her around. She could also be charged for knowing what Mel was planning to do and not reporting it to the police. She figured Mel was toast with a twenty thousand dollar bounty on her head, in the world she lived in that kind of money can change someone's life. While she was in bed staring at the ceiling, Janice heard a tap on her window and almost jumped out of her skin. She turned and Mel was staring at her through the glass motioning for her to open the window. Janice went over, removed the stick above the window that prevented it from being raised and slid it up. Mel crawled through.

They talked in near whispers to avoid Janice's mother's keen ears, "What did you do to that woman, it's all over the news?"

"I got that bitch good, you can hang an out of order sign on that pussy for a while," Mel said.

"You can't stay here because momma saw the news and said so. They got a twenty thousand dollar reward out for you. You know somebody's gonna turn your ass in for that kind of money." Janice said. "Damn, your face is all fucked up. She scratched the shit out of you."

"How much money you got?" Mel asked. "I'm gettin the hell out of Dallas, I'll catch an eighteen wheeler to Houston or something, and I got some homies down there."

"I got forty dollars," Janice said. "That's all my money."

"Give it here and maybe I won't tell the police you helped me if I get caught," Mel said.

"Who's gonna pick you up looking like that?" Janice said.

"Look, if I gotta fuck some fat truck driver to get a ride, so what. If her pussy can get her a Benz maybe mine can get me a ride outta this motherfucker. Go get me a wet towel so I can wipe off and get out of here," Mel commanded.

After Janice left the room, Mel was getting uneasy about why it was taking so long when the door opened and a bright light was in her eyes, "Don't move, Dallas Police," the voice commanded.

Mel bolted out of the light and quickly crawled through the window and when she turned to run she was tackled immediately by a police officer who pressed her face down to the ground and had a knee in the middle of her back. She spread her arms out on the ground because she knew the procedure to follow that would spare her an officially sanctioned ass kicking. Her arms were pulled behind her back and cuffs were snapped in place. Then a female voice started reading her rights.

Mel turned and looked at the female officer who was leading her off and said, "Caught by a motherfuckin bitch."

She was placed in the back of the squad car and somehow the top of the roof didn't quite miss her head as she was pushed into the seat. She glared at the officer who flashed a screw you smile back at her. When she looked out of the window at Janice and her aunt, she just figured her aunt turned her in to get rid of her instead of accepting her for who she was.

The next day Monique opened her eyes to the faces of her father and step-mother at her bedside and it made her feel warm all over.

"Hi," she said.

"Monique, I'm so sorry this happened," her father said as he hugged her.

June came over and brushed the hair back on her head and kept stroking her hair and kissed her on the forehead.

"How do you feel dear?" June asked.

"I'm sore all over, and I don't even know if I can walk," Monique said.

"Do you want to come home with us, until you feel better?" June asked. "The doctor said in a few days you can go home, and it would do you good to get away for a while."

"I'll think about it, that might be nice," Monique said.

"Oh, a policeman came by and said they took the person they think did this into custody last night," Monique's father said.

"Really, could you give me the telephone, I want to call the detective that left me his card," she said.

She spoke with the detective assigned to the case for several minutes and finally hung up the phone and held her head back and clasped her hands together,

"They've got her," Monique said. "A DNA sample has already been taken to match against the flesh they took from under my fingernails. He said she had marks on her face that matched the pattern my fingernails would have made."

"Why would this person do this to you," June asked.

"It's a long story and if I go back home with you, I'll fill in all of the blanks," Monique said. "On further thought, it's a deal, I will go back with you. I don't feel like going back to my apartment right now, it's too soon, she was waiting on me in my own home."

Three days later Monique was released from the hospital and she didn't even go back to her apartment but straight to the airport to go home with her parents. Brandy went by her place and packed some clothes and shipped them down to her. Her new regimens were daily walks, dressing changes and applications of anti scarring cream.

Fifteen

Monique settled in to a slower pace in New Orleans. It was even more leisurely due to half of the former population being scattered over most of the rest of the United States. Her bond with her father and June was growing stronger as each day dawned with them under the same roof. As fate would have it her Uncle Albert had flown into town to make his peace with his former home, say a symbolic goodbye to his birthplace and have a proper home going service for his mother. Albert came by the house to visit Monique. He also talked to the man that got his sister pregnant when she was a teenager and didn't acknowledge his daughter until confronted. After visiting with Monique, Albert and John sat on the porch and there weren't any minced words.

"John, you know I've never had much respect for you from the time you took advantage of my sister. On that front my mind will never change, even though the bible teaches forgiveness," Albert said. "She was a child and you were a well grown man in a position of trust, her doctor, and I consider that to be one of most sacred boundaries to cross."

"Look Albert, I know what I did was reprehensible and I have tried to become a different person and make amends," John said.

"That damaged that girl for life. Margaret never had any normal relationships with men again and was always looking for someone to take care of her. That left her open to be used."

"Albert we can't change the past and…" John said before Albert cut him off.

"No, you need to listen to this, that girl was sixteen and pregnant and the shame of it caused her to drop out of school, her life ended. She chased rainbow after rainbow as one slick hustler after another would promise to give her a pot of gold. All they really gave Margaret was poison to shove up her nose to keep her strung out so they could have their way with her. They used her up and threw her away and you need to accept your role in causing that to happen."

"I deserved that. I'm sorry for what I did and if I could change things I would. Right now, I'm trying with everything in my power to make things right with Monique. I wasn't there for her when she was young, but she needs me now and I intend to do all I can for her. She's just been kicked around like a football the last six months from barely getting out of here alive after the city was ripped apart. Now she's been assaulted in her own home. It was even worse for someone from here to do this to her. She said it was like a curse was following her and waiting until she was at her highest point so the fall would be even longer when she was knocked down," John said.

"She said that?" Albert said. "Get her well and then get her back home. The longer she's out of her normal environment the harder it's going to be for her to catch up to the pace of what she was used to. Think about it, her life was fast paced, and she had a full schedule. One day she came home, just like any other day, and instantly she's on the sidelines. The world is passing her by right now and even more every day she loses contact with her old life. That happened once when she left here the first time. She won't mentally survive a second round of starting from nothing."

"I think I know what you're saying. I'll give it a week. When she's able to get around on her own and do for herself, I'll start dropping hints about not letting everything she's accomplished slip away," John said.

"I'm leaving town tomorrow. I think I'll go to the French Quarter and get one last feel for this place and maybe get a good bowl of Gumbo or some Jambalaya,"

Albert said. "I need a good memory to take back with me after seeing the destruction around my mother's house, it's like the storm hit yesterday."

He stood up, shook John's hand, went into the house and said goodbye to Monique.

Two weeks into her convalescence, Monique was feeling much better and moving around at about seventy-five percent of her normal pace. She was longing for a return to her life of work, friends and home. Her father never had the chance to bring up the subject of her returning home when she sprung it on them at dinner.

"You know I'm starting to feel much better and I thought it may be time for me to, you know, get back home and try to get back into my old routine. Besides some of the court proceedings for what happened to me will be starting and I need to be there for the beginning of those," she said waiting for a response.

"Well, if you don't over do it, I guess that may be a good idea, what do you think June?" John asked.

"A person's body and mind work together and if yours is telling you it's time to get back in the swing of things then who are we to argue," she replied.

A broad smile came across Monique's face and she said, "Great."

"I'll make arrangements for Saturday morning," June said.

A new excitement was at hand. Monique was aware of how difficult it was to go back the scene of her attack and sleep in the same bed she was tied to as she was assaulted. Then she had to face her assailant face to face in court.

Friday night was her last dinner with two people that had truly become her parents during this period of healing. She went to bed and thought about how she would remember the time spent in their loving care. That is why she had enough strength to go back to take her life off pause.

"Monique, it's time to go," June said Saturday morning.

John carried her bags outside and when Monique exited the house she was surprised to see a car with a chauffeur standing by its side. He opened the trunk and placed her luggage inside and Monique was clearly puzzled by this development. She approached the vehicle and the chauffeur opened the back door and Monique peered inside and looking out at her was Stan.

"Surprise, I thought I would escort you back home personally," he said as he got out of the car and hugged her and kissed her lightly on the lips.

"Stan what are you doing here?" Monique asked.

"I told your father to call me when you were ready to come home and I would come and get you personally. It would give me all of that time to have you to myself on the trip back home and I have missed you," he replied.

"Can I ride that far?" she asked.

"Have a seat," he told Monique.

When she sat down, Stan adjusted the seat to lean back in almost a reclining position with her feet elevated.

"Oh my goodness, what kind of car is this?" Monique asked.

"This is a Maybach, and I think it will be comfortable enough for our trip back plus we will stop often enough so you won't get worn out," Stan said.

Monique got out saying goodbye and June hugged her and said, "I think this guy wants to marry you, he has that gleam in his eyes when he looks your way."

"I'm not so sure, and I've got a lot of things to sort out," Monique whispered back to June.

Soon she was adjusted just right in her seat and the massive vehicle drove off. She took one last look at the city and when they drove the almost twenty-four miles across Lake Ponchatrain a shiver went through her body. Since she didn't have a particular deadline to meet, Stan followed a less than efficient route back to Dallas that detoured to the port in Galveston for a relaxing outing on his yacht.

"Stan the sun feels good on my skin and it's so peaceful out here. Thank you for bringing me."

"I wanted to get you completely away from everything so we could talk. How do you feel right now, physically and mentally?"

"I'm starting to feel almost normal physically, about eighty-five percent. I guess, the sutures are about dissolved but the wounds need some more healing. Mentally, I don't know. I don't feel whole right now. The thought of someone doing that to me never crossed my mind. It made me realize how I could be viewed as nothing to another person. She didn't care how much I hurt or if I even died afterwards. It's as if I was less than an animal to be tortured," Monique said. "No one can understand what that does to how you feel about yourself."

"There is no way I can understand exactly how you feel, but what you're telling me makes perfect sense. An individual is the sum of how they look, feel, carry themselves and what others project on them. You know the respect others give them and where they fit in their social circle. When someone goes through something like you have, it attacks every aspect of what has been built up over time that makes you unique and the person you are. That's what she was attempting to do, destroy your self respect and self image," Stan said.

"But why me, I don't know her? I'm not responsible for bad things that happened in her life," she said.

"I know, but in her mind you became a symbol of what's wrong with her. You came to Dallas around the same time and both of you had been stripped down to nothing. Within six months, you're independent, have a great job, live in a nice place and drive a luxury automobile. She on the other hand was still mired in a criminal lifestyle like she was before coming to town."

"What if she's right? It could my appearance and being with you is the reason I'm getting ahead and she's not?"

"When Prentice Grayson first met you, it was a blank slate and she didn't have any idea who you were. The impression you made on her was because you demonstrated potential. You're educated, intelligent and know how to get things done. Let's suppose it was reversed and the person she took out for the day was the woman that attacked you, do you think she would have invited her to stay in her home? No way. That's why you shouldn't have any thought that what happened to you had anything to do with who you are, but everything to do with who she is."

"You sound like something similar to this has happened to you to understand this so well?" Monique said.

"Well, you recall I said my business started when I was living in a trailer park. My father was an alcoholic, and a violent one at that. He wasn't very educated and thought he got a raw deal in life in general and worked minimum wage jobs without much of a chance of advancement. On the weekends he would really get loaded before he came home. We knew it was going to be hell to pay when he got there. My mother took the brunt of most of his frustration and he would knock her around all of the time. When I was about twelve years old, I grabbed his arm when he went to swing at her and told him to leave her alone. Actually, I think I said, 'you'd better not hit my momma again, you son-of-a-bitch', he looked at me as if that was the first time he ever heard me speak out loud. Then his rage shifted from my mother to me, and every weekend he would pound on me but at least my mother was spared."

"What ended up happening?"

"One night he was starting in on me and my mother was fed up with him. She told him to leave me alone. He said to her, if she knew what was good for her, she would keep her mouth shut. She told him again to leave me alone and he turned to her and was staring down the barrel of a shotgun. He said not to pull a gun on him unless she was prepared to use it and was going to teach her a lesson she wouldn't forget for disrespecting him. He lunged for her. All I can remember is the sound and flash of that shotgun when she pulled the trigger. Inside that trailer it sounded like thunder and looked like lighting as he fell to the floor. He died instantly. My mother screamed out his name in a bloodcurdling sound I will never forget.

"What happened to her?"

"Everybody knew how my father was and it was ruled self defense. After I left home, she married a really nice man and they live in one of those adult communities in Georgetown near Austin. She doesn't have to work and I'm so pleased I'm able to provide for her. I tried to get her to live at my place. I was going to build her a separate house on the property but she didn't want to live in the city and loves where she is now."

"I hate that happened to you, but now I understand why you know how I feel," Monique said as she laid her head on his shoulder.

After a relaxing time at sea they pulled back into the port and started the drive back to Dallas. When they finally pulled into the parking area of her apartment complex, she felt a knot in the pit of her stomach. Could she actually reenter the place where so much pain and degradation was inflicted upon her? Once the keys unlocked the door and she turned the knob to open it, she paused. Then she entered into the room and felt the need to survey the apartment for any intruders.

"Look at this, I had the manager install a security system," Stan said and showed her a keypad and how to use it.

She kissed him on the cheek and said, "This will make me feel so much better, thank you."

"I'll be okay, I just have to get readjusted to being here again," Monique said.

Stan stayed for about thirty minutes and said, "I guess I'll be going. Are you sure you don't want to stay with me?"

"No, I need to stay here and get past this now instead of later. It may take awhile, but I'll be fine. Again, thank you for bringing me back home. I'll talk to you soon."

When Stan left, Monique was in her apartment alone with her thoughts, anxiety and fears. Any evidence of her struggle had been erased by a thorough cleanup and the blood stained sheets had been taken by the investigators as evidence. If it was not for her physical and emotional scars she would never know a crime took place here.

Then a knock came on her door and she jumped from being startled at he sound. Honestly she did not know who could be at her door and went to look out of the peephole. She opened the door and Moses came in and hugged her.

"It's good to see you back," he said.

"I never got the chance to thank you for being concerned enough to check on me. Who knows how long it would have been until someone found me if you hadn't came by."

"When your cars were still in the garage, my instincts were telling me something wasn't right because you're always gone when I leave so I decided to see what was going on."

"Given our last conversation before that and what happened between us, I'm surprised you were so concerned, you know with Brandy and everything."

Moses then hugged Monique as if he was going to leave but then he planted a kiss on her lips and she recoiled and pushed him away.

"Moses, what the hell is wrong with you?"

"Look I thought we had gotten past the Brandy thing. Look I'm sorry I guess I got carried away."

"I can't believe you would put a move on me right after I get back home. What kind of asshole are you? Get out of my apartment."

"Look I thought we could start over fresh."

"Get the hell out."

Moses slinked away and then she sat down and tried to gather herself. The nerve of this guy was beyond her belief.

Monique looked in her refrigerator and besides some canned drinks; all of the fresh food was spoiled. She went to her pantry and there were a couple of cans of tuna, some saltine crackers and it turned into an old fashioned meal that reminded her of her college days. A trip to the supermarket was a must tomorrow, but for now this simple meal with a cold cola was as good as it gets.

Sixteen

Two weeks had passed since Monique had returned home and she was ready to get back to work and was going to meet Prentice for lunch. Then she was off to the airport to pick up a surprise visitor, her sister Jenny, who was in town for an interview with a law firm in downtown Dallas.

When Monique arrived at Prentice's house for lunch she detected something different about her demeanor and asked, "Prentice is something wrong? You seem a little sad."

"Nothing gets by you does it. A couple of weeks ago Harry wasn't feeling well and went to the doctor. They found signs that pointed to prostate cancer and immediately took a sample. Three days ago it was confirmed," Prentice said.

"Oh my god, no," Monique said. "I'm so shocked. I'm sorry. Can they do anything to stop it?"

"It had already spread and it doesn't look good," Prentice said and Monique went around the table to comfort her with an embrace as she fought back tears. "Next week they start a round of aggressive radiation treatment. I'm so scared," Prentice said in a trembling voice.

"Harry is a strong man and if anyone can beat this he can," Monique assured.

"I know he's strong, but this is really bad, the doctors are talking about less than a year for him. I don't know what I'll do if something happens to him."

Monique was of as much comfort to Prentice as she could be under these circumstances of impending loss of someone dear and almost worse, the potential suffering he would endure. After a couple of hours of frank conversation Monique gave Prentice a final heartfelt embrace and headed to the airport to meet her sister.

Monique met Jenny at baggage claim and directed her to the car. They stopped by a fast food restaurant for her to get a take out meal because she was hungry after not eating for a few hours. When they were settled in at Monique's apartment they caught up on events both good and bad that had occurred since the last time they were together.

"It looks like you're doing well considering what happened to you," Jenny said.

"I really don't have much choice but to go forward and that's what I've decided to do," Monique replied.

"Next week I have a court date and will see the person that did this to me for the first time since it happened. I'm not looking forward to it." Monique said.

"Do they have any evidence," Jenny asked.

"Yeah a direct DNA match between the suspect and skin I had under my fingernails. My lawyer said it should be a slam dunk case. He thinks she'll plead guilty to avoid a stiffer sentence if it goes to a jury trial."

"That's awful, it's hard to believe people like that are walking around with the rest of us. Hey, I brought something for you," Jenny said.

"You brought something for me? It's not something gross is it?"

"No, why would you think that. Here," she said giving Monique a box.

Monique opened it and inside was a stuffed bear with a nose that had the paint rubbed off the end.

"There has to be a story behind this," Monique said.

"Dad gave this bear to me when I was a baby and I took him everywhere. I rubbed my nose against his nose until the paint came off. Our father used to rub his nose against mine when I was a baby. This bear became the substitute nose when dad wasn't around and made me feel safe. I want you to have it and think it will help make you feel a little safer as well," Jenny explained.

"Oh Jenny, this is wonderful, thank you. He is getting a place of prominence in my room," Monique said as she placed him on her dresser.

The next day Monique drove Jenny down to her interview and had a visit with her own attorney about the hearing coming up in two days.

"We expect there to be a guilty plea and if that happens the next step will be sentencing and its over. You really won't have any other dates to show up for unless you want to make a statement to the court and your assailant when sentence is passed," her attorney said.

"I think I want to make a statement, I have to say something to this person," Monique said.

"I've made a note of that and will inform the judge," he said. "Thank you for coming in Miss Devareaux."

Monique left his office and went to meet Jenny and they had lunch before going back home. Soon Jenny would be flying back out, but thought her interview went extremely well and she just might be moving to Dallas. The thought of having a sister in town really appealed to Monique and gave her a smile inside.

Two days later Monique was sitting in a courtroom with her lawyer when two guards walked Mel into the room. She was in handcuffs and had a short chain around both ankles causing her to walk in a shuffling manner. An orange county issued jumpsuit completed the ensemble.

"All rise," the bailiff ordered and the people in the courtroom stood.

The public defender had to pull Mel to her feet.

"The honorable Judge Mary Robbins presiding," the bailiff continued.

"Be seated," the judge ordered.

"This is a preliminary hearing in the matter of an aggravated sexual assault, the State of Texas versus Melina Hawkins. Would the defendant please rise," Judge Robbins said. "How do you plead in this matter?"

Mel rose to her feet and her attorney spoke, "The defendant pleads guilty your honor."

"Let the record show a plea of guilty was entered in the case of the State of Texas versus Melina Hawkins, unless there is something additional, this court will be adjourned until sentencing is rendered and a date will be set for that session. Yes Mr. Smith," the judge said when the District Attorney stood.

"Your honor may I approach the bench?" he requested.

"Yes you may," the judge said as he approached the bench and said something to her in whisper.

"I have a request from the victim's attorney through the DA that is highly unusual, and I have decided to allow it. She would like to make a statement to the court and address the defendant. Miss you can sit in the witness box," the judge said.

Monique gathered herself and walked up and took a seat in the witness chair. She turned and looked directly at Mel and spoke.

"My name is Monique Devareaux and I was brutally attacked in my home by this woman sitting in front of me. I don't know exactly why she did this to me except to make her own state in life seem better by trying to destroy me. I was uprooted from my home by a hurricane and then attacked and brutalized by somebody from own area who ended up in Dallas in the same shelter I was in. I want you to know that you've failed. I'm not destroyed and while you rot in jail, my life will go on. If you want to know why your life is a sea of misery, then look in the mirror. Thank you your honor," Monique said as she started to leave the courtroom.

Mel suddenly bolted from behind the table and lunged towards Monique shouting, "You fucking bitch!"

Monique turned towards her and instinct took over. Mel stumbled from the chains around her ankles as Monique stepped back and drove a knee into the side of her face. Mel fell in a heap on the floor and the guards picked her limp body up and removed her from the courtroom.

"Court adjourned," the judge said as she pounded her gavel.

She looked at Monique and gave her a wink of the eye. Monique turned and left with her head high and felt better than she had in months.

Seventeen

Monique returned to work after a couple of weeks and one of the first things she found out was that Brandy had dumped Moses. It seemed she caught him advising another client on the floor of a model home.

Her new job was waiting for her and she dove in head first and worked with Stan to identify key needs of his new venture. Then she directed her team back at Grayson to build the prototypes and set up plans for testing and implementation. She felt as if she had regained her former footing and everything was humming along smoothly.

After a few of months a watershed moment occurred. Harry Grayson her benefactor, friend and mentor started to succumb to the ravages of his disease and entered the hospital. Monique and others supported Prentice as much as they could. The final vigil was held by Prentice and Harry's adult children. On a Friday morning the reports went out that a business giant was no more and a veil of sadness descended on all of those who knew and loved him.

His services were grand and the list of tributes and accolades rivaled those of any head of state. One thing was certain. The landscape of the social circle would change as it always did when a power broker exited the scene. Prentice continued at the stately manor for a while but after the estate was settled, she decided to move away to an area to the south of town. She bought a luxurious home on a hill overlooking Joe Pool Lake. She was well taken care of in Harry's will and he left the rest of his assets to his children. Prentice was only a thirty minute drive away and Monique would visit her often.

Monique continued on and got one of her wishes as Jenny was hired by the law firm in Dallas and moved to a condo near downtown. On her personal front there was one aspect of life that had been put on hold and not tested since her attack. She knew it was time to go there again, but was afraid of what her reaction would be.

It was a Tuesday and Monique was flying high above the clouds in Stan's Gulfstream G550. They had just went over some reports from their latest visit with a potential business client when Monique took Stan's hand and led him back to his private sleeping cabin. She pulled him in and closed the door and turned on some soft music from the sound system.

"Stan it's time for this to happen again," Monique said as she kissed him deeply.

"Are you sure?"

"Yes, I'm positive."

Monique started by removing Stan's shirt and tie and then ran her hands over his shoulders and chest and proceeded to plant soft kisses on every sensitive spot she could find. He slowly unbuttoned the blouse she was wearing and brushed it off her bare shoulders and deftly unfastened the front release of her lacey bra. Then he gently caressed tender flesh untouched by his hands for over six months. He felt the apprehension and tenseness in her body due to the trauma from her attack and he was very reassuring and started to feel her tensions ease as she slowly relaxed. His mouth then became reacquainted with the most sensitive spot on her body and he understood this was akin to turning the second key on his sports car to unleash the raw energy stored within. Monique began to moan and juices flowed from a spring long damned up by pain, fear and frustration. Stan continued to increase the rush of water over the dam by releasing her from her skirt and letting it drop to the bed, Monique threw her head back and surrendered her body for him to do with as he wished. He pulled down the thong panties that did a poor job of covering her most private parts and gently rolled her back on the bed. Stan then administered a gentle probing of this once dry reservoir that now overflowed from the abundance of a fresh flood.

Stan continued to stir her waters and removed his remaining clothing and she gazed upon his manhood and pondered what this would be like. This was a rare occurrence for someone to get a second chance in life to feel the excitement of their first encounter of a carnal nature. Monique was at a fever pitch and now was the time. She not so gently pulled Stan up to her by the hair on his head and tried to find the measure of the depths of his throat with her tongue. In one move she became complete once more as the woman that captured his curiosity and then fulfilled his fantasies.

They were cruising at thirty-five thousand feet but in their minds and state of desire they were in orbit and didn't care when they landed. The flight had two more hours until touchdown and thirty minutes ahead of landing, they emerged drained of their energy and pent up desires. Monique was like a woman newly introduced to the world of adult love. She curled up into Stan until it was time to fasten her seatbelt for final approach.

Monique was approaching her thirtieth birthday and reflected on a year in which her experiences would have taken most people a lifetime to amass. Her last birthday was spent in a shelter among hundreds of other displaced souls and today anyone would be hard pressed to determine if she had gone through experiences worse than any other normal citizen. Stan was taking her out on the town for a night of dinner and dancing to celebrate and she was eagerly anticipating the occasion.

When Saturday night came and they were on their way, Stan announced he had forgotten something and headed towards his home to retrieve whatever it was. Once he pulled up outside the front entrance he told Monique to come in because it would take him a few minutes to retrieve the item from the upstairs of the house. She reluctantly followed and when she entered the house was pitch black inside.

"Stan why is it so dark in here," she commented.

"Just then lights came on and people popped out from every corner yelling, "Surprise."

Monique was in shock and started laughing uncontrollably saying, "I'm going to kill him."

Then she scanned the faces and was absolutely stunned, there was her father, stepmother, her sisters, brother and even her Uncle Albert and Aunt Gracie.

Prentice ran up to her and said it was all Stan's idea. Then Stan came back into the room.

"I see you found what I had forgot at home, all of these people that love you came over to celebrate your birthday," he said.

"This is the most unbelievable thing anyone has ever done for me. I can't believe all of you are in the same room, thank you for coming."

The party was officially started. It became a birthday celebration and family reunion all rolled into one. Then it was time to give and open gifts. The last gift was from Stan and it was a large box. Monique tore into it and found layer after layer of gift paper and way at the bottom she fished out a small box and started to open it. Her eyes widened when inside was a flawless five carat yellow diamond perched atop a wide platinum band.

Before she could speak, Stan stood facing her and dropped to one knee and said, "I didn't know how to do this, so I decided to arrange for all of the people that love you and have been touched by your spirit to be here. Monique Devareaux will you be my wife and stay with me until I grow old, or older as my life partner, I love you."

Monique was speechless and looked at the crowd wide eyed and Jenny, Kendra and Prentice all gestured with their hands to her with motions of "snap out of it". She looked at Stan and said, "Yes."

The assembled group cheered and applauded. Stan kissed Monique and lifted her and they swung in a circle with her arms tightly clasped around his neck. All of the women rushed the new bride-to-be to gaze at the massive ring and the men were shaking Stan's hand and slapping him on the back.

"Wow, Monique look at that ring and this house," Jenny said. "This is where you will be living? You've hit the jackpot."

"Well, I love Stan and this is the kind of life he leads," Monique said.

"Does he have a brother, just kidding," Jenny remarked.

"We've got to give you a good bachelorette party, isn't that right Kendra?" Prentice said.

"Oh yeah and we know just the place, Las Vegas, and your sisters are coming too," she said looking at Jenny and Meagan, "It's on us. We know you're not rich yet."

"Yeah, sure," Meagan replied eagerly.

"I am really overwhelmed by this," Monique said.

"We need to have a good long visit and talk," Prentice said. "Come over tomorrow about two o'clock and you, Kendra and I can catch up on things."

Eighteen

The next day Monique took the leisurely drive to visit Prentice and Kendra, her two friends who now lived together after divorce and death left them single again. They were far more than mere roommates. She wondered what Prentice wanted to talk to her about.

After arriving they sat upstairs in an area Prentice had added to the home to relax in as she could look out over the hills to the lake and drink in the beauty of the setting. Her home was on one of the highest points in Dallas County overlooking Joe Pool Lake in the suburb of Grand Prairie. She could see the boats cruising across the surface of the water in the distance beyond the treetops below.

"Have a seat, have a drink and relax," Prentice said.

Kendra soon joined them.

"First, I wanted to share something with you, Kendra and I are going to be parents. She's pregnant," Prentice said as Kendra rubbed her belly area.

"How did this happen?" Monique asked.

Kendra and Prentice looked at each other and laughed, "Actually that's a logical question since we're both women, we have a friend that acted as a donor."

"Did you do in-vetro fertilization?" Monique asked.

"No we did it the old fashioned way, although I told Prentice I didn't enjoy it at all," Kendra said. "I won the coin flip so I had to do the dirty work."

"Well, whatever," Prentice said. "It worked and she's one month along and we're so excited."

"I've got a confession to make to you. When I was staying in the pool house, I heard a noise and woke up early one morning. I looked out of the window from the bathroom and saw you two in the hot tub, I never said a word," Monique admitted.

"Oh shit, that was when both of our husbands were out of town, "Kendra said.

"And all that time you never let on you knew a thing, while we went on like nothing was going on," Prentice remarked.

"You, my friend are a sneaky little bitch, but you kept your mouth shut," Kendra said.

"Well I didn't want to get thrown out on my ass," Monique said.

"Thank you for being discrete," Prentice said. "That would have blown the lid off of the country club."

"You know it's not like any of those other women haven't eaten a little pussy now and then. Come on, they probably got wasted in college at parties and did all kinds of shit they couldn't remember the next day," Kendra said and they all had a good laugh.

"This is all fascinating, but the reason I asked you to come over today is to talk about your engagement and upcoming marriage. We thought as your friends and semi big sisters we could give you a little bit of background on what we experienced in that whole environment you're about to enter," Prentice said.

"I had the same thought myself. I'm excited but a little frightened as well. Stan has been in this world for a long time and just got out of a long term relationship. I kind of go in and out of this surreal life he leads, but to be in it full time worries me a bit," Monique said.

"Well don't be too afraid, but two things will help you to no end. First, don't assume anything and second, stay grounded in reality. By don't assume anything, I mean discuss how things are going to be once you become Mrs. Brickman, will you still work, are you having children, how often will he be away from home and other issues. Those things are important on a personal level," Prentice said. "When I married Harry, I had no idea how much time I would spend alone because of his travel schedule."

"That's why we formed this social group, of women like us, to have something to keep ourselves occupied with different projects," Kendra said.

"I guess I just assumed I'd still work. But we haven't had time to discuss it," Monique said. "As far as children, yes I want children."

"Stan may be different, he and Doris didn't have any children," Prentice said. "You're thirty and how old is Stan," Kendra asked.

"Stan is almost fifty," Monique said.

"Your clock is starting to tick and his has struck midnight, by the time you're married, get pregnant and have a child, he'll be on his way to fifty-two years old. When his kid is ten he's sixty-two and at the high school graduation Stan's seventy if he's still with us and you're forty-nine or fifty years old," Prentice said.

Monique sat there as if a cold pail of water had been poured over her head. The idea of being married to a seventy year old man while she was still vibrant was a starkly sobering thought.

"I love Stan, but the things you're telling me, if it was coming from someone else, I'd be suspicious of their motives, but you two have lived this life I'm embarking on," Monique said.

"We're not trying to discourage you at all, because very few people on the planet get a chance to live the dream life they see on the shows about the rich and famous. Let's face it, how many people can you call on your speed dial that have been driven in a million dollar car right onto the deck of a yacht. Don't knock the life, just realize the other consequences," Prentice said.

"He did that with you, drove onto the yacht," Kendra said. "He really wanted to impress you because no one did that for me."

"No, yours just bugged the hell out of you for five years until he wore you down," Prentice said.

"I guess you're right," Kendra said.

"But seriously Monique, Stan probably loves you to death, but part of him is a cold calculating business man. That's why he's worth a billion dollars. The business part of him will show up seemingly in the middle of all of the planning and romance of your engagement with a piece of paper for you to sign, a prenuptial agreement. If you're not prepared for it, you'll feel crushed. He could love you enough to crawl over broken glass, but if you don't sign he will not marry you," Kendra said.

"How do you know he wouldn't marry me without a prenuptial agreement?" Monique asked.

"Did Doris have a prenuptial agreement?" Prentice asked.

"Yeah he did mention that and said it was ironclad," Monique answered.

"She helped him build the business," Prentice said.

"Did you both have one?" Monique asked.

"Everyone we know has one that was married to someone that had a lot of wealth before they met. The husbands married to wealthy women also signed agreements," Kendra said. "It's not personal, it's business and they are advised by attorneys to protect themselves and their assets. Look at reality, over fifty percent of marriages end in divorce, at that rate someone could be wiped out after three or four failed marriages and divorce settlements. You know Texas is a community property state."

"When this happens, just be rational about it, he still loves you, but get a lawyer to look it over and negotiate for you, he'll have the best money can buy," Prentice said. "When you sit across the negotiation table from him, smile, hold hands and let the lawyers argue not you, keep emotion out of it."

"How can you keep emotion out of it when some says I love, but I only love you this much," Monique said.

"Monique, I love you, I'm your friend, but just over a year ago you were sitting on a rooftop in New Orleans waiting to be rescued," Kendra said. "If a guy loves you ten million dollars worth, is that so bad?"

Monique looked at Kendra like she had been stabbed in the heart and tears welled up in her eyes. Kendra went over and hugged her.

"I'm sorry, but I was running a ballet studio and next thing I know I'm in the lap of luxury and going to the opera. I was a poor girl from Chinatown, born of immigrant parents," Kendra said. "Prentice grew up in the West Dallas housing projects. All I'm really saying is, don't let misplaced pride and hurt feelings cloud your judgment and ruin things."

"I understand what you're saying now, I'm sorry, it's just when you said that, it sounded so cruel," Monique said.

"It wasn't meant to be, we're on your side, but you're going to hear it again from people that want you to have an emotional reaction and run away so they can take your place. Get ready for it, your past is gone, but it will be thrown in your face at the worst times from people hoping to make you doubt yourself and drive you away." Prentice said. "Once you say I do to a man like Stan you, your world and how others view you will never be the same."

"What was the most difficult thing for you to adjust to after marrying your husbands?" Monique asked.

"Honestly for me it was how large his world was and how fast it moved," Prentice said. "I felt lost for the first three months and had a hard time regaining my bearings. His normal was being anywhere in the world at a moments notice and feeling perfectly comfortable wherever it was. Imagine for me, a trip to California or Las Vegas is exotic. I was lost, unless you grew up doing that kind of thing it's almost impossible to get used to. I learned to step back and watch him and slowly it became more comfortable, but it was hard, I almost couldn't find myself for a while."

"That was the same problem I had, compounded by being of Asian descent, I felt completely isolated. At least Prentice has family here. That's probably why we gravitated to each other and formed kind of a two person minority clique. Some of the snide remarks from the other wives about us being the affirmative action members or the African and Asian connection were horrible," Kendra said.

"Just be ready for that kind of thing, but don't let it get to you," Prentice said. "Unfortunately we didn't have anyone to let us in on what to expect and it was a trial by fire. And get ready to be called a trophy wife, that one is coming as sure as the sun rises."

"I can see how lucky I am to have friends who care enough to tell me like it is, whether my feelings were hurt or not," Monique said.

"Have you set a date yet?" Kendra asked.

"We're thinking the fifteenth of June," Monique said.

"That's only nine months," Prentice said. "A lot of planning needs to go into this and you need to get busy."

"I know, but his mother is getting older and he doesn't want to wait too long," Monique said.

"Well Kendra, it looks like we need to get busy planning that party out in Las Vegas," Prentice said.

"We'll set that up and tell you the date," Kendra said. "You just need to put your party shoes on.

"Thanks guys, after talking to you I'm approaching this with my eyes wide open and hopefully won't fall into some potholes along the way," Monique said as she left.

"Were we too harsh," Kendra asked.

"I don't think so, if someone had told me what we just told her, I'm not sure I would have gone through with it," Prentice said. "Then maybe I wouldn't have had to watch Harry die the way he did."

Nineteen

Nine months is a long time for most things in the lives of ordinary people, but when you are about to become the wife of one of the richest men in America it goes by like the blink of an eye. The planning was enormous and there were logistics involving invitations, guest list, travel and unexpected surprises of every kind imaginable. Stan had given Monique a blank checkbook for the affair, but she needed a wedding planner. Her range of experience didn't allow her to think on a grand enough scale to do an event of this magnitude justice. Prentice and Kendra helped expand her vision of what was expected when your guest list would include some of the prime business and political movers and shakers on the scene today. In the midst of this flurry of activity came the inevitable discussion about a premarital contract. What she came to discover is the most frequent wedding date delay in most high profile marriages was getting consensus on acceptable terms for the prenuptial agreement. The level of complexity has moved far beyond simple payouts for a divorce to penalties for infractions from infidelity to spousal abuse and sliding payout scales based upon time accumulated in the union.

Since her conversation with Prentice and Kendra, Monique had not been complacent in the area of the prenuptial agreement. She enlisted her sister Jenny to create a formula based on multiple factors to come up with terms for a counter offer if the arrangement presented by Stan's counsel was inadequate. Monique had Jenny factor in her age, education and remaining working years. Companionship value based upon a formula that used data from some unique research sources. If children were a product of this union then there was a separate category for that circumstance. Once this was compiled it was adjusted for inflation and elevated based upon the lifestyle she would live in if the union dissolved. Of course there was a portion that was guaranteed after the vows were spoken and rings affixed on respective fingers. The result of this exercise gave Monique an enhanced view of what she was worth. Of course Jenny was instructed not to reveal her counter offer unless Stan's position was untenable and the gap couldn't be bridged with reasonable negotiation over a short period of time. Love was at the core of their relationship, in spite of the contractual elements.

As it turned out Stan valued Monique far more than she imagined. If the marriage somehow ended in divorce she would never have to be concerned for her financial well being and would be a very wealthy woman. He told her there was no need for that part of their life to cast doubt upon how he felt about her. Unfortunately in today's world these types of things are par for the course.

Two months out from the big event she took a break from nonstop planning and flew to Las Vegas with her friends Kendra, Prentice and Brandy. Meeting them there were Meagan and Jenny. Meagan and Jenny had never been to Las Vegas and were wide eyed at the sights and sounds of this adult playground. Kendra, Prentice and Brandy were veterans and Monique had been once on a quick three day trip when she was in college and really didn't venture out much at all.

When they hit the strip they settled into their rooms at an exclusive villa Prentice had reserved. This property had five bedrooms, two whirlpool spas and a steam room. The party immediately started as Prentice had rented a gigantic stretched SUV limo complete with a monster sound system and packed with drinks and food. As they were driving around partying the vehicle stopped and a couple of muscular policemen stepped into the back and closed the door.

"We have an arrest warrant for a Monique Devareaux," one of them said.

Immediately all of the other women pointed her out and the music started blasting and the cops ripped off their uniforms and were down to g-string thongs. They started a wild sandwich lap dance with Monique in the middle and the screaming and laughing continued for hours. After the limo party the vehicle pulled up in front of the main hotel property and everyone streamed onto the casino floor. Kendra immediately went for baccarat. Monique was not a big gambler and gravitated towards the simplicity of the slots. Jenny and Meagan decided to try their luck at blackjack and Brandy was testing the craps pit. Monique noticed a couple of guys chatting up her sisters at the blackjack table. Meagan was bantering with a handsome guy about thirty with a polished continental look, clean shaven, six feet tall with Italian shoes and a slim angular build. Jenny was with a gym buff and he showed it with a muscular build laid out on a six foot two frame. Meagan was showing casual interest in her pursuer, but Jenny was displaying more than a passing level of attention to her guy.

Monique looked over again to the blackjack table and Meagan was still there but Jenny and her companion had vanished.

Monique went over to Meagan and told her she was turning in for the night and Meagan said she would join her and they wound their way through the hotel to the exclusive area where the villas were located. Soon after watching a little television the rest of the crew came in except for Jenny and they all retired to their rooms. Sometime in the middle of early morning Monique got up and made her way to the kitchen for a drink and heard noises out by one of the whirlpool spas. She cautiously approached and peeked around the corner and spotted Jenny in the hot tub with her head laid back against the side of the spa and her hair was hanging down with her face towards the ceiling. Monique was about to walk up to her when suddenly a man's head and torso rose from the water in front of Jenny and her ankles were resting on either side of his head on shoulders pulsing with muscular bulges. Monique froze in her tracks and gazed at the sight in front of her. The unknown man advanced towards Jenny and her legs elevated and bent backwards with each step. Soon her knees were pressed back against her chest and she emitted a gasp as he obviously struck a pleasure center right below the water line. This site transfixed Monique as it was a voyeur's delight.

Soon Jenny was expressing her approval of his activity with loud moans and the splashing was more intense and then one loud expression came from Jenny of, "Yes, oh shit, yes!"

Monique crept back to her room and left this scene to the two performers involved. She went to bed with fresh images in her mind that served to spark a quick session of self pleasuring and then a sound sleep. The next day hangovers were had by all except for Kendra who sipped on non alcoholic drinks due to her pregnancy.

Monique was having the time of her life and this was a needed break from the pressures of planning for the wedding. The rest of the trip was spent in general bonding with her sisters and enjoying the companionship of her friends. To her knowledge there was not a repeat performance in the whirlpool and Jenny never mentioned her encounter to anyone. She didn't know she had been accidentally discovered in her early am passion fest.

All too soon the time was upon them and the grand event had arrived and Monique embodied the vision of the beautiful bride. She would be led down the isle by her father, which was something beyond her imagination during the early years of her life. Her sister Jenny was her maid of honor while Meagan, Prentice and Kendra were bridesmaids. When the wedding march was struck up, her heart raced and she was the center of attention. When the bride entered the church all eyes were focused on this person that was rescued from oblivion in New Orleans. Her wedding gown was strictly custom designer issue and was sewn on in the dressing area to hug each curve perfectly and her lithe frame was encased in white with a slit up each side with the train attached from her waist trailing as she walked. If there was a more stunning bride, she had yet to be captured on film. She could feel her mother walking on one side and her grandmother on the other.

After music, promises and vows of love everlasting, Monique became Mrs. Stanley Brickman and fulfilled a chapter in her life unforeseen in her own mind.

The honeymoon was something out of her wildest fantasies and Stan fulfilled every desire of her mind, body and spirit but, Monique was to find out the reality of being married were far different than her perfect vision.

The first year of her journey with Stan as a married couple was glorious and within two months she became pregnant with her first child and feeling that maternal glow put a new purpose in her life. After six months Monique decided to take a leave of absence from work in order to concentrate on making sure their unborn baby was given every opportunity to be as healthy as possible. It was then she noticed a change in Stan or was it just a perception.

When she no longer was involved in his daily business life she noticed how absent he was from her on a regular basis. It was then she realized exactly what Prentice and Kendra meant by some of what they told her. With her baby not even born yet, she made a decision of sacrifice and she would not return to her work life in order to give her child the love and support of at least one parent on a consistent basis. This would not be a checkbook upbringing by way of nannies and boarding schools.

Stan was a good man, but sadly he had a major flaw she didn't understand until after she became his wife. He was a goal seeker and once he achieved his goal it no longer held his interest as much. His goal of gaining her was satisfied and although his interest was still keen, it never rose to the same level it was during his pursuit and over time a degree of complacency crept into the relationship.

"Stan, can we talk?" Monique said.

"Sure, what's on your mind?" he asked.

"Do you love me as much as before we were married?" Monique asked.

"Of course I do, what kind of question is that?" he asked.

"I just feel different. You seem to be preoccupied with other things now and don't pay as much attention to me anymore."

"Well you know, the company is really getting off of the ground and my scheduled is packed tight, it's just a matter of only so much time in a day, but that doesn't mean I don't love you as much."

"I guess I just felt a little ignored I guess, I love you too," she said and went to bed.

Soon she gave birth to a beautiful little girl and she named her Margaret after her mother, in fact little Margaret had eyes like her grandmother. Monique was the ever proud parent and basked in the glow of motherhood. This was an energetic bundle of joy and Monique decided to breast feed so she could build the closest bond possible between mother and child. Then one day her world was changed by a fateful chance meeting.

Twenty

Monique was shopping while pushing little Margaret in her stroller when a ghost appeared in front of her. She didn't know how to react when Doris Brickman spoke to her.

"Hello, its Monique isn't it?" she said.

"Yes, how are you?" Monique answered.

She looked down at Margaret, "You have a beautiful baby, congratulations."

Shocked at her pleasant attitude she answered, "Thank you."

"I don't want this to sound strange but could I buy you a cup of coffee so we can talk?" Doris asked.

"Well, I don't know, I'm running late," she answered. "Frankly given what happened between us, I don't see the point."

"Please?" Doris asked.

Monique agreed and they went to a restaurant and sat in the back corner for a little privacy and by this time the baby was asleep in her stroller.

"I know our last meeting was a bit rough and I shouldn't have been involved in that e-newsletter mail out. I want to apologize to you for that. My marriage to Stanley was over whether you had come along or not," Doris said.

"Well I don't quite know what to say," Monique said.

"I understand. Stan and I had stopped being truly husband and wife years before we officially ended our relationship. We stayed together to keep up appearances and for the sake of our families," Doris said.

"Why are you telling me this? I'm his wife now and frankly it doesn't seem right for you to be talking to me about my husband," Monique said.

"Just hear me out, this is so hard," Doris commented.

"There were certain details of our divorce settlement I am not supposed to talk about under court order. It's been eating me up inside not to be able to talk to you and tell you about it," Doris said.

"Okay, we're sitting here now and even though I'm going against my better judgment, go ahead and tell me what's on your mind."

"I was with Stan for quite a few years as he grew his business and was a few years older than he was. When we were married it was a union of two people that knew and trusted each other and was good for both of us. Well we never had children and a few years ago Stan became concerned he didn't have an heir to continue his legacy. It was too late for me to have a child and he didn't want to adopt. That was the fatal blow to our marriage together because he wanted to have children and I couldn't give them to him."

"So you're trying to tell me Stan married me because I could give him an heir. Doris, Stan loves me."

Doris' eyes welled up with tears, "Initially we didn't have any children because Stan is gay."

Monique's face went blank and any blood in her body rushed to her heart, "What, you're lying."

"I wish I was. That's why I married Stan. I'd known him for years and when he sold his company and became this noted, powerful businessman he made an arrangement with me. I know it's hard to believe, but my prenuptial agreement amounted to a compensation package to marry him so his secret wouldn't come out. He felt it would help him in future business ventures to be seen as this married business tycoon. I'm so ashamed; I should have come to you sooner."

Monique just sat there and her vision seemed to go black and suddenly she struck out and slapped Doris with the palm of her right hand, "You bitch!"

Doris recoiled at the impact and got up and left as Monique started sobbing and the resulting commotion jolted the baby into a crying frenzy. She hurriedly left the restaurant as the manager rushed to the back to see what was going on. This was a disaster and if Doris was telling the truth then her life was a lie. The one thing she did know is this child was hers and real regardless of the circumstances of how she came into the world.

Would the curse of her conception and childhood be generational? This had to be a cruel joke by an embittered woman to take her joy away. For now Stan was out of town for four more days and she decided not to let her emotions run wild. Monique called her sister Jenny and said she needed to see her as soon as possible.

Jenny told her to come over to her place that night around eight o'clock. When Monique arrived Jenny could detect by the expression on her face something was terribly wrong. When she told her this fantastic tale Jenny could not believe it.

"You have got to be shitting me. How could he be gay and you not know it. You've been with him and have a baby by him. Let's say it is true, what do you want to do?" Jenny said.

"Isn't that fraud, deception or something like that, for me to think he loves me as a woman when he is really gay?" Monique said.

"If, and this is a big if, he is gay then it could rise to the level of fraud," Jenny said.

"I don't know if this is true, but I want to be prepared in the event it is. That would mean I have been used to meet his needs and his love for me was a lie and he will pay for that. I don't care what my prenuptial agreement says. There is a different price to protect his prized reputation that was built on hiding his true identity and using me to continue the charade. I love my child but I'm not going to be a brood mare for hire, used to provide him a made to order inheritance pool."

"Monique, aren't you concerned about what he will do when you confront him?" Jenny said.

"I've survived much worse than him, and you know that for a fact. This is what I want you to draw up and make triplicate copies for me, him and his attorney. If what Doris said is fact, then Stanley Brickman will regret the day he deceived me into this marriage."

Monique gave Jenny a document she had drafted before coming over.

"What if he doesn't care and refuses to sign?" Jenny said.

"I'm sure the national tabloids, talk shows and newspapers would love the story about the gay billionaire businessman who tricked a Hurricane Katrina survivor into marriage to be used for breeding stock."

"I'll write this up, but you need to be careful, someone who would do something like this could be capable of worse," Jenny said.

What Jenny said gave Monique something to think about and she decided to also prepare a will specifying what should take place if she died including funeral arrangements and care for her daughter. By the time she left Jenny's condo, this task of confronting Stan was taking on a serious tone and how it would be handled was now on her mind. Monique planned to have everything ready when Stan was back in town before the weekend.

Stan was back home Friday night and Monique had prepared a dinner so they could spend a quiet evening at home. When it was time to sit down for a hearty meal Monique got right to the heart of the matter.

"Stan when you asked for my hand in marriage, you told me you loved me, what made you fall in love with me?" Monique asked.

"Why are you asking something like that?" Stan asked.

"I would just like to hear it, every woman needs affirmation occasionally from her life partner of his love for them."

"Well, I think you are an intelligent, beautiful and strong woman and your spirit won my heart."

"Is there something else about me that moved you to the point of wanting to have me as your wife?"

"Monique what exactly do you want me to say? I love you of course."

"If I asked you a question will you give me a straight answer?"

"Why wouldn't I, of course I will? Is something wrong?"

"I don't know yet, but it's time to lay this on the line. Did you marry me so you could have someone to give you a child, so you could pass on your legacy?"

"Don't be absurd, of course I wanted a child but it's not the reason I married you, how could you think that. A man and his wife having children is the most natural act in the world. What's gotten into you?"

"I don't know, I've been feeling neglected lately and even more so since Margaret was born."

"I'm sorry for all the travel, I'll try to slow it down some," he said.

"We've only been intimate together three times in the last couple of months. I miss you and need you."

"I've just been so drained by all of this activity and stress of the business. Other things have just distracted me. I didn't mean to neglect you in that way."

"Look, Stan I know your marriage to me is a cover to conceal your sexual preference for men. You're gay and married me to protect your reputation."

Stan froze and looked at Monique in silence not quite knowing how to answer or if he should answer. This moment of silence seemed to last an eternity until Stan spoke.

"Monique, how did you find out? Did you find Henry's phone number and call him?"

Monique felt a shiver run through her body with his confirmation of this awful truth, her wedding, marriage and current life were all an elaborate illusion. It was all staged for the sake of deceiving others, however the grossest of those deceptions were those perpetrated on her and her heart and spirit. Deep inside of her something broke and might never come back together again. Monique dropped her head and cried.

Stan walked around to console her, "Don't put you're hands on me!" she seethed. "How dare you do this to me, I don't care if you're gay, just don't pretend to be otherwise to marry me and steal my life with a lie. You're no different than that monster that raped me, except you hid behind a stack of lies instead of my bathroom. You were even willing to betray yourself by sleeping with me to make the deception complete."

"I didn't mean to hurt you."

"You didn't mean to hurt me, well what the fuck did you think was going to happen, no, you didn't mean to get caught. Now, who the hell is Henry?"

"Henry is someone I met in this little club type thing I belong to, kind of a network and we hit it off and continued to see each other outside of that environment. He lives in Austin, and works for the company," Stan said while clearing his throat.

"So you put you're lover on the payroll, to make it look official and hide the fact that you're his sugar daddy. How old is this Henry?"

"Monique, why do you want to know…" he said and then she cut him off.

"Because I think I have a right to know who my husband is fucking when he's not in bed with me."

"He's twenty-nine and was an actor and had couple of television shows in his background," he said and then suddenly stood as if hit by a bolt of lightning.

Stan walked towards her with a scowl and hand on his chin as if he had unraveled the secret of life.

"That double crossing bitch! It was Doris, wasn't it, she told you?" he said as he towered over her with clenched fists.

"I think you need to step back and sit down," Monique said slowly and measured looking at him intently with her hand on the handle of a steak knife that was on the table.

Stan, surprised at her request sat and said, "You didn't think I was going to harm you? I would never do that, how could you think that?"

"I don't know you, after what has happened, you're capable of anything. Why did you do this to me? Am I just dirt to you, just a hired surrogate to produce a child for you to continue your bloodline?" she said removing her hand from the table.

"Monique, this may sound harsh, but after I met you I thought you had a lot of qualities I would want the mother of my children to have. You were attractive, strong and very intelligent and had a survivor's spirit. I came to deeply care about you and decided to pursue you and asked you to marry me. I felt you would agree to be my wife and it was less complicated than any other way to approach the issue."

"You fucking piece of shit!" Monique said as she unleashed her full furry with a closed fist swing that landed flush with Stan's left jaw. "I'm not some god-damned womb for hire, you stole from me and you're going to pay for that."

She proceeded to reach into the china cabinet and Stan became quite appre-hensive concerning what she had concealed there and said, "Monique what are you doing?"

"Don't worry, I didn't hide a gun, that would be way too easy," she replied as she pulled out a brown envelope and threw it to him. "These are my terms for what you have done to me."

"What is this, terms, we have a prenuptial agreement?" he said.

"This is not about that, I'm not leaving you or our marriage," she said. "These are the terms for you to remain in the eyes of the public, Mr. Stanley Brickman, respected business tycoon with his lovely wife Monique and precious daughter Margaret."

Stan opened the envelope and proceeded to read the twelve page document with a look of concern on his face.

"This is outrageous, why do you think I'll agree to this?" Stan asked.

"I have press releases prepared to go to the major wire services, news networks, business publications and all members of the board of directors, and potential investors. I don't think you want that kind of publicity with plans to take the company public and the IPO scheduled in a few months," Monique said. "I need an answer by the end of the day tomorrow, Margaret and I will be somewhere else tonight."

"I will let you know by five o'clock tomorrow," he said.

Monique left and headed over to Jenny's where she had left Margaret and would spend the night with her and related the shocking news that Stan had con-firmed her worst fears. Jenny offered an ear to listen and a shoulder to cry on and regardless of what Stan did the next day. Monique already had the feeling of being alone with her child in the world. To top it off, she had a feeling Stan met

Henry through this network that Prentice and Kendra were involved in running. She only hoped they had no idea he was a participant.

The next day while she was still visiting with her sister, Monique's cell phone rang and it was Stan and he wanted to meet with Monique at his attorney's office that afternoon. Monique said she would. Jenny would be going with her. She made arrangements to leave her daughter with Prentice, then the two sisters now attorney and client made their way to Stan's lawyer's north Dallas office.

"Mrs. Brickman I have read your request of Mr. Brickman. In light of the obviously disturbing developments in your marriage, I'm authorized to double the terms of payout in the prenuptial agreement for dissolution of your union," he said.

"Monique, I know how shocking this was to you, so I want to be more than fair on this matter," Stan said.

"Fair would have been for you to be the person I thought I married, my terms are non negotiable," she said.

Stan and his lawyer glanced at each other and his attorney, Frank Wiseman, said, "Mrs. Brickman why do you insist on my client continuing in this marriage when clearly it was not entered into in good faith from his obvious deception."

"It was entered into in good faith on my part and I conceived and gave birth to my child in good faith, I gave up my career in good faith and I loved him in good faith. Stan Brickman may be whatever he wants to be when he is away. He is going to be a good father to our daughter and he will appear to be a good husband to me in the eyes of my child and the rest of the world. He can continue to steal those moments for his other life just as he has been doing all along. As for me I will be the loving wife for the world to see, but my personal life is my own, but my daughter will not grow up without a father like I did. I don't think you have enough money to pay for that circumstance."

Stan took the pen and signed the papers like he was signing a death sentence. Jenny looked over the documents and Monique signed. Then Jenny and Stan's lawyer witnessed the signatures and they would be sealed and locked away.

At that moment Stan entered into an arrangement that would keep his true sexual preferences a secret but denied him the free reign to express who he was publicly. Monique became a ceremonial wife with a man she no longer loved, but for the sake of their child she would make the sacrifice.

Stan went about complying with the terms of the agreement. One of those was to construct a separate living area adjacent and connected to the master bedroom so when Margaret was of age she could see her parents go into the bedroom together. Sharing of the same bed was a thing of the past. A door from the master bedroom would lead into Monique's living area complete with master bedroom and full living quarters. In total an additional three thousand square feet would be added for her living comfort, apart from the man she walked down the isle with only a year ago.

In addition Monique was added to the board of directors of the company with a direct line of succession in the event of Stan's death while they were still married. There were no restrictions on either party for romantic relations they may form during the balance of their marriage as long as these relationships were not publicly flaunted. Both parties would portray to their daughter the appearance of a normal committed family unit at a minimum of until she reached twenty years of age. Monique still had every monetary provision of her prenuptial in place but it was increased by one hundred percent given the circumstances that brought them to the table. The prenuptial payout commenced if Stan breached the conditions of the agreement even if the marriage union survived. Of course the provisions for Margaret were very generous as she was the biological daughter of Stan. He was also required not to seek retaliation against Doris because Monique felt she reached out in a noble manner when she informed her of his deception. Doris had received an apology from her for the slap she had delivered out of anger.

As they left the table, husband and wife shook hands and parted ways. Monique would live in a separate wing of the home until her quarters were completed in about nine months given design and construction time. She would never have imagined this situation happening in the second year of her marriage but given the circumstances this was the best accommodation she could find.

No one was the wiser as this unique arrangement went into effect and the coming out party for the new public Mr. and Mrs. Brickman was at hand. A charity ball was coming up next weekend and they had agreed to the role play and personal interaction between them.

In spite of everything it's difficult to hide something so personal to good friends and family. Outside of the immediate parties involved and their legal advisors, no one else knew what was taking place, in fact Stan didn't even tell his lover, Henry about what had transpired. But all good things must come to an end, including secrets.

Monique was visiting with Prentice and lounging by the pool in her much cozier five thousand square foot home, compared to her former residence at least, when she shocked Monique with a question.

"How long has it been since you had sex with Stan?" Prentice asked.

"Why would you ask a question like that, Stan and I are married, why do you assume we're not having sex?" Monique replied.

"Do you remember when we all went to the jazz club and you met that guy and took a little ride around Dallas with him?" Prentice asked.

"Yes, I remember and what does that have to do with Stan and me?" she asked.

"I thought I would never tell you this, but Kendra and I could tell you needed a man's attention and we kind of arranged for him to be at the club," Prentice said. "You have that same, look about you now."

"First of all, I can't believe you set me up with that guy and secondly there's no way you can tell if I haven't been getting laid."

"I'll just spell it out for you, there's one part of your body that shouts to the world when you are overdue for some attention in the sexual area. When we went to that charity auction, all eyes were on your headlights, and right now you're about to poke holes through the top of that swimsuit. You've hardly said a word about Stan the last few times we've been together, so what's going on?" Prentice asked.

Monique broke down and cried, "Stan has a sexual performance issue and hasn't been able to perform recently and I don't know what to do about it. It's been three months since we have been intimate and it very hard to handle."

Prentice looked at Monique and had a disbelieving stare, "Monique, I'm afraid of what I'm about to ask and don't be angry with me. When I was married to Harry, there were rumors about Stan, how can I put it, about his sexual preferences. I mean it was said that he may have been what black people call on the "down low".

"What's the down low?" Monique asked.

"The down low is when a married man is secretly gay but doesn't want to come out of the closet and continues in his marriage as if nothing is going on. When Stan started dating you and you told me how you two were together, I just blew it off as gossip. Monique, it's not true is it?"

"Oh my god, it's true," Monique said choking out the words. "I ran into Doris in the mall and she confronted me with this. I told her she lied, but she wasn't spiteful at all. I think she felt sorry for me in some way, knowing I had been misled into this marriage so he could have a child."

"Wait a minute, so you're saying he tricked you into marrying him just so he could have a child to pass along his inheritance. That's despicable. Why didn't you tell me about this?"

"I was too embarrassed. I didn't want anyone else to know what a mess I was in."

"You're leaving him, aren't you?"

"No, he's not getting off that easy," Monique said and she explained the complicated arrangement between herself and Stan.

"The only problem is, I'm the one hung out to dry, Margaret gets her two parent family and Stan already has his little love nest set up. So what do I do? I can't cruise the bars, I'm Mrs. Stanley Brickman, married lady of society. It's not a good situation to be in and I created it for the sake of my daughter. He said he met this guy he's seeing in some kind of network he belonged to. Have you heard of anything like that?"

"I guess it's possible, but that has nothing to do with him deceiving you. This is going to sound odd, but you have to use your head in this situation. You need a man to give you what you need, love, companionship and someone to go to when you need a shoulder to cry on. Someone will find you, so don't push them away because of your marriage."

"How is somebody going to find me? I could be recognized, it's a problem."

"Stop thinking like a woman, look at what Stan did, he set his lover up in another city and that reduces the chance he will be spotted by someone locally that will recognize him. This is what men do all of the time."

"Thanks Prentice, I know you understand this needs to be kept private."

"Of course I do," Prentice said.

Twenty-One

Monique was enjoying a rare day out and was browsing through a rack of dresses in a department store when a voice said, "Excuse me Miss, I wanted to compliment you on your sense of style. I'm trying to find something for a friend of mine and she is about your size but not nearly as beautiful, what do you think of this?"

"I don't usually talk to strange men in the women's department," Monique said.

"I'm Larry Martin, and who do I have the pleasure of speaking to?" he said.

"I'm Monique," she said.

"My friend, she dresses a little conservative, and I told her she should go for a more sophisticated look. We've known each other for years and she's been having a little trouble with her relationships and has a big date coming up. I told her I would get her some clothes that would really accentuate her best features," Larry said.

"So you're doing this to help out a platonic friend?"

"Yeah, but I may have gotten in over my head."

"Okay, I'll help you out, what color are her eyes?"

"Thank you, I actually have a picture of her," he said as he pulled out a photograph.

Monique gave him suggestions on what to look for and eventually he settled on something and thanked Monique profusely.

"Listen, I've taken up a lot of your time and want to thank you, can I buy you lunch?"

Monique was about to give a knee jerk response of no, when a voice in her head said, 'Don't push him away', "Sure, that would be nice."

Monique was surprised to find out how interesting Larry was as a person. He was a realtor by trade but wrote music and was an exercise buff. His twenty-six year old body showed the results. Larry was a feast for her eyes at about six foot one, very handsome with a caramel skin tone and chiseled body sculpted by many days in the health club. He had a neatly trimmed moustache and deep brown eyes that caused her to stare deeply until she became aware of what she was doing and would break her gaze. As the conversation continued she began to experience some stirrings that had been absent for months.

"So how did you get into real estate?"

"It wasn't something I planned on. I thought I was going to be a sports superstar. You could say I was the hero around town. I was all everything in three sports."

"What happened?"

"I started believing what people were telling me and stopped studying. My theory was if I'm good enough, grades didn't matter. Well I found out grades did matter and I couldn't get into any of the division one schools and went to junior college first. Then I kind of fell off of the radar screen, but I decided to get an education anyway and didn't stop until I got a four year degree. My uncle had a real estate company and that's how I got into the business. Monique I couldn't help but notice your wedding ring, it's beautiful. Your husband is a lucky man. Have you been married long?" he asked.

"About eighteen months," she said.

"Okay, that almost still qualifies for newlywed status, so the honeymoon must still be going on," he said.

"Well he's gone a lot on business," she said.

"You don't travel with him? How could he leave a woman like you behind?" he said.

Monique decided to give this conversation a boost by saying, "Exactly what kind of woman am I?"

"From our brief meeting, you're very attractive in a smoldering fashion, extremely intelligent, independent and exude a sophisticated sex appeal," he said.

"What exactly is a sophisticated sex appeal?" she asked

"That's when you see a woman that is obviously well groomed, probably well to do financially, dressed very well with a little of a model's aura and very beautiful and fit. The effect is those layers of sophistication have to be peeled away individually as she transitions into a state where all of the trappings are gone, but the essence of that sophisticated woman is there as a purely sexual being. Even though she is now at her bare essence, you still expect that grace to come through in her lovemaking and that heightens the erotic effect."

Monique's received more of an answer than she expected and was becoming a little flustered being in the company of this man.

"Monique is your husband out of town now?"

"Yes, he is."

"I don't want to be too forward, but would you like to take in a movie with me?"

"A movie, in the middle of the day?"

"Sure, why not? The theatre is on the next level."

"Sure," she said as Margaret was with a sitter for the next four hours.

They entered the theatre to see a feature that had been out for a few weeks and there was no one else there but them. It was a mystery with a few heated sex scenes. They watched and munched on popcorn and drank soda. Thirty minutes into the showing Larry eased his arm around Monique's shoulder and she made no effort to resist or remove it. He slowly moved his hand down to slide under the arm opening of her loose top and pulled her bra aside and caressed her breast with his fingers. Her breathing became deeper and she was responding to his ministrations with quick gasps.

Larry, in the darkness of the room, placed his other hand on her left thigh and moved her dress up towards her waist. Then he pulled the crotch of her panties aside as she parted her legs to allow better access. Now Monique had shifted her body down into the seat so her buttocks rested at the edge. He moved from his place and positioned himself between her thighs while lowering his head as she her hands gripped the back of the seats in front of her for support as the waves of pleasure washed through her. She contained several verbal outbursts to mask her physical releases. She saw he had risen to her face level and kissed her deeply and then moved in one motion and she felt the essence of a man for the first time in many months. She was less than ladylike in her response to his urges. Larry was amazed at the raw energy she was releasing to meet her need to satiate her sexual desires. Then with a final shudder they both relaxed and released their pent up tensions. For Monique this was a movement to a new beginning, the first step out of her sexual prison and permission to enjoy what had been denied her by marital entrapment.

After a brief period of regaining their composure they both proceeded to attempt to put themselves back into some kind of order so they could properly exit the facility. They still had to traverse the mall without presenting a noticeably disheveled appearance. Larry pulled out a business card and circled his cell phone number.

"Monique, call me when you can so we can talk, I really want to get to know you. This was sudden, but I've never been with anyone like you. I understand you're married and this was risky, and I don't mean to place you in an awkward position."

"I'm not placing the blame on you for what happened, I was here of my own free will. This is not something I normally do. There are some complicated circumstances at play in my life and maybe if we meet again, I can share a little more. You were great," she said as she kissed him lightly on the cheek and placed her hand on his face.

Monique quietly left the room and paid a visit to the nearest bathroom to freshen up. She then heard someone else enter. When she looked in the mirror it was Larry and she turned to face him and he proceeded to pull her close to his body and kissed her long and deep. Monique could barely catch her breath as he lifted her by her waist and she wrapped her legs around his torso. He used the strength of his body to carry her into the last stall and closed the door behind them.

In this less than elegant setting, he turned her so she could brace herself with her hands against the back of the wall and she presented all of her glory to him. This time their pure animal lust was satiated with her full strength pressing back, meeting his forward surges. Then unlike the earlier silence they both verbalized their pleasure with muted low outbursts.

When the carnal ballet was completed they quickly washed up and Monique stepped out of the bathroom and upon confirming the coast was clear, she motioned for him to exit. He grabbed her hand and pulled her around a corner.

"I couldn't just let you leave like that without, well without doing what we just did, but I have to see you again, whenever and wherever you want. It could be in the middle of the night, another city, you name it."

Monique was buoyed by this ego boost, smiled and said, "I'm flattered and have a lot to think about, I'll call you and let you know how I feel, but I've got to be careful about my activities."

She kissed him on the cheek and left the theatre by walking down the long hallway and Larry was transfixed by that glide she employed as she walked away.

Monique knew liaisons in the back of empty movie halls and bathrooms were not something she could engage in on a regular basis. As much as she enjoyed her tryst with Larry, she was far beyond being swept off her feet by a superior display of sexual prowess, regardless of how skilled the practitioner. She had other considerations to keep in mind, namely her daughter, reputation and this sham of a marriage she was determined to maintain for the sake of her child. Even if Larry turned out to be just an afternoon matinee without a repeat showing, it was certainly a worthwhile screening.

Construction of her home within a home was underway and she was meeting with the construction supervisor and architect to make sure the reality was lining up with her plans. Due to dry weather the project was ahead of schedule and would be completed three months early and Monique was thrilled. Even with the less than joyous reason for the building activity, it would also be the first time anything of this magnitude was created for her needs and desires only. Soon she would no longer adapt her tastes to something that was someone else's character expression. The more she thought about it, this would have been a good undertaking even if her marriage had been genuine. If possible, everyone should be able to live in an environment designed to reflect their personality. When she finally completed the final layout, the space had expanded to five thousand square feet from the original three thousand.

Little Margaret was six months old now and showing she was a very bright baby who loved the attention of both of her parents. At this tender age she had no inkling of the situation her mother and father were enduring. Stan had his own issues as his companion, Henry, was also growing weary of being regulated to the background. It seems he was expecting for Stan to sever his marital bonds with Monique sometime after the birth of his child, but was not getting any signals of an impending separation.

Two months passed and Monique was shopping for furniture and had a thought of someone she hadn't seen since that day at the theater, Larry. She pulled his card out of her purse and stepped around a corner and dialed and held her breath. She was careful to punch in a code to conceal her phone number.

"Hello, this is Larry Martin may I help you?" he answered. "Hello, is anyone there?"

"Larry, this is Monique, do you remember me?"

"Do I remember you, where have you been, I'd given up on hearing from you."

"I'm sorry. I should have called you sooner. Can we meet tonight? Of course if your schedule is free?"

"Sure we can, do you have somewhere in mind?"

"It has to be away from the north side of town, so I won't be so easily recognized."

"I know just the place," he said and gave her directions to a jazz club and restaurant in the southern part of Dallas in the Oak Cliff area. They would meet there at eight o'clock.

She felt a bit guilty about meeting with Larry. Regardless of her relationship with Stan, she stood in front of friends, family and God vowing to be faithful to her husband for better or worse. She wondered if the word worse in her vows was meant for her current predicament.

Margaret was spending the night with her aunt Jenny so Monique didn't have to worry about rushing back home to meet any particular deadline. She was trying to decide how to approach the night and decided to go low key in order to draw the least amount of attention to herself. These days she shepherded little Margaret around in the vault like confines of a Mercedes S600. She had held onto her Toyota Camry Hybrid and would drive it tonight, as well as tone down her wardrobe. Last but not least she would relegate her flamboyant five carat wedding ring to the vault at home. It was like a beacon signal to anyone around of not only her marital status but invited speculation as to the financial and social position of the members of said union.

Monique chose to simply place her hair in a ponytail and selected a smart strapless black dress that came to right below knee length, a simple top jacket and three inch heeled sling back sandals. Her small stud diamond earrings were the only jewelry that adorned her this evening. Even in a toned down mode, she still had failed to grasp the effect her appearance had on men as well as the intimidation it created in other women. Monique had a diminished view of herself due to the rejection she felt in her marital relationship, but that didn't affect the impact she had on others in reality.

When she arrived at the dinner club it was obvious this was a different environment than her north Dallas hangouts. This area had texture and a feel of history as she entered. She was noting the clientele was comprised of fashionable attired mostly African American men and women and among them in a booth near the rear of the club sat Larry.

Upon spotting Monique, he went to the front and escorted her back to their seats, "It's good to finally see you again," he said as they walked to the turned heads of several patrons.

"Again, I want to apologize for not calling you sooner. I've been very distracted and busy the last couple of months."

"All that really matters is that we are here now. What would you like to drink?"

"I'll take a white wine."

Larry signaled for the waitress, ordered drinks and then excused himself to go use the men's room. While he was gone Monique noticed the sharp looks from a booth across from theirs from two very attractive black women. She tried not to look and concentrated on the music that played in the background. Then when she turned around, one of the women was walking her way and she prepared for what could come next. To her surprise the woman was coming over to intercept Larry right as he reached the booth.

"I just wanted to complement you on something," the woman said.

"Excuse me," Larry said.

"Where are my manners? I'm Keisha. My friend and I were just commenting on how refined you look and we would be honored if you would join us at our table."

Monique was stunned at the boldness of this woman's actions, but given the circumstances she dared not make a move. Her position was too tenuous to risk any kind of altercation that could lead to exposure, negative or otherwise.

"I'm very flattered, but as you can see, I'm with a guest, and you are being very rude," Larry said.

"Oh, you mean Miss Snow White here, I'm sure she's just looking for a little black Mandingo meat for the night. When you're through with this skinny bitch give a real woman a call. Unless you're one of these brothers that prefers those submissive white women," Keisha said as she placed a piece of paper with her phone number in his hand.

Larry put the paper back in Keisha's hand and said, "No thanks, I'm with a real lady."

This made Keisha furious and she spewed, "That's what wrong with you black men. You think you've made it and get a taste of white pussy and sisters aren't good enough for you anymore. See how fast she'll leave your black ass when you're broke."

She stormed off to her seat obviously agitated and expressing as much to her friend.

"I don't know what to say, that was uncalled for," Larry said. "I hate you had to witness that."

Monique was taken aback by this display and said, "This wouldn't be so awful if she knew my mother was black."

Monique smiled and picked up her wine glass and made a toast with Larry and said, "To the sisters of all shades and colors."

She couldn't help but smile at the irony and absurdity of this situation. Keisha saw no humor in their revelry and stormed out of the club with her friend in tow.

"Larry I want to be as honest with you as possible. I'm not going to leave my husband or home, but there are things I need that my current relationship doesn't provide. We had an encounter, albeit, a great encounter, but we didn't get to know each other and that's what I would like to do now."

"Monique, I appreciate your attitude and I want to be as straightforward with you as possible also. I'm single and not looking to get married anytime soon, but a relationship with a married woman does have some complications. There will be times I want to be with you and can't because you will have other obligations. Although I'm not presuming we will have a relationship past tonight…" he said until Monique cut him off.

"I understand, and I wouldn't expect you to put you're life on hold until we can get together, that's not fair for anyone to ask of another person. If we did this, I just don't want to know about anyone else. At least the illusion of being the only one is better than knowing other women are in your life," she said.

"Monique, what is going on with your husband to cause you to be here with me?" Larry asked.

Monique looked down and said, "He has a sexual performance problem that prevents him from being intimate with me physically or emotionally."

"I know that must be difficult to live with, look let's talk about whatever you want," he said.

That night Monique and Larry forged a mutual understanding they would have a relationship based upon personal intimacy built around separate public lives. Later that night they consummated their agreement with a release of unbridled passion. For the first time Monique slept in bed with a man other than her husband since leaving New Orleans. In his bedroom there was no need to hold back and they were physical, insatiable and vocal.

"Monique you are an amazing lover. I have to really stretch my imagination to understand how any man is not able to be intimate with you," Larry said as he ran his hand down the length of her bare back. "You should be bottled as an impotence cure."

"Now that's a line I've never heard, and I've heard a lot of lines."

"I reached deep to come up with that."

"I have to go," Monique said. "Here is my phone number. Just call and I will call you back."

"Monique, I don't know your last name, is there a reason you haven't told me?"

"My last name is Brickman."

"Brickman, like Stanley Brickman?"

"Yes, like his wife."

"Oh shit."

"Is that a problem?"

"No, it's not a problem, it places things in perspective, we'll be careful, and I'll be discrete."

"I appreciate that."

She soon left and was on her way to pick up Margaret from Jenny and thought about the circle of deception she was caught in and wondered how long could she keep it going. There was a god somewhere and she wondered when he would give her peace of mind.

Twenty-Two

Her time with Larry became her special Wednesdays, and she looked forward to them like a mini vacation she took every week. It was an escape from her daily routines of motherhood, business meetings and happily married couple acts which were rare. A grand performance was coming up soon. There was a dinner party planned for some of the top sales performers in the company and she was the hostess.

When Saturday night came and the guests began to arrive, both Stan and Monique greeted them at the door. For these visitors, to be in the home of the CEO and his wife who also is a member of the board of directors, was a rare privilege and a chance to get a peek inside their life. It was important for them to leave with a positive impression and not detect dissention between the top executive in the company and his board member wife.

They were on their best behavior and even posed with the couples for photographs that would be incorporated into an award piece commemorating attendance at the event. When the couples left Stan and Monique posed at the front door and waved a farewell with arms encircled around each other's waist. Once they were back inside their separate lives resumed.

"So, what have you been up to?" Stan asked.

"I don't see how that's any of your business," Monique replied.

"Well, we are man and wife in the eyes of the law and we could at least be civil to each other," he said.

"Stan, don't lecture me about marital etiquette, you forfeited that right when you perpetrated this fraud by standing with me before god and repeated vows with no basis in truth. You were in love with another man when you pledged your love to me, slept with me and when we conceived our child. I haven't brought this up, but did you at least practice safe sex when you were intimate with him, did you at least think that much of me?"

"Of course I did, I didn't want to expose you to any undue risk. I know with what has taken place I shouldn't expect you to be thrilled to be with me and carry on as if nothing has happened. I guess I didn't realize how deeply this has hurt you."

"Hurt me, Stan this was devastating to me, my foundation was ripped from under my feet. I'm just now trying to get my bearings. You destroyed my world as I thought I knew it. Don't you get it?" Monique said as she stormed off.

Stan stood there in silence and then he understood what happened to Monique was like the shotgun blast going off when his mother killed his father in front of him. There was no way to put her world back together again after it had been shattered into a million pieces.

Monique soon signed off on her newly completed living quarters and proceeded to bring in an interior decorator so she could adorn the space with personal touches that reflected her personality and tastes. She decided to host a private showing as a housewarming party to a few close friends and the small group consisted of Prentice, Kendra, Jenny and Brandy. Kendra brought their son Kendrick to the event and he occupied himself by playing with Margaret who was over a full year younger than he was.

"Prentice if I didn't know better, I would swear Kendrick looks like you," Monique said.

"Well it's not just a coincidence, my brother was the donor, so he does have my family genes," Prentice said.

Monique looked at Kendra and said, "You did it with her brother? Doesn't that feel kind of weird?"

"Well we really wanted this child to feel like both of us were a part of it and this was as close as we could get. It hasn't been hard, he's a good guy and knows we will be good parents," Kendra said.

"My brother's a really cool guy and did this for me out of love. And besides look at Kendra, I didn't have to ask him twice," Prentice said.

Monique showed her home within a home to her friends and it was a sleek interpretation of her with soft fabrics and surfaces in the living areas. One room was dedicated to her mother and the style she recalled from her memories. She had a steam room and took a page out of Kendra's book with her closet design. If anything this place was a slice of New Orleans with little hints throughout of Mardi Gras with masks and beads strategically located.

"Why did you build this? Your house already had everything?" Brandy asked.

"I know but it was everything someone else wanted. I know this seems extravagant, but I needed something that was just me," Monique replied.

As it turned out, Brandy was the only person there that didn't know about Stan and Monique's relationship.

Given her situation Monique had everything she needed to settle into her routine and that was a place to call her own, a child to nurture and a man to provide what her nature required. Over time it became apparent her relationship with Larry was developing beyond a way to quell her physical desires.

She was becoming acquainted with his family and friends through photos, videos and stories. He became familiar with people in her life in a similar fashion and in some way they became friends after becoming lovers and now the danger of real feelings developing was rearing its head.

Jenny would take Margaret on vacation for a week once a year. Monique used this time to take a trip with Larry. They selected out of the way locations to avoid raising any suspicions. One of their favorite spots was a cabin in the hills of New Mexico.

On one of these breaks Larry looked at her and asked, "What is the hold your husband has that causes you to stay with him and take these risks to be with me? I'm a little puzzled."

"I know you don't understand it and I can't tell you everything. I don't want to lose you, but please don't press me on this."

"I can't just walk away from you, we have too much history. I worry about you when we're not together."

There were no answers and they just embraced each other and looked out over the valley below.

Monique was staring at herself in the mirror one morning before getting dressed. She was alone in her five thousand square foot living quarters and didn't recognize who was looking back at her. This is when she decided her life had to change and it was time to let Larry know how she felt.

After two years of them being together Monique asked Larry, "I told you I didn't want to know, but do you have someone that you would want to marry and start a family with?"

"There was someone, but I have a problem, no one can measure up to you as a woman, and if I married someone else we would be over and I don't want that to happen," he said.

"Larry, you can't do that, flush you life away because of me, you know what I'm involved in and don't let someone get away because of me," Monique said.

"Monique, I will wait for you, I know it sounds silly, but I have fallen in love with you and it's worth the chance, but be honest with me how do you feel about me. I need to know?" he asked.

"I never thought I would say this, but over the last two years our relationship has grown and being with you is my greatest pleasure. I have to tell you something else. I have a young daughter and she is the reason I'm staying with my husband, there's nothing between us and we live separate lives. He deceived me into marrying him so he could have a child. It turns out he was gay all along but wanted a child to continue his legacy and a wife to protect his reputation. I found out about his secret lifestyle and this is why I'm where I am today because I didn't want my daughter to grow without a father as I did and forced this arrangement," Monique replied.

"Come here," he said as she lay on his shoulder. "It's unthinkable that he could do that to you. I'm sorry."

"Larry, I fell in love with you over a year ago, but have held back because I didn't want to break my promise to you regarding what this relationship was about, but I can't deny what I feel. I didn't want to make things any more difficult than they were. Why have two things I can't possess, a true husband and you?"

"I will wait on you," Larry said again.

That day they made love as two people that knew they were in love with each other and not there just for a physical encounter. Afterwards Monique showed Larry pictures of Margaret and he remarked about how much she looked like her mother and asked about her personality and temperament.

When Monique left she felt she had reached a watershed moment in their relationship and now they were true kindred spirits due to both having desires beyond their reach.

Over the years Monique would cry on Larry's shoulders and he would cry on hers. When her father passed away she shed tears of a daughter denied her father for the second time. Larry consoled himself in her arms when his beloved mother was called home to glory.

She also would look in his eyes and wonder if she was robbing this man she loved of his life and future for her own selfish purposes. What would his life have been if he hadn't met her? Would he have had a family and children? Would his son or daughter have heard him cheering from the sidelines as they followed in his footsteps in some sporting endeavor? Monique wept in private to think she may have been the reason for Larry to miss his chance at a family life.

Monique came home one day and Stan was there and he was sitting in the family room with the lights out and Monique felt compelled to find out what was going on.

"Stan is something wrong?" she asked.

"My mother just died and I wasn't there. She had a sudden heart attack and was gone."

Monique went to him and embraced him and he started to cry and sob onto her shoulder.

"Come on, let's get ready to go to the airport so we can get things in order," Monique said.

"You're going with me?" he asked.

"Of course I am. You're my husband and our daughter's grandmother just died. We have to be a family for each other now."

"I don't deserve you. Thank you."

The Brickman family took the company jet to Georgetown, set the funeral arrangements and was there for a week until Stan's mother was laid to rest. On the trip back while Margaret was asleep in the bed, Stan looked at Monique and poured his heart out to her.

"Now that my mother is gone, I can feel my own mortality closing in on me. I want to thank you for not doing the easy thing and leaving when you found out about my lifestyle. You forced me to be a real father and not just some drop in weekend parent."

"Stan, I never thought we would have a conversation like this again. Thank you for saying what you did."

"I have to ask you something and I hope you don't get offended. Have you found someone special to be with?"

Monique sat silent for a minute and said, "Yes. I did find someone."

"Is he nice to you?"

"Yes, he's very nice to me. Why are you asking me this?"

"Well, if he wasn't nice to you, I'd have to kick his ass."

"Stan, I can't believe you said that."

For the first time in many months Stan and Monique shared a laugh.

"He's a lucky man. I think I'm jealous."

Monique actually blushed and then Margaret came from the sleeping area and bounded into the lap of her parents.

From that day forward Monique and Stan's relationship changed from venom to more like a cup of tea. They focused on Margaret's upbringing and even conspired to give each other away time with their respective lovers by splitting duty looking out for Margaret when requested. As strange as it seemed, this husband and wife evolved from lovers into friends that shared a home and child.

Then one day she was having coffee and Margaret was already off to school. She looked at her watch and thought Stan needed to get it in gear or they would be late for the board meeting.

After thirty more minutes Stan still hadn't appeared and she went to see what was going on. Stan was laying in bed and Monique approach him and noticed he was not moving and she touched his forehead and he was cold and clammy and his mouth was twisted.

"Stan," Monique said as she shook him.

She grabbed the phone and called 911. And the paramedics came within ten minutes.

Incredibly they couldn't revive him and he was pronounced dead on the way to the hospital.

Monique was in shock as Stan seemed to be as healthy as a horse and she ordered an autopsy. As it turned out Stan died from a brain aneurism which often happen without warning or any leading symptoms.

Monique wept tears of remorse for his death and life not fully lived, tears of sorrow for her thirteen year old daughter and tears of grief for her husband of fourteen years. She also shed tears of shame for feeling this part of her ordeal was ending. Stanley Brickman was sixty-five years old at his death.

Monique had to console her heartbroken daughter once she found out her father was gone. The following week was extremely difficult and the funeral services were attended by business leaders and dignitaries from around the world. At the graveside she noticed a man standing in the back of the crowd and approached him.

"Are you Henry?" she asked.

"Yes, I am," he said.

"Come with me," she said and led him to seats near the graveside.

After the services were over she pulled him aside, "Is there a memento you would like as a keepsake of his to remember him by?"

"Well there was a watch, not expensive, it was gold with a silver band and a black face, I gave it to him as a gift," he said.

"Yes, I know the one, I'll send it to you, just give me your address," she said.

"I know this is an awkward time, but he admired you so much, he told me of any woman he ever met, you were the best person he could have as the mother of his child. He could only hope she turned out to be like you," Henry said. "I know things didn't turn out the way you thought they would, and it didn't for any of us, but he loved you in a way beyond physical."

"Do you want to come back to the house to maybe get something or talk," Monique asked.

"No, that's very kind but I wouldn't want to intrude. You have a lot to deal with and Stanley and I had our time and it's time for me to move on with my life," he said. "Monique, I wish you all of the best, you're free now also, because things happen but not always the way we expect them."

Henry shook her hand, kissed her cheek and left the cemetery and Monique never laid eyes on him again. She wanted to hate him but realized he was just as much of a victim in this as anyone and now at the age of forty-five she was single again.

Monique went home to reflect. This house this man had built using a fortune made from a business started in a trailer park never felt as empty as it did now. Regardless of how it turned out, Stanley Brinkman was a larger than life character and his presence could fill this place. He took this woman from the poorest part of New Orleans on adventures she could never have imagined and was the reason she was where she was now. She lay across the bed where he was stricken and wept all night.

Now the real work started after the funeral, there were estate issues, company matters, Margaret's well being and her personal issues to be resolved. By unanimous vote of the board of directors and control of a trust that controlled fifty-one percent of common stock of the corporation, Monique succeeded her husband as CEO of the company. She would formally take her post in six months and effective control of all of Stan's assets went to Monique as trustee of Margaret's inheritance. Stan was a masterful businessman and Monique was a very wealthy woman because of the agreement she had structured. Stan also expressed his regret for the pain he caused her generously in his will.

After two weeks Monique was able to see Larry again and she took the lead.

"Larry, I don't know where this is going. Stan was just buried and I'll be expected to have a period of mourning before being seen with anyone else," she said. "Plus I have to deal with my daughter's emotions about the idea of her mother being with someone other than her father."

"Take it slow, Monique," he said. "First of all, I'm sorry about Stan, he was your husband and the father of your child. That's a big loss. We have time to bring our lives together and out into the open, it's not the way I wanted it to happen but my patience may have paid off because the woman I love is in front of me and available. A little more time is worth it."

"You have no idea of the range of emotions I've been through in the last two weeks and trying to keep Margaret together. She adored her father and was devastated when he died. I have to be careful with her feelings at this sensitive stage in her life," Monique said.

They didn't make love but talked and expressed how loss can create new beginnings and considered what it would mean to be together as a couple without hiding under a veil of secrecy. Monique left and returned to her life as a widow of one of the most powerful men in America and knew a certain level of scrutiny would be directed her way concerning her personal life.

Three months after Stan's death Monique received a call from the parole department from the State of Texas, "Mrs. Monique Brickman?"

"Yes this is Mrs. Brickman," she said.

"This is John Tolman with the State of Texas Parole Board. I was calling because we're obligated to inform you that Melina Hawkins, who was incarcerated for a crime against you, is being released on parole in two weeks. Its just standard procedure to inform victims when the person institutionalized for an offense against them is released. Do you have any questions regarding this matter?" he asked.

"Where is she being released from?" she asked.

"She is being released from the Huntsville State Penitentiary in Huntsville, Texas, any other questions Mrs. Brickman?" he asked.

"No, I don't have any other questions, thank you," she said.

This was a ghost from her past resurfacing at a time when she didn't have any room to add another thing to think about. Monique shoved thoughts of Mel into the back of her mind. After over fifteen years in prison, surely she had flushed any thoughts of Monique out of her mind.

Twenty-Three

Eight months after Stan's death Monique asked her daughter the strangest question a mother ever has to ask their children, "Margaret, if a nice man wanted to take mom out to lunch or dinner, would it make you feel bad?"

Monique clearly was behind the curve on what modern fourteen year olds knew and was taken by surprise when Margaret said, "Mom, you need a boyfriend, you're not too old yet, on television they said women are vital into their sixties these days. You're not sixty are you?"

"No, I'm not sixty yet, I'm over thirty. A nice man named Larry wants to take me to dinner Saturday night," Monique said.

"Have fun mom, just be smart and use protection," Margaret said.

Monique stood up stunned by what her daughter just said, "What have you been watching young lady, to hear talk like that?"

"Mom, I'm fourteen, sex education in school," she said and left the room.

Obviously she was paying a visit to that school to review the curriculum content. Now with her daughter's blessing she was going out with Larry. There would be no concern for where they went and who saw them. After two months they were a couple of note. Margaret told her mother she liked her new boyfriend because he had muscles and Monique knew she had to keep an eye on her precocious daughter and the boys she associated with.

Eighteen months after Stan's death Monique was married to Larry to sounds of the gossip mill as background music. Outsiders perceived this as a quick rebound relationship but only the bride and groom knew of the more than decade long love affair.

While on their honeymoon Monique asked Larry, "Not that it matters, but was there anyone you almost left me for over all of these years?"

Larry replied, "There never really was anyone else. Those Wednesdays we had were enough for me."

"Do you want to have a child with me?" Monique asked.

"I've always wanted to be a father, are you sure?"

"I'm in my forties and today women have babies into their fifties. I would love to have our child. For all of those years of waiting on me, it would be my greatest gift."

"You would do that for us, that would make me the happiest man alive. I thought my chance to have a son or daughter had passed, but I didn't care because I had you."

They were sitting looking out at the blue Caribbean waters from high above the earth suspended in a posh suite at the most exclusive resort property in the Bahamas. They had come to the island in Monique's private yacht which was docked right in front of the property.

Monique looked at Larry and said, "There's only one way I want to make a baby, the old fashioned way, so what are you waiting for?"

Larry didn't need a second reminder and took his bride in his arms and ran his fingers through her hair. Then he traced his tongue down her long neck and pushed her dress off her shoulders and kissed them individually. Monique responded by unbuttoning his shirt and running her fingernails through the hairs on his chest. She felt like she did the first time he touched her in the movie theatre. She moaned as his lips and tongue touched all of the right places on her upper body. With her eyes in a half closed state the waters of the ocean below served to amplify the mood she was feeling. Larry managed to extricate himself from his pants and underwear and with one swift movement lifted Monique. With one maneuver he pulled her dress down below her waist and she lifted her legs out of the garment and kicked it to the floor. With the strength of his sculpted arms he lifted her up until her thighs rested on his shoulders. She braced her upper body weight with her hands against the windows.

Monique gasped as he performed tender expressions of love until she screamed in ecstasy for the man she loved. Then in one swift smooth motion he elevated her body with his hands around her waist. She then slid down his torso with her lips meeting his in a molten kiss and they joined completely and became flesh and bone of each other.

This was the love she had longed for and thought she had found only to discover an illusion and vapor, but out of that came her beautiful daughter. This time she knew the act of creating this life was in mutual love that couldn't be questioned. She would bear his seed, their offspring with gladness in her womb. Now she could be complete in her journey as a woman knowing her baby was from a man who loved her enough to risk not having a living legacy to be with her.

Larry tensed and poured himself into her and Monique screamed, "Oh baby, yes!" and collapsed on him panting.

Monique wiped the sweat from his brow and kissed him tenderly and then tested his manhood and stamina again and again until neither could respond further. The rest of this honeymoon was largely devoted to procreation and this was an activity they both enjoyed immensely.

Within two months it was confirmed that Monique was pregnant. The smiles on both of their faces seemed to be a permanent fixture, but it wasn't that simple as she miscarried after a few weeks. It would take six months and many visits to a fertility specialist before she was confirmed to be expecting again. She took every precaution to ensure this pregnancy went to term.

Twenty-Four

Monique was as contented as she had been in many years, the marriage she thought she had initially, finally materialized seventeen years later. Her family, business and personal life all seemed to be in perfect harmony and nothing seemed to be horizon to dampen her mood. She was on top of the world with a new addition to the family on the way, but what came next was enough to shake the faith of the most ardent optimist.

She was on her way home from the office when she received a call from her housekeeper, "Mrs. Brickman, Miss. Margaret hasn't come home from school yet, was she going home with one of her friends?"

"No Juanita, she was supposed to come straight home, have you called the school?" she replied.

"Yes, I called the school and they said the driver picked her up as usual and Joe hasn't made it home either and I saw him leave to pick her up and now they're both not here," Juanita said.

Monique began to panic and called Larry and he was coming straight home from his real estate company office to meet her when she arrived. By the time Monique got home there was a beehive of activity and the police were there also. They took the information and were about to issue an Amber alert for a missing child when the main house phone rang and what she heard on the other end of the line sent chills down her spine.

"You remember me bitch, yeah that's right, it's Mel and I've got something you want, 'Mom, it's me, help me...' What you gonna say now? I got your precious little daughter," she said.

"Don't you hurt my little girl, what do you want?" Monique asked frantically.

"I'll let you know that later, you just chew on this, you took my freedom from me and I'm going to take something from you. I'll be calling you later, you keep your fucking ass by the phone," Mel said as she hung up.

"No, no, nooo!" Monique screamed into the phone and collapsed into Larry's arms crying hysterically.

"Monique, Monique who was that?" he asked.

"It's that psycho Mel, she's got Margaret," Monique sobbed.

"Mel, the Mel that attacked you?" he asked.

After a few minutes she calmed down enough to tell everyone Mel was out of prison and the police put out an all points bulletin for her. They set up a command center with phone trace at Monique's home. Monique was really frantic because she knew first hand what Mel was capable of doing. The thought of her precious daughter in the hands of this vicious criminal now hardened even more by years in prison made her blood run cold. Frankly she wanted her daughter back and she wanted Mel dead.

Mel's soul had become dark in prison as she spent much of the first year in solitary confinement. After that, she suffered the same fate she dealt out to Monique when the dominant female gang member assaulted her in the shower. She had her underlings hold Mel while she ravaged her body and left her in a pile on the tiled floor. That experience was not one that built compassion for others but burned revenge lust in her heart. Six months after her attack Mel exacted revenge when she sunk a sharpened fork into the jugular of her enemy and like a female hyena took over leadership of her pack. Mel assumed all of the rights and privileges from the deposed queen and reigned until she was released years later. At least once daily Mel thought of Monique and how she could exact her revenge when she was back in the free world.

Prentice, Kendra, Jenny and all of Monique's family and friends gathered to lend moral support. The news stations broadcast the posting of a one million dollar reward for Margaret's safe return. Prentice reached out to a select few people with certain kinds of connections that could give them some insight into this situation.

Prentice pulled Monique into a backroom and called her cousin Rodney who was what would have been called a thug in his earlier days but now he ran a youth after school program. He still had street credibility because he was the founder and most ruthless of one of the gangs in the city and knew all of the major players in the underground drug and crime scene. Rodney was six foot four inches tall and a chiseled steel two hundred and thirty pounds with a tattoo across his back reading South Side.

"Hello."

"Rodney, how are you?" Prentice replied as she called from a bathroom and turned on the speakerphone.

"I'm doing fine little cuz, how're you doing?" he asked.

"Not so good, a friend of mine is in trouble, her daughter has been kidnapped," Prentice said. "Have you heard about it on the news?"

"You know some of the kids came in here talking about a girl with a million dollar reward for her return."

"Yeah, that's it, she's sixteen and the woman that took her was released from prison and was on parole for assaulting her mother about eighteen years ago," Prentice said.

"Wait a minute, that was right after that hurricane ripped up New Orleans and she was there, I remember now," Rodney said. "So she gets out and comes back and snatched the kid this time. That's fucked up, pardon my French, cuz."

"Rodney I know you're out of that street life, but I'm scared to death for that girl and thought you might be able to see what you could find out for me. I hate to ask. I'm here with here mother, Monique."

"Hello, Rodney I know you don't know me, but Prentice is my closest friend. If she has faith in you, then I trust her judgment.

"Hey, I might be dead by now if it wasn't for her bailing me out of some of those jams I used to get into. Looking back on it, I used think I wouldn't live past twenty-five. Now I'm forty-five, have a family and she helped me see past all of the bad stuff out here in the streets. Where did she get released from?"

"Huntsville and her name is Melina Hawkins, but she goes by Mel. She's gay, really butch and used to be in some of the old girl gangs." Prentice said.

"If she got out of Huntsville, then somebody's sponsoring her up here, and helping her out," he said. "I'll see what I can find out."

"Thanks, Rodney?" Prentice said.

"Thank you and call this number if you find out anything and Prentice will pull me aside."

Rodney Jenkins was a hard nosed, no nonsense guy. He understood some things change very little and crime and criminals was one of those things even in the year two thousand and twenty-three. While the official police effort was in full swing from the posh confines of Monique's compound in north Dallas, he hit the streets and wore his former gang banger colors just to let people know he meant business. His first stop was to the minister of information his old friend Donald Jones who knew when things happened and when people moved in and out of the prison system.

Back at Monique's home they had yet to hear from Mel again and thought this was a bad sign when the phone rang and Monique answered, "Hello."

"Yeah, it's me again," Mel said.

"Where's Margaret?" she asked.

"She's here, keep you're panties on, 'I'm scared mom'. You hear that don't you bitch. I want you to get together two million dollars and put it in a suitcase. I'll tell you where to bring it to later on, don't cross me on this or your little girl will get the same treatment I gave to yo ass. I've even learned a few more tricks since I had all that time to practice on those hos in the joint. Your precious little girl looks like she ain't even been broke in yet. If you don't do what I tell you to and keep the police out of it, I'm gonna have a good time with this little piece of fresh meat, you gittin my meaning bitch. You do what I say or I'll turn this little white bitch out," Mel said as she hung up.

Monique was speechless and turned to Larry for support.

"Get the two million," Monique said.

"Mrs. Brickman, we can't give in to her demands," detective Waller said.

"Get the goddamned money she screamed, this is my daughter we're talking about," Monique said.

The bank was called and they said, "Mrs. Brickman we have to go to the main bank downtown, we don't keep that kind of cash at the branch."

"Do what you have to do, I have the money so get it now and have it delivered to my house as soon as possible," Monique ordered. "I don't know what to do? I'm so scared for her and she didn't do anything to anybody, why is this happening?"

Prentice had her cell phone on vibrate and when it went off she recognized Rodney's number and motioned for Monique to follow her. Prentice answered as they walked to the bathroom.

"Hello."

"It's Rodney. I have a pretty solid lead I'm tracking down."

"Do you think you know where she is?" Monique asked.

"Yeah, I think so. I just need a little more time to confirm it. I need to know how far to take this. This is your daughter. Do you want me to find her and let you know so you can tell the police or do you want me to try to get her out?"

Monique paused and remembered Mel saying to keep the police out of it or she would hurt Margaret.

"Use your best judgment. If you get an opening, get her out," Monique said.

It had been over twenty-four hours since this nightmare began. Police preparations were being made, for hidden surveillance and a sniper. Undercover officers were working their informants to try to locate Margaret before the drop time.

Prentice's cell phone went off again and they hustled off again.

"I've found her. A friend of mine went into this old hotel that's a drug hangout. One of the women there told him Mel was holed up with a young girl. He said a guy in a Benz dropped her off out front. I think I can get her out, but it would have to be tonight. I just wanted to check back in. Is it still a go?" Rodney asked.

"Yes please. If you can't get her tonight, what the police have planned for tomorrow just scares me to death," Monique said.

"We're praying for you Rodney," Prentice said.

"I'll be in touch," Rodney said.

The two women embraced and went back up front.

A few hours later the phone rang and Monique picked it up, "Hello."

"Mom, it's me," Margaret said.

"Baby, where are you?" Monique asked.

"A man got me out and we're driving away from that place. He's says he's Mrs. Grayson's cousin," she said.

"Prentice, he got her out. Thank god," Monique said.

"Oh thank God," Prentice said. "Give him directions on how to get here."

They filled the rest of the group in on what had happened.

Twenty minutes later Rodney pulled into the circle and Margaret jumped out and ran into the arms of her mother for a tearful reunion. Rodney told them the whole story about how he used some old contacts to track Mel down to an abandoned drug house called the Gallery. Soon the full force of the Dallas Police Department descended upon the Gallery but Mel was on the run, but it didn't last long because early the next morning she was cornered in a condemned house.

In a move that could be considered suicide by cop, she ran out with a handgun and pointed it in the direction of a wall of policemen crouched behind squad cars. They unleashed a rain of automatic gunfire that ripped her body for ten seconds then she fell. Her life rolled before her eyes in reverse and when she took her last breath she was not a hardened career criminal. She had a smile on her face as the final image in her mind was her playing in the streets of New Orleans with other children in the neighborhood. A life largely wasted and used to cause pain to others ended sadly.

The driver Monique had trusted was found in a hotel room in Oklahoma dead from a self inflicted gunshot wound with a suitcase filled with twenty thousand dollars in cash sitting on the floor. Mel's girlfriend ran the Gallery and confessed to setting the kidnapping up while Mel was still in prison and paid Margaret's driver Joe off to bring her there. She was charged with being an accessory and conspiracy. She will spend the best years of her life behind bars.

Rodney was hailed as a hero and became a bit of a national celebrity and the irony of an ex hardcore gang banger sharing stages with politicians and stars wasn't lost on the children he counseled. He was awarded the one million dollar reward by Monique and the Chief of Police in a ceremony hosted by the Mayor. He used a portion of the money to expand his youth outreach program and also improved his family's situation.

Because of this ordeal, Monique's faith in her fellow man was restored because a complete stranger risked his life to save her daughter. She also embraced and almost squeezed the life out of Prentice who once again proved to be a friend beyond measure. She stepped up and did something she would have never imagined to help a stranger that was plucked from a rooftop and dropped off at a shelter.

Twenty-Five

Monique went back to work and somehow the regular routine of running the company served as therapy as she regained her bearing when the unthinkable happened. A monster hurricane named Noah was marching through the Gulf of Mexico and it was headed straight for Galveston and Houston. Comparisons to Katrina were everywhere and the evacuation disaster of hurricane Rita was on everyone's mind. It looked like the storm might miss the heavy population centers when a high pressure system collapsed and the storm move up the coast and slammed into Galveston.

This was a replay of the horrors of eighteen years ago and Monique replayed those images in her mind of the terror of those days during and after New Orleans was devastated by Katrina.

"Monique, are you okay?" Larry asked

"No, I'm not doing so well. This is bringing back all of those memories. It feels just like it was yesterday."

Larry held Monique and she clutched onto him a tightly as she had the man that pulled her from that rooftop many years before. She could also feel the signs of life in her abdomen as the baby would kick heartily to let her know he was around. She felt in many ways Larry pulled her from another rooftop the day they met in that department store many years ago. Soon she was able to breathe a little easier and reflected on how a response to stimuli created by an event eighteen years ago could still be so strong. This storm was hundreds of miles away but she could swear she could hear the howl of the wind and sound of the rain hitting the house sideways. Those in the direct path seemed to have a direct connection to her, she not only knew how they felt, but could sense how they felt.

The seawall in Galveston put up a brave fight but this was the first category six storm to hit the United States since this new classification was added. The seawall was built after the worst natural disaster in U.S. history hit when an unnamed Hurricane hit September eighth in the year nineteen hundred and killed over six thousand people. The gulf swelled twenty feet above the ten mile long, seventeen feet high wall and swamped the island which is only eight feet above sea level. Noah brought to them what the area dodged when Rita missed the island in two thousand five as it turned and destroyed areas of the Texas and Louisiana coast to the east of them. The new construction along the beachfront was devastated and the entire island was under water as the bay and gulf merged into one body of water.

Now Houston was in the crosshairs of the storm and at less than fifty miles inland there was not enough time for the storm to lose much of its punch. Water from the ship channel was driven up into the city and then the monster storm stalled dumping almost immeasurable amounts of water swept up from the gulf onto the low lying city. The flooding was unprecedented, except for the levee breaches following Hurricane Katrina. The roads were still jammed with late evacuating cars and city buses going north, there simply was not enough highway capacity to evacuate millions with a week.

Monique's cell phone went off and it was time to see if her late husband's vision would make a difference in the aftermath of this event. She was called to go to the command center in Boise, Idaho where all of the back up system that supported the City of Houston was located. All of the news channels and satellite stations were in full swing as images of the destruction flooded into homes worldwide. She had flashbacks of being stranded on that rooftop years ago as this human drama unfolded in front of her eyes.

The government emergency response system was one seamless resource pool that responded to crisis of all types from wars to wildfires. This had broken down the lines of bureaucracy that hampered the recovery effort after the hurricanes eighteen years ago. Monique just hoped Stan's vision would help people in this catastrophe avoid the suffering she endured after Katrina. But right now in her mind she could feel the sun beating down on her just like she was still waiting on a rescuer, those memories remain vivid.

The massive three hundred and sixty degree display screen in Brickman's operations center lit up with displays of data and communications connections to the Houston area as the local, state, federal and corporate backups systems kicked in. Unlike Katrina where everyone was flying blind, this was not the case and resources were on the move in a coordinated fashion. She looked up and remembered that business mixer years ago when Stan announced the formation of Brickman to assist in such a disaster.

Help was pouring in within hours instead of days, central command was in touch with all elements of the force and coordinated activities were taking place instead of chaos. Because of the transportation issues, the Coast Guard was pressed into service for non water based rescues.

"Mrs. Brickman, there's a call for you," her assistant said.

"Hello," she said.

"Mrs. Brickman, this is President Lawson and I wanted to let you know my emergency offices are reporting flawless operations from your backup systems and the country is indebted to you for your assistance."

"Thank you, Madam President," she replied.

"I wanted to ask if you could get out to Washington as soon as possible to join an advisory panel to plan for recovery efforts and how we deal with the aftermath and the wave of displaced citizens?" President Lawson requested.

"Of course, Madam President, I'll leave for Washington today," she replied.

The human toll was staggering with two thousand dead and countless others injured and maimed. The systems Monique's company had in place prevented the resulting confusion caused by a lack of communication and loss of critical data. Families were able to reconnect quickly and criminals were not able to disappear into the general population and cause problems later.

Temporary housing was quickly mobilized and local companies were already identified that could help in the recovery effort which helped put people back to work rebuilding their local communities. Monique was elected chairperson of the Texas Gulf Coast recovery advisory panel. Once the initial shock of the disaster passed it was time to care of the three quarter of a million people housed in all of the other forty-nine states, Canada and Mexico.

Monique was participating in a panel interview when a reporter asked her, "Mrs. Brickman-Martin, how can you identify with the people around the country that are housed away from their loved ones and in strange cities? They have nothing and your company is profiting greatly from this tragedy," she asked.

Monique looked into the camera and her face was being broadcast worldwide when she said, "I can identify personally with their plight," she said and pulled out a photo and held it towards the camera. "Someone sent this picture to me three years after Hurricane Katrina hit New Orleans. At first I couldn't tell who the woman was in the arms of the Coast Guard rescuer pulling her off of the rooftop up to the helicopter. But I still have the dress I was wearing that day in my closet at home. I'm the woman being pulled from the roof of my home in the lower ninth ward in New Orleans in two thousand and five. I identify personally with the displaced souls out there in three countries. I also know you can recover and rebuild your life, it may not be the same life but it can be a good one."

"Thank you Mrs. Brickman-Martin, this session is ended," the moderator said to the assembled press.

In one instant everyone viewing that broadcast took Monique as a symbol of hope and of what could be done with their shattered lives. It was time to go home and the last few weeks had been very stressful. Old emotions came flooding back as the wave of people streamed across the country into shelters, family homes and hotels.

Twenty-Six

When Monique returned, her daughter was reaching a milestone and going out on her first date with a young man with his newly minted driver's license. His name was Kendrick Chen Grayson and the parents of both children were giving instructions on the ground rules for the evening.

Prentice said, "Kendrick you know how to behave."

"You'd better or you know what's good for you," Kendra said.

"He'll be okay, or he'll have to deal with me," Larry added.

"Mr. Martin, you said I was the man, just last week," Kendrick said.

"That was before you were going out with Margaret, now I might have to lean on you if you mess up," Larry said jokingly.

Margaret came downstairs and Monique almost gasped at what she had on, "Don't you think that dress is a little short?"

"Come on mom, you're just out of touch," Margaret said.

"Let's get out of here," Kendrick said. "You look hot."

The two teenagers left the house and all of the adults just looked at each other in disbelief.

"How old are we?" Monique asked.

"I called the shelter set up at the football stadium in Arlington and asked the director if there were three women she could select for a day of relaxation and beautification this Saturday and she said there were some she had in mind," Prentice said. "Do you want to join us in giving these ladies a break from the routine of that environment?"

"Of course, I'll come by your house Saturday morning and follow you over there," Monique said.

"Good, we'll see you then, and let me know if Mr. Romeo doesn't have Margaret back home by eleven," Prentice said as she and Kendra left.

Then Monique received a phone call that shook her to her core, "Hello, this is Monique."

"Monique this is Sonja Lacy and I was on a bus with you from New Orleans after the hurricane, I saw you on television and had to call, do you remember me?"

"Oh my god, Sonja, I can't believe it's you, how are you?" she asked.

"I'm doing fine," Sonja said. "I just wanted to let you know you got me through those first days because I was scared to death, and I never really told you how much I appreciate what you did for me. Now I realize you were in the same situation I was and could have pushed me away. When I saw you on television I was so proud to have known you and to see what you've done in your life. I'm living in New Orleans now."

Monique wiped tears from her eyes as she and Sonja briefly caught up on years of living and renewed a friendship forged in tragedy.

The next day Monique was walking through the cavernous interior of the football stadium. The volunteer introduced them to three women. Monique was drawn to a young woman about twenty-five and walked up to her.

"Hello, I'm Monique," she said with her hand outstretched.

"I'm Juanita Gomez," she said.

"Nice to meet you Juanita," Monique said.

"Are you ready to go?" she asked.

"Yes, I'm ready," Juanita said. "I didn't know you were going to have a baby. Congratulations."

"Thank you. It shouldn't be too much longer."

They left and after three hours of treatment and new clothing Juanita stepped out. She looked at herself in a full length mirror and smiled at the reflection looking back at her. She was a diamond in the rough that was now polished and sparkling. Her long black hair was swept back and neatly cut at her shoulders. Her bronzed skin glowed. Juanita's near perfect figure was showcased beautifully in the strapless dress that showed off her toned thighs and calf muscles.

"I can't believe it's me," she said.

"You look amazing," Monique said and marveled at the sheer beauty of youth.

"What did you do back in Houston?" Monique asked.

"I had finished my degree in Electronic Marketing and started my job at Gulfcoast Global Industries when the Hurricane hit," she said. "Everything is gone, my parents didn't make it out and I was stranded for a day on top of my apartment building. All I had were the clothes I was sleeping in when they rescued me."

"Do you have any family here?" Monique asked.

"No, I just have to find a way to start over," she said.

"You're the lady from the New Orleans hurricane aren't you?" Juanita asked. "I saw you on television at the shelter."

"Yes, I was in Katrina and ended up in Dallas after the storm was over," Monique answered.

"How did you survive to become who you are now?" she asked.

Monique looked at her and didn't answer as she pulled into the circular driveway of her home and invited Juanita inside. Juanita was awestruck by the sights inside of Monique's palatial estate.

Monique picked up the telephone and dialed the shelter and told the administration desk, "This is Monique Devareaux Brickman-Martin, Miss Gomez will be staying at my home tonight and not returning to the shelter."

She hung up the telephone and gave Juanita a tour and showed her where she would sleep. After the tour and talking late into the night Juanita went to her room and Monique prepared for bed.

Once she was in her night clothes she looked at herself in the mirror and noticed the gray streak of hair that ran from her right temple and ended with the rest of the neatly cut hair at her shoulders. She had a couple of small wrinkles at the corners of her mouth. Then she looked at her mother's picture and placed the photo of her being pulled off the roof in New Orleans on the corner of the mirror. While she looked in the mirror the image of her husband's strong hands resting on her shoulder came into view. Larry leaned over and kissed her neck and ran his hands down and rubbed her bulging abdomen ripe with their son who would be making his debut in a few weeks. She glanced at her mother, the rescue picture and lastly her image in the mirror, turned out the lights and went to bed.

The next day Monique was having breakfast out by the pool and watching the sun rise when Juanita came out to join her and Monique said, "Good morning Juanita, how did you sleep last night?" Monique asked.

"I haven't slept that well in weeks," Juanita answered. "Is this your real life, everyday? How does someone get to live like this?"

Monique heard those words as if they came from her mouth years ago and she hesitated and then said, "Juanita, would you like to go to the art exhibit with me tonight, there're some people I would like you to meet?"

"What would I wear to something like that?"

"I've got just the thing."

Juanita was a hit at the art exhibit and tongues were wagging about this Latina diva that showed up with the Martins. Most of the uproar was lost on Juanita but she handled herself just as Monique had instructed and made quite an impression. She never returned to the shelter and moved into the quarters Monique had constructed during her marriage to Stan.

Margaret was quite fascinated with Juanita and talked her head off about all sorts of things that a sixteen year old wanted to know from a twenty-five year old like men for instance.

Juanita's stock answer was "You should ask your mom about that" and the usual response was "She's too old to understand what I mean".

Then on a Thursday night Monique sat up in bed and announced to Larry, "It's time to go to the hospital. I'm having contractions."

He grabbed the packed bags and ushered her to the car and headed to the maternity ward. Eight hours later with one final push and a viselike grip hold on her husband's hand Monique presented the world with Lawrence Martin, Jr., her son.

This was more than just the birth of her son, when he exited her birth canal all of the pain and sadness from the betrayal of her first union were expelled with him. The afterbirth was the remnants of her other sorrows over the years being removed forever.

She then held her son in her arms and looked upon his face and a deep warming glow resonated throughout her being. Larry kissed her forehead and touched the tiny finger of his hands. LJ as he would be called had a light tan skin tone and his father's eyes and nose.

After leaving the hospital Monique was taking a break from running the company and spending the first months of her son's life bonding with him. Her family had come to town to visit their new nephew as Meagan, Jenny and John Jr. and their families came when the baby was one month old.

Larry who fancied himself somewhat of an outdoor chef had invited all of their friends and family over for a poolside cookout the coming Saturday afternoon. The Friday night before the gathering Monique had visions during her sleep.

She walked into a room and was greeted by her mother who embraced her, "Monique, look at you, you have become such a woman, and you are who I would have been."

"Hello baby, don't you recognize me? I'm your grandmother. I'm so proud of you," she said.

"You're not in your wheelchair and you're younger than I am," Monique said.

"We don't keep those crippled bodies over here," her grandmother replied.

She then talked with her father, stepmother and uncle and aunt.

Then her mother said, "It's time for us to go now. Be nice to your family and we'll wait for you over here."

Monique woke up and then drifted back to sleep with a sense of peace.

The next day her compound was filled with family and friends and her husband was holding court at the grill. Margaret brought little LJ over to her with Juanita close behind.

"Mom I think he's hungry," Margaret said placing him in her mother's arms.

Monique then lowered her top and place LJ up to her breast and he started to nurse.

Margaret was shocked, "Mom, you can't just pull those out like that in front of everybody!"

"She's just feeding the baby," Juanita said.

"This is good for him and will make him strong," Monique told her red faced daughter who went over and brought a towel to cover her mother's bare breast.

"My god mom," Margaret said as she and Juanita walked back to the group.

Monique looked out at the gathering and at her son receiving nourishment and thought this is more than she ever imagined her life would become. After all, she was just a woman pulled from a rooftop wearing everything she owned in the world.

Two weeks later Monique's private jet landed at Louis Armstrong airport in New Orleans. She was here to visit an old friend. Thirty minutes later she pulled up in front of a modest home and knocked on the door and a slender young girl answered the door.

"Hello. Is your mother here?" Monique asked.

"Momma, there's a lady here to see you," the girl said.

"Monique, get away from that door," a voice said in the background.

Then her mother came to the door.

"Oh my god, it's you," the woman said.

"Sonja, come here."

The two women hugged and cried.

"You named your daughter Monique?"

"I had to. You just don't know what you meant to me."

"I'll be right back," Sonja said as she went inside and then returned.

Then they went back to where they were rescued almost two decades before.

"Can you believe we were here and sitting on those rooftops," Monique said.

"Well I've been here for many years and I have seen this area change into something completely different than it was back then. A lot of people never came back and new people came in. You have to see this plaque below the levee wall," Sonja said.

There was a plaque stating the time and date of Hurricane Katrina's landfall and a reference to those lost in the storm.

"How has your life been?" Monique asked.

"My life has been good overall, but the first few years after the storm were rough. Moving to Houston with my cousins was fine at first. You know everyone is glad to see you and all, but after a while everyone started to get on each other's nerves. There were ten people in a three bedroom house. The job market was flooded with so many new people in the city. Some of the native Houstonians resented us because they felt we were getting first choice ahead of them for work. It got pretty ugly sometimes. It was my decision to leave. I was grown and didn't see much opportunity. I left Houston and came back because there was a lot of work here and I've been here every since. I went to college at night until I got my degree. My husband is a wonderful man and my two kids keep me busy. How about you, obviously you did well for yourself?"

"Sonja, I have to tell you, inside of every silver lining there is a cloud. I'm going to choose to just show the silver lining this time. Next time we can really talk."

"By the way did you ever get the dress that was in the window?"

"Yes, I went back and got the dress and I still have it. I can still get in it if I hold my stomach in," Monique said.

The two women laughed and went back to the car.

Sonja and Monique left and went to a nearby park along the river and they walked hand in hand. Monique looked at Sonja and decided to tell her some things she was going to hold back.

"Sonja, after you left the shelter I met a woman who became my best friend and she was very wealthy. She allowed me to stay with her and helped me get a great job. I met a man who would later become my husband. Everything was going great. Then I was sexually assaulted by someone I met when I was in the shelter. It took me a long time to get over that, but I did manage to pick myself up and move on with my life."

"Oh, my god Monique, I'm sorry."

"Well, I went on to get married, had a daughter and that marriage had some problems because my husband wasn't who he represented himself to be. Out of all of this I've found a wonderful man that I love and he loves me. After first husband died, I married the love of my life and we had a son less than two months ago. It has been a strange journey but I'm as happy as I can ever remember. Those are the clouds, but the lining is pure silver."

This time Sonja embraced Monique and comforted her like she was during that bus ride out of New Orleans all of those years ago. Then they sat on a bench along the banks of the Mississippi River, watched the water flow by, embraced each other and shed tears of joy.

About the Author

The author D.T. Pollard was born in the small town of Henderson, Texas and currently lives in the Dallas/Fort Worth, Texas area. Married with one son, he is a career business professional with a passion for the written word and found a way to blend real world events with steamy fiction in Rooftop Diva. Incorporating scenes taking place in some of his favorite locations that he has visited, vacationed and lived helps bring this novel to life.

978-0-595-40234-2
0-595-40234-8

8158332R0

Made in the USA
Lexington, KY
11 January 2011